A PLUME BOOK

AN ELM CREEK QUILTS COMPANION

Steven Garfinkel

JENNIFER CHIAVERINI is the author of the *New York Times* bestselling Elm Creek Quilts series and the historical novels *Mrs. Lincoln's Dressmaker* and *The Spymistress*. A graduate of the University of Notre Dame and the University of Chicago, she lives in Madison, Wisconsin, with her husband and two sons.

Also by Jennifer Chiaverini

The Spymistress
Mrs. Lincoln's Dressmaker
The Giving Quilt
Sonoma Rose
The Wedding Quilt
The Union Quilters
The Aloha Quilt
A Quilter's Holiday
The Lost Quilter
The Quilter's Kitchen
The Winding Ways Quilt
The New Year's Quilt
The Quilter's Homecoming
Circle of Quilters
The Christmas Quilt
The Sugar Camp Quilt
The Master Quilter
The Quilter's Legacy
The Runaway Quilt
The Cross-Country Quilters
Round Robin
The Quilter's Apprentice

Elm Creek Quilts
Quilt Projects Inspired by the Elm Creek Quilts Novels

Return to Elm Creek
More Quilt Projects Inspired by the Elm Creek Quilts Novels

More Elm Creek Quilts

Sylvia's Bridal Sampler from Elm Creek Quilts

Traditions from Elm Creek Quilts

Loyal Union Sampler from Elm Creek Quilts

An
Elm Creek Quilts
Companion

New Fiction, Traditions,
Quilts, and Favorite Moments
from the Beloved Series

Jennifer Chiaverini

A PLUME BOOK

PLUME
Published by the Penguin Group
Penguin Group (USA) Inc., 375 Hudson Street,
New York, New York 10014, USA

USA | Canada | UK | Ireland | Australia | New Zealand | India | South Africa | China
Penguin Books Ltd, Registered Offices: 80 Strand, London WC2R 0RL, England
For more information about the Penguin Group visit penguin.com

First published by Plume, a member of Penguin Group (USA) Inc., 2013

 REGISTERED TRADEMARK—MARCA REGISTRADA

CIP data is available.
ISBN 978-0-14-219670-0

Printed in the United States of America
10   9   8   7   6   5   4   3   2   1

Set in Garamond Premier Pro Std
Designed by Victoria Hartman

To Marty Chiaverini and Jerry Niedenbach,
who were with me when I set out upon this journey,
and to Denise Roy and Mana Massie,
who joined me early along the way.

CONTENTS

Introduction: A Journey Through the World of Elm Creek Quilts ◆ ix

The Elm Creek Quilts Library ◆ 1

Timeline ◆ 22

Residents and Visitors ◆ 29

The Bergstrom Family Tree ◆ 158

Places ◆ 160

Elm Creek Manor ◆ 192

Artifacts, Souvenirs, and Associations ◆ 194

Quilt Blocks ◆ 234

A Stitch in Time: Behind the Scenes at Elm Creek Quilt Camp ◆ 270

INTRODUCTION

A Journey Through the World of Elm Creek Quilts

"When I think of all the winding ways the path of my life has followed," Sylvia said as she and Andrew strolled arm-in-arm back to the manor, "I believe it's a miracle that I ended up back in this beautiful place, surrounded by so much love and friendship. I could have followed my winding ways anywhere, and yet here I am, exactly where I am meant to be."

—*The Winding Ways Quilt*

Ever since I learned to read, I've wanted to create stories and share them with readers the way my favorite authors shared their stories with me. For as long as I can remember, I have also admired and appreciated quilts—but I never could have imagined that one day, my twin passions, storytelling and quilting, would come together and allow me to fulfill my lifelong dream of becoming a novelist.

I became a quilter almost two decades ago, in 1994. I was living in State College, Pennsylvania, where my fiancé, Marty Chiaverini, was working toward his Ph.D. in mechanical engineering at Penn State. While he studied rocket science, I taught writing for the English department—and tried to launch my writing career.

Although my part-time teaching position allowed me time to write, I made many false starts and had only a handful of pages to show for my efforts. I knew, at least vaguely, what I wanted to write about; I knew the mood, the theme, and in my mind's eye I could glimpse two significant characters, a young woman and her older and wiser friend with a secret, tragic past. And yet somehow I struggled to get beyond the first few paragraphs of any story I began.

I wanted to write about women and their work, and about valuing the work women choose to do. I've always believed that if our work is worth the time, energy, and talent we commit to it, we ought to value it, especially if we expect other people to do the same. If we don't value the work to which we commit so much of our lives, then we ought to devote ourselves to something else. Friendship was another theme I wanted to explore, especially women's friendships and the way women use friendship to sustain themselves and nurture one another. But time after time, my attempts to persuade those two disparate themes to live together harmoniously within the same novel failed. I tried writing about jobs I'd had and enjoyed, as well as jobs that had been somewhat less than satisfying. Regardless of what I attempted, I couldn't wrestle those two themes into a coherent story.

Fortunately, I was able to ignore my writer's block in the excitement surrounding our wedding. As our wedding day approached, I longed for a beautiful heirloom wedding quilt to decorate the apartment where Marty and I would make our first home together. Unfortunately, none of my friends or relatives quilted, and we couldn't afford to purchase an heirloom wedding quilt on our tight budget. I soon realized that if I wanted a beautiful heirloom wedding quilt, I would have to make it myself.

At that time State College didn't have a quilt shop where I could take lessons, so I found an instruction book titled *Teach Yourself How to Quilt,* bought some fabric from a discount store, and taught myself to quilt. My first project was a simple nine-block sampler, not the elaborate king-sized bed quilt I had envisioned, but I was proud of my handiwork and eager to attempt a more challenging project. I bought more pattern books, browsed through quilting magazines, and sought advice from more experienced quilters on the Internet, learning through trial and error.

My passion for quilting grew, and as soon as I saved up enough money for a sewing machine, I taught myself machine piecing and rotary cutter techniques. My second quilt was a Lone Star wall hanging for Marty's mother, and after that, I made a Jacob's Ladder quilt for my mother's Christmas present. In the years that followed, I made many more quilts, some large, some small, some to ward off the winter chill, and some to cuddle my cousins' newborns.

Two years later, with several quilts to my credit, I resumed the pursuit of my lifelong goal to write a novel.

In all that time, my interest in those two compelling themes—friendship, and valuing our work or working at something we value—had not waned. Beginning writers are often given the advice "Write what you know," and I knew quilters—their quirks, their inside jokes, their disputes and their generosity, their quarrels and their kindnesses. Quilters, who invest so much of themselves into their creations, usually discover the intrinsic value of their work. Perhaps even more importantly, quilting is a wonderful form of artistic and creative expression that draws the quilter into a wider community of talented, supportive women and men who teach and encourage one another. Novices find themselves warmly embraced by more experienced quilters who are eager to pass along their traditions. Quilters form enduring bonds of friendship that time, distance, and hardship can't overcome.

At long last, I realized that I should write about quilters. Anyone who works on a quilt, who devotes her time, energy, creativity, and passion to that art, learns to value the work of her hands. And as any quilter will tell you, a quilter's quilting friends are some of the dearest, most generous, and most supportive people she knows. Two quilters who have just met will be strangers only until their mutual passion for quilting is revealed, and then they can talk for hours like the best of friends. Quilting joined together my two themes more seamlessly than any other subject could—and so I began writing the novel that became *The Quilter's Apprentice*.

After working on *The Quilter's Apprentice* for so long in solitude, and after struggling to get it into print, I was gratified to discover how much readers from around the world enjoyed the book. I had hoped readers would be touched by the characters I had created, and I was absolutely thrilled to discover that many had come to look upon Sarah, Sylvia, and the Elm Creek Quilters as friends. Even so, I never intended to write a series or even a sequel to *The Quilter's Apprentice*. Like most authors, I assumed I would move on to new settings, characters, and themes in my subsequent novels. But the reaction to *The Quilter's Apprentice* was so positive that I decided to continue the story of the Elm Creek Valley in a second volume, *Round Robin*.

In *Round Robin,* I explored two questions that remained unanswered from *The Quilter's Apprentice*. First, I wanted to see if Sarah and Sylvia had been able to fulfill their grand plan to turn Elm Creek Manor, Sylvia's ancestral home, into a retreat for quilters. All Sarah and Sylvia have at the end of *The Quilter's Apprentice* is a plan and the desire to bring it to fruition—that's a great beginning, but still, it's only a beginning. I thought it would be interesting to return to Sarah and Sylvia two years later to see if they had been able to accomplish their goals. Secondly, I was intrigued by the friends Sarah met when she moved to Waterford— Gwen, Summer, Judy, Bonnie, Agnes, and Diane—and I was eager for the chance to explore these characters more thoroughly. I wanted to learn about their goals, their dreams, the challenges they faced, and their perception of Elm Creek Quilts, their fledgling business.

To my delight, *Round Robin* was also warmly received by readers eager to see more of the Elm Creek Valley. Quilters, especially, found the idea of quilt camp very appealing. Wherever my book tour took me, invariably a reader would ask if Elm Creek Manor was a real place, and if so, how to sign up for quilt camp. "Can't I register online?" plaintive or curious readers inquired time and time again. "I keep searching for Elm Creek Quilts on the Internet, but all I ever find is *your* website." There's a reason for that: While real quilt camps do indeed exist, Elm Creek Quilt Camp can be found only within the pages of my books.

I couldn't give these eager would-be campers a week at Elm Creek Manor, but I could write a novel that would allow them to experience the excitement and camaraderie of quilt camp through my characters' eyes. *The Cross-Country Quilters* features five women who attend camp at Elm Creek Manor and become dear friends despite their differences in age, race, and life experience. The novel traces their friendship as it is tested by time, distance, and conflict until they reunite the following year at Elm Creek Quilt Camp. *The Cross-Country Quilters* was both a special gift for true Elm Creek Quilts fans and a worthwhile challenge for me as a writer, to exercise my imagination by creating characters as rich and as real as the ones I already knew so well. To my delight, my readers embraced Donna, Megan, Grace, Julia, and Vinnie as warmly as they had the Elm Creek Quilters.

It was while I was working on the first draft of *The Cross-Country Quilters* that I realized I must have been writing a series—and after that, one book naturally led to the next as a particular character or plot twist inspired a new story. Instead of proceeding in a strict linear fashion, always and invariably following the same thread of the same character's life, I often took a secondary character from an earlier story and made her the protagonist of a new book. In other stories I delved into a familiar character's past, creating entirely new settings and characters that were still tied in some way to the Elm Creek Valley. Because I haven't been constrained by the traditional series format, I've enjoyed the creative freedom to write novels that stand on their own while still satisfying readers eager to read more about the people and places they have already come to know and love.

Quilters and the wonderful works of art they create inspired me to write *The Quilter's Apprentice,* the first of what has grown into an enduring, beloved series twenty volumes strong. Sarah, Sylvia, and the Elm Creek Quilters will always occupy a special place in my heart, but an even greater place is reserved for my readers, whose affection for my characters and enthusiastic support of my work never fail to inspire me. Your requests for family trees, quilt block illustrations, and character lists encouraged me to create *An Elm Creek Quilts Companion,* your guidebook to the people and places we visit together in our imaginations. It has been my great privilege to welcome you into the world of Elm Creek Quilts, and whether you're a new reader or a longtime fan, I hope that you've enjoyed the journey and that you'll return often. The residents of Elm Creek Manor will be waiting for you, happy to welcome you home.

Within gray stone walls just down the road and across the creek, Sylvia Compson and the Elm Creek Quilters were congratulating themselves on another week of camp successfully concluded, and preparing to welcome the next group of quilters, friends, and friends-to-be.

—The Cross-Country Quilters

An Elm Creek Quilts Companion

The Elm Creek Quilts Library

"People need stories." With some effort, Sylvia pushed herself out of her chair and beckoned for Linnea to accompany her to one of the bookshelves. "We use stories to teach, to learn, to make sense of the world around us. As long as we need stories, we will need books, and as long as there are books, there will be libraries."

—*The Giving Quilt*

NOVELS

The Quilter's Apprentice (1999) (TQA)

After moving with her husband, Matt, to the small college town of Waterford, Pennsylvania, unemployed accountant Sarah McClure struggles to find a fulfilling job. In the meantime, she agrees to help seventy-five-year-old Sylvia Bergstrom Compson prepare her family estate, Elm Creek Manor, for sale. As part of Sarah's compensation, the curmudgeonly Sylvia, a master of the craft, teaches her how to quilt.

During their lessons, the intricate, varied threads of Sylvia's life begin to emerge. It is the story of a young wife living through the hardships and agonies of the World War II home front; of a family torn apart by jealously and betrayal; of misunderstanding, loss, and a tragedy that can never be undone. Her stories force

Sarah to face uncomfortable truths about her own alienation from her widowed mother, and as their friendship deepens, Sylvia confides in Sarah the truth about why she wants to sell Elm Creek Manor. In turn, Sarah seeks a way to bring life and joy back to the estate so Sylvia can keep her home—and Sarah can embark upon a fulfilling new path. *The Quilter's Apprentice* teaches deep lessons about family, friendship, and sisterhood, and about creating a life as you would a quilt: with time, love, and patience, piecing the miscellaneous and mismatched scraps into a beautiful whole.

Round Robin (2000) (RR)

Round Robin reunites readers with the Elm Creek Quilters in a poignant and heartwarming follow-up to *The Quilter's Apprentice*.

The Elm Creek Quilters have begun a round robin, a quilt created by sewing concentric patchwork or appliqué to a central block as it is passed around a circle of friends. Led by Sarah McClure, the project is to be their gift to their beloved fellow quilter Sylvia Bergstrom Compson. But like the most delicate needlework, their lives are held together by the most tenuous threads of happiness . . . and they can unravel.

As each woman confronts a personal crisis, a painful truth, or a life-changing choice, the quilt serves as a symbol of the complex and enduring bonds between mothers and daughters, sisters and friends. In weaving together the harmonious, disparate pieces of their crazy-quilt lives, the Elm Creek Quilters come to realize that friendship is one of the most precious gifts we can give one another, and that love can strengthen understanding, lead to new beginnings, and illuminate our lives.

The Cross-Country Quilters (2001) (TCCQ)

Readers of *The Quilter's Apprentice* and *Round Robin* have been enchanted by Elm Creek Quilt Camp, where women gather each year for quilting, friendship, and fun. The third in the Elm Creek Quilts series introduces the Cross-Country Quilters, a group of far-flung friends who pledge to complete a "challenge quilt block"—symbolic of each woman's personal goals—in one year's time.

These five women arrive at Elm Creek Manor hoping to find in their quilt lessons an escape from the problems they left at home. Julia Merchaud, an aging starlet, has pinned her hopes to a plum role in a historical epic whose director is under the mistaken impression that Julia already knows how to quilt. Megan Donohue is a successful engineer who has won prizes for her one-patch quilt design, but the one challenge she has yet to master is single motherhood. Donna Jorgenson, a mother of two, must hasten to teach her daughter independence and self-esteem, lessons she too must take to heart. Grace Daniels is a renowned curator of antique quilts, whose creative flair is waning for reasons she is unwilling to reveal even to her closest friends. Vinnie Burkholder, the senior member of the group, is a sunny soul with a tragic past. Her overwhelming desire is to bring happiness into the lives of those she loves.

Although the Cross-Country Quilters share a common creative goal, as the year goes by their bonds are tested by the demands of daily life. But despite differences in age, race, and life experiences, the friends' love for quilting and affection for one another unite them in a patchwork of caring and acceptance. The quilt they make reminds them of an everlasting truth: Friends may be separated by great distances, yet the strength of their bond can transcend any obstacle.

The Runaway Quilt (2002) (TRQ)

The fourth book in the Elm Creek Quilts series explores a question that has long captured the imagination of quilters and historians alike: Did stationmasters of the Underground Railroad use quilts to signal to fugitive slaves?

Alerted to the possibility that her family had ties to the slaveholding South, Sylvia searches her attic and finds three quilts and a memoir written by Gerda, the spinster sister of clan patriarch Hans Bergstrom. The memoir describes the founding of Elm Creek Farm and how, using quilts as markers, Gerda, Hans, and Hans's wife, Anneke, came to beckon fugitive slaves to safety within its walls. When a runaway named Joanna arrived from a Virginia plantation pregnant with her master's child, the Bergstroms sheltered her through a long, dangerous winter—imagining neither the impact of her presence nor the betrayal that awaited them.

Gerda's memoir raises new questions for every one it answers, leading Sylvia ever deeper into the tangle of the Bergstrom legacy. Aided by the Elm Creek Quilters, as well as by descendants of others named in Gerda's tale, Sylvia dares to face the dark secrets of her family's past while reaffirming her own moral center. A spellbinding fugue on the mysteries of heritage, *The Runaway Quilt* unfolds with all the drama and suspense of a classic in the making.

The Quilter's Legacy (2003) (TQL)

In *The Quilter's Legacy,* a daughter's search for her mother's treasured heirlooms illuminates life in Manhattan and rural Pennsylvania at the turn of the last century.

When precious heirloom quilts hand-stitched by her mother turn up missing from the attic of Elm Creek Manor, Sylvia Bergstrom Compson resolves to find them. From scant resources—journal entries, receipts, and her own fading memories—she pieces together clues, then queries quilting friends from around the world. When dozens of leads arrive via the Internet, Sylvia and her fiancé, Andrew Cooper, embark on a nationwide investigation of antiques shops and quilt museums.

Sylvia's quest leads her to unexpected places, where offers of assistance are not always what they seem. As the search continues, revelations surface about her mother, Eleanor Lockwood Bergstrom, who died in 1930, when Sylvia was only a child. Burdened with poor health and detached parents, Eleanor defied her family by marrying for love. Far from her Manhattan home, she embraced her new life among the Bergstroms—but although warmth and affection surrounded Eleanor at last, the Bergstroms could not escape the tragedies of their times.

As Sylvia recovers some of the missing quilts and accepts others as lost forever, she reflects on the woman her mother was and mourns the woman she never knew. For every daughter who has yearned to know the untold story of her mother's life, and for every mother who has longed to be heard, *The Quilter's Legacy* will resonate with heartfelt honesty as it reveals what tenuous connections bind the generations and celebrates the love that sustains them.

The Master Quilter (2004) (TMQ)

As *The Master Quilter* opens, the Elm Creek Quilters can hardly believe that their own Sylvia Bergstrom Compson planned her holiday wedding to sweetheart Andrew Cooper in complete secrecy, without the help of her friends. Eager to honor the newlyweds, the Elm Creek Quilters hasten to stitch a bridal quilt for their favorite master quilter. Until the time comes to unveil the surprise gift, Sylvia will be the one in the dark for a change.

Such little white lies seem harmless enough, especially in service of future happiness. Yet Elm Creek Manor, and the quilting retreat established there by the Elm Creek Quilters, thrives on the strength of women sharing their creativity, their challenges, and their dreams. Somehow, in their race to commemorate in Sylvia's bridal quilt all that they hold dear about her wisdom, skill, and devotion, they forget to give honesty its pride of place.

As the quilt blocks accumulate, the Elm Creek Quilters celebrate the joy of new beginnings and the ongoing success of their business—until forces conspire to threaten their happiness and prosperity. Two among them falter in their personal relationships, but are too proud to share their pain. The financial problems of another leave the quilt project vulnerable to a malicious act that may prevent its completion. And as two others weigh the comfort of the present against dreams of a future far from Elm Creek Manor, closely guarded secrets strain the bonds of friendship with those who may be left behind.

The Sugar Camp Quilt (2005) (TSCQ)

In the years leading up to the Civil War, friends and neighbors in Creek's Crossing, Pennsylvania, are set against one another and an extraordinary young heroine passes from innocence to wisdom against the harrowing backdrop of the American struggle over slavery.

A dutiful daughter and niece, Dorothea Granger has her dreams of furthering her education thwarted by the needs of home. A gifted quilter, she has a hope chest full of quilts that is lost in a tragic flood. A superior student, she is promoted from pupil to teacher, only to lose her position to the privileged son of a town benefactor. But the ultimate test of her courage and convictions comes about because of her stern uncle Jacob, who inexplicably asks Dorothea to stitch him a quilt with four unusual patterns of his own design. After his sudden, unexpected death, Dorothea discovers that the quilt contains hidden clues to guide runaway slaves along the Underground Railroad. Emboldened by the revelations about her uncle's bravery, Dorothea resolves to continue his dangerous work. Armed with the Sugar Camp Quilt and its mysterious symbols, she must evade slave catchers and outwit unscrupulous neighbors, embarking upon a heroic journey that allows her to discover her own courage and resourcefulness—unsuspected qualities that may win her the heart of the best man she has ever known.

The Christmas Quilt (2005) (TCQ)

The eighth Elm Creek Quilts novel offers readers a holiday tale filled with the memories and traditions of Elm Creek Manor's indomitable master quilter, Sylvia Bergstrom Compson.

It is the morning of Christmas Eve, and Sylvia is resisting the efforts of Sarah McClure, her young business partner and friend, to infuse Elm Creek Manor with Christmas cheer. Sylvia thinks that Sarah and her husband, Matt, should spend the holiday with Sarah's intractable mother, but Sarah insists that Sylvia should not be on her own. Reluctantly, Sylvia allows Sarah to decorate a few rooms, but when the women retrieve the boxes of Christmas ornaments from the attic, it opens an unexpected floodgate of memories and emotions for the aging matriarch.

Among the decades-old Christmas decorations, they find a long-forgotten, unfinished Christmas quilt. With bittersweet nostalgia, Sylvia admires the work her great-aunt Lucinda and her mother, Eleanor, contributed to the project—including intricate Feathered Star blocks and graceful appliquéd clusters of holly leaves and berries—but derides her sister Claudia's second-rate additions. Only two years apart in age, the sisters always had a fractious relationship, which becomes a focal point of Sylvia's memories of Christmases past.

Her reminiscences begin during the Great Depression, when the once-grand Bergstrom traditions needed to be curtailed for the first time. The ensuing years will witness the premature death of her kindhearted mother, the loss of a beloved cousin, and the disruption of World War II. Throughout, the domestic arts handed down to each generation of Bergstrom women remain a sustaining constant, including quilting, knitting, and baking—especially their unrivaled Christmas strudel.

As the years pass, Sylvia and Claudia remain locked in battle, until a final family tragedy separates them forever. Now, as the only surviving Bergstrom, Sylvia comes to terms with her emotional ambivalence, brought to the fore by the Christmas quilt that inextricably ties her and Claudia together. But while it is too late for a Bergstrom rapprochement, Sylvia realizes it is not too late for Sarah and her mother to avoid making the same mistakes.

Circle of Quilters (2006) (COQ)

Elm Creek Quilts, the thriving artists' retreat at Elm Creek Manor, stakes its sterling reputation on the creative energy and collective goodwill of its teachers and students. But when two of its founding members decide to leave the fold, the Elm Creek Quilters face untold changes. Who could possibly replace their cherished friends and colleagues? An Elm Creek Quilter must possess not only mastery of quilting technique, but also teaching experience, a sense of humor, and that intangible quality that allows an individual to blend harmoniously into a group.

With high hopes, the Elm Creek Quilters announce an open call for applicants. Suddenly, quilters everywhere are vying to land one of the prestigious posts. Among the candidates are Maggie Flynn, whose love of history shines through in all her projects; chef Anna Del Maso, whose food-themed quilts are wonderfully innovative; Russell McIntyre, a widowed male practitioner of the predominantly female art form whose pathbreaking style could lend Elm Creek Quilts an intriguing aesthetic departure; Karen Wise, a novice quilter whose preternatural gifts complement her deep understanding of the mission of the Elm Creek Quilts; and Gretchen Hartley, the soulful veteran with a legacy steeped in traditional quilting.

"We must evaluate all of the applicants' qualities," advises Master Quilter Sylvia Bergstrom Compson. "Our choice will say as much about us and what we want for Elm Creek Quilts as it says about those we decide to hire." In the course of the members' careful deliberations, cherished memories resurface and inspiring visions for the future take shape. Only by understanding the meaning of what their own labors have wrought can they select the ones who have earned a place among their circle of quilters.

The Quilter's Homecoming (2007) (TQH)

In 1925, newly wed in a festive yet poignant ceremony at Elm Creek Manor, bride Elizabeth Bergstrom Nelson takes leave of her ancestral Pennsylvania home. As she sets off with her husband, Henry, on the adventure of a lifetime, the couple's trunks are packed with more than the wedding quilts Elizabeth envisions them dreaming beneath every night of their married lives. They are landowners who hold the deed to Triumph Ranch, one hundred twenty acres of prime California soil located in the Arboles Valley north of Los Angeles.

"Triumph Ranch," says Mae, a traveling companion to whom Elizabeth has confided the promise of the Nelsons' bright future. "That sounds like a sure thing." But in a cruel reversal of fortune, the Nelsons arrive to the news that they've been swindled and that they are suddenly, irrevocably penniless.

They hire on as hands at the farm they thought they owned, and Henry struggles mightily with his pride. Yet clever, feisty Elizabeth draws on her share of the Bergstrom women's inherent economy and resilience and vows to defy fate. As her life intertwines with that of Rosa Diaz Barclay, a fellow quilter native to the Arboles Valley, their blossoming friendship sheds light on many secrets that have kept these quilters and their families from their rightful homes.

When Elizabeth discovers in her cabin quilts belonging to Rosa's mother, she sees in their exquisite patterns a misplaced legacy of love, land, and family. But her newfound understanding of the burden of loss that Rosa shares with the reticent Lars Jorgensen—and why they dare to shed it—places her in mortal danger. Only by stitching the rift between the past and the future can the inhabitants of Triumph Ranch hope to live in peace alongside history.

The New Year's Quilt (2007) (TNYQ)

As each holiday season approaches, some revel in welcoming the New Year ahead, but others quietly mourn the passing of time gone by. "We can't hold on to the past," says Master Quilter Sylvia Bergstrom Compson, "but we can keep the best part of 'Auld Lang Syne' in our hearts and in our memories, and we can look forward to the future with hope and resolve." As Sylvia, a late-in-life newlywed, has discovered, love can enter one's life at any age. Yet before she can truly delight in her present happiness, she must face the sorrow hidden in her past—her own role in the tragic circumstances that left her estranged from her sister, Claudia, until it was too late to make amends.

Vowing not to repeat the mistake with her new stepdaughter, Amy, who opposed Sylvia's marriage to her father, Sylvia must convince Amy that family is more precious than pride. As Sylvia takes up a quilt for the season, begun and abandoned over six years, she recalls the New Year's Eve festivities of her youth at Elm Creek Manor as a member of the Bergstrom family. She titles the quilt *New*

Year's Reflections, after her belief that year-end reflections ought to precede the making of resolutions. The quilt blocks she chooses commemorate the wisdom that no one can ever be truly alone if she keeps the memory of those she loved and those who loved her alive in her heart.

The Winding Ways Quilt (2008) (TWWQ)

Year after year, quilters have flocked to Elm Creek Manor to learn from Master Quilter Sylvia Bergstrom Compson and her expert colleagues. There's Sarah Mc-Clure, Sylvia's onetime apprentice, who has paired her quilting accomplishments with a mind for running the business of Elm Creek Quilts; Agnes Emberly, who has a gift for appliqué; Gwen Sullivan, who stitches innovative art quilts; Diane Sonnenberg, a passionate advocate of traditional quilting; and Bonnie Markham, with her encyclopedic knowledge of folk art patterns.

But with Judy DiNardo and Summer Sullivan, two founding members of the Elm Creek Quilters, departing to pursue other opportunities, will the new teachers be able to fill in the gaps created by the loss of their expertise—and more importantly, their friendship?

As Sylvia contemplates a tribute to the Elm Creek Quilters, past and present, she is reminded of a traditional quilt pattern whose curved pieces symbolize a journey. Winding Ways, a mosaic of overlapping circles and intertwining curves, would capture the spirit of their friendship at the moment of its transformation.

Will Sylvia's choice inspire the founding members to remember that each is a unique part of a magnificent whole? Will the newcomers find ways to contribute, and to earn their place? *The Winding Ways Quilt* considers the complicated, often hidden meanings of presence and absence, and what change can mean for those who have come to rely upon one another.

The Quilter's Kitchen (2008) (TQK)

For the Elm Creek Quilters, sharing recipes and dishes is a natural extension of the fellowship of their craft. Yet even the fondest of traditions can benefit from innovation, so Master Quilter Sylvia Bergstrom Compson endeavors to "clear out the old and make way for the new" in Elm Creek Manor's kitchen, which hasn't been renovated for decades. At her side is Chef Anna, one of the newest members of the circle of quilters, who has accepted the position on the condition that the kitchen be upgraded. She's hoping to elevate her own status, too, from colleague to trusted friend.

"We need to find a way to make this kitchen serve up the spirit of Elm Creek Quilts just as it serves delicious meals," Anna muses to Sylvia as they begin the project. "I want to honor all the traditions of the Bergstrom family as well as all the people, Elm Creek Quilters and campers alike, who make Elm Creek Quilt Camp such a unique place."

The historic manor, dating to the mid-nineteenth century, houses a trove of all that its inhabitants have held most dear. As Sylvia and Anna explore the long-neglected corners of the kitchen's cabinets, the details of events long since transpired spring to life. An old gingham tablecloth, Great-Aunt Lydia's handmade aprons, a cornucopia made by Sylvia's sister when she was a schoolgirl, their mother's favorite serving dish—each unearthed treasure prompts memories of times past, when celebrations throughout the year were steeped in good food and good company. These include not only Christmas, New Year's, and Thanksgiving, but days special to those who have lived at Elm Creek over the years—the annual harvest dances that brought the community together before World War II, the family picnics, the happily shared potlucks. Anna learns, too, of a holiday that has more recently captured the Elm Creek Quilters' collective heart—National Quilting Day, celebrated on the third Saturday in March since 1991.

As each celebration is considered, Anna contemplates the recipes she would serve: some traditional fare, such as the German Christmas cookie recipes handed down by the Bergstrom family, others her own unique creations. The actual recipes—one hundred in all—are included, created by renowned cookbook writer Sally Sampson especially for *The Quilter's Kitchen*.

A much-anticipated addition to the Elm Creek Quilts series, *The Quilter's Kitchen* is a delicious, captivating tale of family, friendship, and holiday traditions.

The Lost Quilter (2009) (TLQ)

Master Quilter Sylvia Bergstrom Compson treasures an antique quilt called by three names—*Birds in the Air,* after its pattern; *The Runaway Quilt,* after the woman who sewed it; and *The Elm Creek Quilt,* after the place to which its maker longed to return. That quilter was Joanna, a fugitive slave who in 1859 traveled by the Underground Railroad to reach safe haven at Elm Creek Farm.

Though Joanna's freedom proved short-lived—she was forcibly returned by slave catchers to Josiah Chester's plantation in Virginia—she left the Bergstrom family a most precious gift, her infant son. Hans and Anneke Bergstrom, along with maiden aunt Gerda, raised the boy as their own, and the secret of his identity died with their generation. Now it falls to Sylvia—drawing upon Gerda's diary and Joanna's quilt—to connect Joanna's past to the present of Elm Creek Manor.

Just as Joanna could not have foreseen that, generations later, her quilt would become the subject of so much speculation and wonder, Sylvia and her friends never could have imagined the events Joanna witnessed in her lifetime. Punished for her escape by being sold off to her master's brother in Edisto Island, South Carolina, Joanna grieves the loss of her son and resolves to run away again, to reunite with him someday in the free North. Farther from freedom than she has ever been, she nevertheless finds allies, friends, and even love in the slave quarter of Oak Grove, a cotton plantation where her skill with needle and thread soon becomes highly prized.

Through hardship and deprivation, Joanna's dreams of freedom and memories of Elm Creek Farm endure. Determined to remember each landmark on the route north, Joanna pieces a quilt from the cast-off scraps of the household sewing, concealing clues within the meticulous stitches. Later, in service as seamstress to the new bride of a Confederate officer, Joanna moves on to Charleston and to other secrets that will affect the fate of a nation, where Joanna's abilities and courage enable her to aid the people she loves most.

The knowledge that scraps can be pieced and sewn into simple patterns, beautiful both in and of themselves and also for what they represent and what they could accomplish, carries Joanna through dark days. Sustaining herself and her family through ingenuity and art during the Civil War and into Reconstruction, Joanna leaves behind a remarkable artistic legacy that, at long last, allows Sylvia to discover the fate of the long-lost quilter.

A Quilter's Holiday (2009) (AQH)

For the Elm Creek Quilters, the day after Thanksgiving marks the start of the quilting season, a time to gather at Elm Creek Manor and spend the day stitching holiday gifts for loved ones. This year, in keeping with the season's spirit of gratitude, Master Quilter Sylvia Bergstrom Compson is eager to revive a cherished family tradition. A recent remodeling of the manor's kitchen unearthed a cornucopia that once served as the centerpiece of the Bergstrom family's holiday table. Into it, each member of the family would place an object that symbolized something he or she was especially thankful for that year. On this Quilter's Holiday, Sylvia has invited her friends to continue the tradition by sewing quilt blocks that represent their thankfulness and gratitude.

As each quilter explains the significance of her carefully chosen block, stories emerge of love and longing for family and friends, feelings also expressed in the gifts they work on throughout the day. Diane is thankful for her two sons, who've outgrown their youthful troubles into fine young men, but she wishes they cherished their family traditions as much as she does. Anna, in her first holiday season as an Elm Creek Quilter, creates a quilt for her best friend, even as she begins to question her feelings for him, which may have grown beyond friendship. Sylvia reflects upon holidays past spent with her beloved, long-lost cousin Elizabeth and wonders whatever became of her. Sarah, pregnant with twins, determinedly sews a Christmas gift for her father-in-law, whose insistence that Matt come to work for his construction company has created tension in their marriage. And as Gretchen pieces a quilt for charity and Gwen completes a project begun by her graduate school mentor, both women lend their talents to those in need.

As an early winter storm blankets Elm Creek Manor in heavy snow, each quilter finds new meaning in their cherished traditions, and more than one finds new reason to be thankful. *A Quilter's Holiday* is a story of holiday spirit, in its truest, most generous sense.

The Aloha Quilt (2010) (TAQ)

Another season of Elm Creek Quilt Camp has come to a close, and Bonnie Markham faces a bleak and lonely winter ahead with her quilt shop out of business and her divorce looming. A welcome escape comes when Claire Duffield, a beloved college friend, invites her to Maui to help launch an exciting new business: a quilter's retreat set at a bed-and-breakfast amidst the vibrant colors and balmy breezes of the Hawaiian islands.

Soon Bonnie finds herself gazing at sparkling waters and banyan trees, helping to run Claire's inn, planning quilting courses, and learning the history and intricacies of Hawaiian quilting. As her adventure unfolds, it quickly becomes clear that Claire's new business isn't the only excitement in store for her. Bonnie's cheating soon-to-be ex decides he wants her stake in Elm Creek Quilts, which threatens not only her financial well-being but also her dearest friendships. Fortunately, she has the distraction of the artistic challenge of creating her own unique Hawaiian quilt pattern—and new friends like Hinano Paoa, owner of the Nä Mele Hawai'i Music Shop, who introduces her to the fascinating traditions of Hawaiian culture and reminds her that love can be found when and where you least expect it.

The Union Quilters (2011) (TUQ)

In 1862, the men of Water's Ford, Pennsylvania, rally to answer President Lincoln's call to arms, spurring the women of the Elm Creek Valley into their own battle to preserve the nation. Dorothea Granger, dismayed by her scholarly husband's bleak descriptions of food shortages and illness in the soldiers' camps, marshals her friends to "wield their needles for the Union" and provide for the men's needs. Her friend Constance Wright staunchly supports her husband as he is repeatedly turned away from serving in the Union army because of the color of his skin, determined to help him secure both the privileges and the responsibilities of citizenship. Anneke Bergstrom's pacifist husband does not enlist, but his safety becomes her shame—one that compels her to work ceaselessly for the Union cause to prove her family's loyalty. A gifted writer committed to hastening the end of the war, Gerda Bergstrom takes on local southern sympathizers in the pages of the *Water's Ford Register,* risking the wrath of the Copperhead press—and the jealous wife of the regimental surgeon she loves.

While the women work, hope, and pray at home, the men they love confront loneliness, boredom, and harrowing danger on the bloody battlefields of Virginia and Pennsylvania. Anxious for news, the women share precious letters around the quilting circle, drawing strength and comfort from one another as they witness from afar the suffering and deprivation their husbands, brothers, sons, and sweethearts must endure. It falls to the Union Quilters to provide for the soldiers at the front and the wounded veterans who have come home, to run farms and businesses, and to protect their homes and families when the Confederate army threatens the Elm Creek Valley. Their new independence will forever alter the patchwork of town life in ways that transcend even the ultimate sacrifices of war.

The Wedding Quilt (2011) (TWQ)

Sarah McClure arrived at Elm Creek Manor as a newlywed, never suspecting that her quilting lessons with Master Quilter Sylvia Bergstrom Compson would inspire the successful and enduring business Elm Creek Quilts, whose members have nurtured a circle of friendship spanning generations. As the wedding day of Sarah's daughter, Caroline, approaches, Sarah's thoughts are filled with brides of Elm Creek Manor past and present—the traditions they honored, the legacies they bequeathed, the wedding quilts that contain their stories in every stitch.

Because Sarah learned the craft after her marriage, she had no wedding quilt, only one to commemorate her anniversary. When the young bride confides in her mother a single, fervent wish—"I wish I had a wedding quilt, one I made myself"— Sarah yearns to grant it.

A wedding quilt is a symbol so powerful that even the most talented novice would be daunted by the task of stitching in mere days a masterpiece worthy of the couple's bonds of love, commitment, trust, and hope for the future. Sarah turns to the Elm Creek Quilters, cherished friends who help her create a fitting tribute for a beloved daughter who will soon stand beside her husband in the union of their shared lives.

As they pool their creative gifts, memories of Elm Creek Manor—and of the women who have lived there, in happiness and in sorrow—spill forth, rendering a vivid pastiche of family, friendship, and love in all its varieties.

Sonoma Rose (2012) (SR)

As the nation grapples with the strictures of Prohibition, Rosa Diaz Barclay endures loneliness and sorrow on a Southern California rye farm with her volatile husband, John, who has lately found another source of income far outside the federal purview.

Mother to eight children, Rosa mourns the loss of four who succumbed to the mysterious wasting disease currently afflicting young Ana and Miguel. Two daughters born of another father are in perfect health. When an act of violence shatters Rosa's resolve to maintain her increasingly dangerous existence, she flees with the children and her precious heirloom quilts to the mesa where she last saw her beloved mother alive.

As a flash flood traps Rosa and her children in a treacherous canyon, only one man is brave—or foolhardy—enough to come to their rescue: Lars Jorgensen, Rosa's first love and the father of her healthy daughters. Together they escape to San Francisco, where a leading specialist offers beneficence far beyond the requirements of his physician's oath, directing them to a family farm where the children can convalesce while the adults work the harvest of luscious grapes.

Yet even in rural Sonoma County, safety continues to elude the fugitives. New identities offer scant protection from Rosa's vengeful husband, the police who seek her for questioning, and the gangsters Lars reported to Prohibition agents—officers representing a department often as corrupt as the mob itself.

Drawn to the plight of local winemakers whose honest labors at viticulture have, through no fault of their own, become illegal, Rosa aspires to learn their craft. Ever mindful that his youthful alcoholism provoked Rosa to spurn him, Lars nevertheless supports Rosa's daring plan to stake their futures on a struggling Sonoma County vineyard.

Rich with the vibrant detail of one of America's most storied eras, *Sonoma Rose* is a novel of passions—for love and work and family—that yields a generous bounty.

The Giving Quilt (2012) (TGQ)

"Why do you give?" asks Master Quilter Sylvia Bergstrom Compson in *The Giving Quilt,* an artful, inspiring novel that imagines what good would come from practicing the holiday spirit each and every day of the year.

At Elm Creek Manor, the week after Thanksgiving is "Quiltsgiving," a time to commence a season of generosity. From near and far, quilters and aspiring quilters—a librarian, a teacher, a college student, and a quilt shop clerk among them—gather for a special winter session of quilt camp to make quilts for Project Linus.

Each quilter, ever mindful that many of her neighbors, friends, and family members are struggling through difficult times, uses her creative gifts to alleviate their collective burden. As the week unfolds, the quilters respond to Sylvia's provocative question in ways as varied as the life experiences that drew them to Elm Creek Manor. Love and comfort are sewn into the warm, bright, beautiful quilts they stitch, and their stories collectively consider the strength of human connection, and its rich rewards.

Featuring not only well-loved characters but intriguing newcomers, *The Giving Quilt* will remind us all: Giving from the heart blesses the giver as much as the recipient, and while giving may not always be easy, it is always worthwhile.

PATTERN BOOKS

Elm Creek Quilts (2002)

Twelve quilt projects inspired by the first four Elm Creek Quilts novels, including:

- *Sarah's Sampler* from *The Quilter's Apprentice*
- *Elm Creek Medallion* from *Round Robin*
- *Sylvia's Broken Star* from *Round Robin*
- *Cross-Country Challenge* from *The Cross-Country Quilters*
- *The Runaway Quilt* from *The Runaway Quilt*
- *Birds in the Air* from *The Runaway Quilt*
- *Gerda's Log Cabin* from *The Runaway Quilt*
- *Underground Railroad* from *The Runaway Quilt*

Return to Elm Creek (2004)

Features "On the Road with Elm Creek Quilts," Jennifer Chiaverini's book tour diary from April 2003, and twelve new quilt patterns:

- *Castle Wall* from *The Quilter's Apprentice*
- *Megan's Prizewinner* from *The Cross-Country Quilters*

- *Grace's Gift* from *The Cross-Country Quilters*
- *Gerda's Shoo-Fly* from *The Runaway Quilt*
- *Miss Langley's Lessons* from *The Quilter's Legacy*
- *New York Beauty* from *The Quilter's Legacy*
- *Wholecloth Crib Quilt* from *The Quilter's Legacy*
- *Eleanor's Ocean Waves* from *The Quilter's Legacy*
- *Elms and Lilacs* from *The Quilter's Legacy*
- Five blocks from *Sylvia's Bridal Sampler* from *The Master Quilter*
- *Sylvia's Shooting Star* from *The Master Quilter*
- *Odd Fellow's Chain* from *The Master Quilter*

More Elm Creek Quilts (2008)

Includes "The Spirit of Elm Creek Quilts," Jennifer Chiaverini's essay about how the Elm Creek Quilts novels have inspired readers around the world to make positive changes in their lives and their communities, as well as instructions for eleven quilt projects:

- *Authors' Album* from *The Sugar Camp Quilt*
- *Constance's Marriage Quilt* from *The Sugar Camp Quilt*
- *The Sugar Camp Quilt* from *The Sugar Camp Quilt*
- *Christmas Memories* from *The Christmas Quilt*
- *Christmas Greetings from Elm Creek Manor* from *The Christmas Quilt*
- *Violets for Gretchen* from *Circle of Quilters*
- *Mill Girls* from *Circle of Quilters*
- *Lucinda's Gift* from *The Quilter's Homecoming*
- *Road to Triumph Ranch* from *The Quilter's Homecoming*
- *Arboles Valley Star* from *The Quilter's Homecoming*
- *New Year's Reflections* from *The New Year's Quilt*

Sylvia's Bridal Sampler from Elm Creek Quilts (2009)

Sylvia's Bridal Sampler is a 140-block sampler quilt made by the characters in *The Master Quilter,* the sixth in the Elm Creek Quilts series. In the story, the friends of Elm Creek Quilts founder Sylvia Bergstrom Compson secretly plan to make her a special quilt to celebrate her wedding. They ask her many friends, colleagues, and former students to contribute a block that represents what Sylvia means to them—which is why many of the sampler's blocks have a marriage theme, but others focus on friendship and others have meanings known only to their makers.

Instructions for five of the *Sylvia's Bridal Sampler* blocks appeared in *Return to Elm Creek,* and over time, the rest were posted online on the *Sylvia's Bridal Sampler* blog. Quilters from across the country and around the world began making blocks of their own and sending in pictures of their works in progress to inspire and motivate other aspiring *Sylvia's Bridal Sampler* makers. In the years since, the community has expanded to include an e-mail list and numerous block exchanges, with more quilters happily joining in every day. *Sylvia's Bridal Sampler from Elm Creek Quilts* collects all 140 patterns in a beautiful book, complete with a gallery of stunning *Sylvia's Bridal Samplers* from around the world.

Traditions from Elm Creek Quilts (2011)

Features a new behind-the-scenes essay, "Elm Creek Quilts Inspirations," and instructions for thirteen new quilt projects:

- *Winding Ways* from *The Winding Ways Quilt*
- *Springtime in Waterford* from *The Winding Ways Quilt*
- *Welcome, Baby Emily!* from *The Winding Ways Quilt*
- *Anna's Kitchen* from *The Quilter's Kitchen*
- *Joanna's Freedom* from *The Lost Quilter*
- *Mr. Lincoln's Spy* from *The Lost Quilter*
- *Cornucopia of Thanks* from *A Quilter's Holiday*

- *Remembering Victoria* from *A Quilter's Holiday*
- *Holiday Blessings* from *A Quilter's Holiday*
- *Pineapple Patch* from *The Aloha Quilt*
- *The Aloha Quilt* from *The Aloha Quilt*
- *Dorothea's Dove in the Window* from *The Union Quilters*
- *Caroline's Wedding* from *The Wedding Quilt*

Loyal Union Sampler from Elm Creek Quilts (2013)

In the novel *The Union Quilters,* as in history, Union and Confederate women alike made quilts for soldiers to use in camps and in hospitals. They sewed and raffled off quilts to raise funds to support important causes, and they quilted to express themselves artistically during a time of national strife and personal turmoil. On the northern home front, the demands of war thrust women into new roles, for they suddenly needed to support and provide for the men who had always been cast in the role of their protectors.

To raise money for the war effort, Anneke Bergstrom, Dorothea Nelson, and the other Union Quilters embarked upon an ambitious plan to create the *Loyal Union Sampler.* They invited every woman in the Elm Creek Valley to contribute a six-inch patchwork block of her own design, or a favorite traditional pattern that was not particularly well-known. Each participant also provided templates and suggestions for how best to construct her chosen block. The blocks were sewn together into an exquisite sampler, quilted by the finest needleworkers in the valley, and offered up in a raffle. The fortunate winner claimed quilt, templates, and instructions, and thus won a lovely quilt as well as an extraordinary catalog of quilt patterns, enough to keep even the most industrious quilter pleasurably occupied for years to come.

The sixth Elm Creek Quilts pattern book provides instructions for the 121 blocks of the *Loyal Union Sampler* and features a gallery of gorgeous quilts created from blocks contributed by more than two hundred talented quilters and Elm Creek Quilts fans from around the world.

Timeline

So much about Elm Creek Manor had changed, but not the view from the window over the sink. If not for the stiffness in her hands and the way the winter chill had seeped into her bones, Sylvia could convince herself that the past fifty years had never happened. She could imagine herself a young woman again, as if any moment she would hear her younger brother whistling as he came downstairs for breakfast. She would look up and see her elder sister entering the kitchen, tying on an apron. Sylvia would gaze through the window and see a lone figure trudging through the snow from the barn, returning to his home and his bride after completing the morning chores. She would leave her work and hurry to the back door to meet him, her footsteps quick and light, her heart full. Her husband was there and alive again, as was her brother, as was her sister, and together they would laugh at the grief of their long separation.

Sylvia squeezed her eyes shut and listened.

She heard a clock ticking in the west sitting room off the kitchen, and then, distantly, the sound of someone descending the grand staircase in the front foyer. For a moment her breath caught in her throat, and she almost believed she had accomplished the impossible. She had willed herself back in time, and now, armed with the wisdom of hindsight and regret, she could set everything to rights. All the years that had been stolen from them were restored, and they would live them out together. Not a single moment would be wasted.

—*Round Robin*

1827   Thomas Nelson is born.

1830   Dorothea Granger is born.

1831   Gerda Bergstrom is born.

1833   Jonathan Granger is born.

Hans Bergstrom is born.

1836   Charlotte Claverton is born.

1838   Anneke Stahl is born.

1847   Jonathan Granger begins his apprenticeship in Baltimore.

1849   Violet Pearson marries Hiram Engle.

Hans Bergstrom immigrates to America.

Abel Wright buys Constance's freedom.

1850   George Wright is born.

1852   Joseph Wright is born.

Dorothea Granger marries Thomas Nelson.

1856   Hans Bergstrom wins Elm Creek Farm from Amos Liggett.

Anneke Stahl immigrates to America.

Gerda Bergstrom immigrates to America.

Hans Bergstrom marries Anneke Stahl.

1858   The original wing of Elm Creek Manor is built.

Jonathan Granger marries Charlotte Claverton on December 24.

1859   Elm Creek Farm becomes a station on the Underground Railroad.

Anneke Bergstrom and the fugitive slave Joanna give birth at Elm Creek Farm within weeks of each other.

The fugitive slave Joanna is betrayed and captured. To protect her son, the Bergstroms pass him off as the twin brother of Anneke's son.

Robert Granger is born to Jonathan and Charlotte Granger.

1861   Abigail Nelson is born to Thomas and Dorothea Nelson.

Jonathan Granger, Thomas Nelson, and other men of the Elm Creek Valley enlist in the Forty-ninth Pennsylvania Volunteers, Company L, organized at Lewistown and Harrisburg.

1862   Albert Bergstrom is born to Anneke and Hans Bergstrom.

Jeannette Granger is born to Jonathan and Charlotte Granger while Jonathan is serving in the Civil War.

The women of the Elm Creek Valley make the *Loyal Union Sampler*.

Union Hall is constructed under the direction of Abel Wright and the Union Quilters.

President Abraham Lincoln announces the preliminary Emancipation Proclamation.

1863   The Battle of Gettysburg is fought .

The Sixth United States Colored Infantry Regiment organizes at Camp William Penn, Pennsylvania.

Abel Wright enlists in the army.

Gerda Bergstrom receives her first letter from Elizabeth Van Lew, a Union loyalist in Richmond.

Gerda Bergstrom hears President Lincoln speak at the dedication of a new national cemetery at Gettysburg, Pennsylvania.

1864   Thomas Nelson is killed in the Battle of Spotsylvania Court House in Virginia.

Abel Wright is wounded at the Battle of the Crater in Petersburg, Virginia.

1866   Abel Wright's first book, an account of his wartime experiences, is published to great acclaim.

1867   Miguel Diaz Sr. is born in the Arboles Valley, California.

Lydia Bergstrom is born.

Abel Wright's second book, an account of his Underground Railroad years, is published.

1868   Gerda Bergstrom finally receives a reply to her many letters to Josiah Chester.

The *Dove in the Window* quilt is returned to Dorothea Granger Nelson.

1870   Isabel Rodriguez is born.

1872   George Bergstrom is born.

1875   The Rodriguez family leaves El Rancho Triunfo.

1876	Lucinda Bergstrom is born.
	A severe drought strikes the Arboles Valley.
	The Grand Union Hotel opens in the Arboles Valley.
1885	Isabel Rodriguez's mother dies.
1886	John Barclay is born.
1887	Abigail Nelson, daughter of Thomas and Dorothea Nelson, gives birth to a daughter.
1888	Frederick Bergstrom is born.
	Lars Jorgensen is born.
1889	Isabel Rodriguez and Miguel Diaz marry.
1890	Eleanor Lockwood is born.
	Rosa Diaz is born.
1892	Oscar Jorgensen is born.
	Carlos Diaz is born.
1895	Gerda Bergstrom writes her memoirs.
1899	Eleanor Lockwood and Frederick Bergstrom meet in New York City.
1903	William Bergstrom is born.
	Henry Nelson is born.
1904	Elizabeth Bergstrom is born.
1905	Clara Bergstrom is born.
1907	Eleanor Lockwood marries Frederick Bergstrom.
1912	Rosa Diaz and John Barclay marry.
1913	Rosa Diaz Barclay gives birth to a daughter, Marta.
	Annalise Jorgensen is born to Oscar and Mary Katherine Jorgensen.
1914	John Barclay Jr. is born to John and Rosa Diaz Barclay.
1916	Angela Barclay is born to John and Rosa Diaz Barclay.
1917	Ana Barclay is born to John and Rosa Diaz Barclay.
1918	James Compson is born.
	Claudia Bergstrom is born.
	Maria Barclay is born.
1919	Pedro Barclay is born.
1920	Sylvia Bergstrom is born.

Isabel Rodriguez Diaz dies under mysterious circumstances.

Lupita Barclay is born.

1923 Miguel Barclay is born.

1925 Elizabeth Bergstrom marries Henry Nelson and the newlyweds move to the Arboles Valley in Southern California.

1927 Richard Bergstrom is born.

Andrew Cooper is born.

Eleanor Lockwood Bergstrom's mother, Gertrude Drayton-Smith Lockwood, dies.

1928 Agnes Chevalier is born.

1930 Eleanor Lockwood Bergstrom dies.

1936 Gretchen Hartley is born.

1940 Sylvia Bergstrom marries James Compson.

1944 Agnes Chevalier marries Richard Bergstrom.

1945 James Compson and Richard Bergstrom are killed in World War II.

Sylvia Bergstrom Compson leaves Elm Creek Manor.

Claudia Bergstrom marries Harold Midden.

1946 Bonnie Markham is born.

1950 Gwen Sullivan is born.

1955 Diane Sonnenberg is born.

1960 Russell McIntyre is born.

1964 Maggie Flynn is born.

1966 Judy Nguyen DiNardo is born.

1970 Karen Wise is born.

1971 Sarah Mallory McClure is born.

Matthew McClure is born.

1972 Anna Del Maso is born.

1975 Summer Sullivan is born.

1981 Michael Sonnenberg is born.

1983 Todd Sonnenberg is born.

1995 Sylvia returns to Elm Creek Manor.

Emily DiNardo-Boyer is born.

1996 Sylvia Bergstrom Compson, Sarah McClure, and their friends found Elm Creek Quilts.

1997 Ethan Wise is born.

2000 Lucas Wise is born.

2001 Sylvia Bergstrom Compson marries Andrew Cooper.

2002 Gretchen Hartley joins the faculty of Elm Creek Quilts.

Bonnie Markham travels to Maui to help Claire Duffield establish Aloha Quilt Camp.

Gretchen Hartley proposes an annual week of winter quilt camp to benefit Project Linus.

2003 Maggie Flynn joins the faculty of Elm Creek Quilts.

Sarah and Matt McClure's twins, Caroline Sylvia and James Matthew, are born.

Aloha Quilt Camp is launched.

Jeremy Bernstein proposes to Anna Del Maso at the Quilter's Holiday potluck luncheon.

The Elm Creek Quilters launch the first annual Quiltsgiving winter camp for charity.

2004 Anna Del Maso marries Jeremy Bernstein.

2005 Gina Del Maso–Bernstein is born.

Ann Del Maso resigns from Elm Creek Quilt Camp because her husband has obtained a faculty position with a university in Virginia.

2007 Jocelyn Ames, Mona Lindstad, Linnea Nelson, Michaela Phillips, Pauline Tucker, and Karen Wise attend the fifth annual Quiltsgiving at Elm Creek Manor.

2008 Bonnie Markham marries Hinano Paoa.

Russell McIntyre joins the faculty of Elm Creek Quilt Camp.

Maggie Flynn marries Russell McIntyre.

2012 Gwen Sullivan is elected to the Waterford city council.

Anna Del Maso rejoins the staff of Elm Creek Quilts when her husband, Jeremy Bernstein, returns to Waterford College as the Abel Wright Professor of American History.

2013   Emily DiNardo-Boyer graduates from high school.

Sylvia Bergstrom Compson dies peacefully in her sleep at the age of ninety-three.

2014   Gwen Sullivan is reelected to the Waterford city council, and later that year, to Congress.

2016   Gwen Sullivan is reelected to Congress.

2017   Agnes Chevalier Bergstrom Emberly dies.

2018   Gwen Sullivan is reelected to Congress.

2019   Emily DiNardo-Boyer graduates from the California College of the Arts.

2020   Gwen Sullivan is reelected to Congress.

2022   Emily DiNardo-Boyer earns a master of fine arts in fiber and material studies from the School of the Art Institute of Chicago.

Gwen Sullivan is reelected to Congress.

2023   Emily DiNardo-Boyer joins the faculty of Elm Creek Quilts.

2025   Caroline McClure graduates from Dartmouth and begins medical school.

James McClure graduates from Penn State and begins working full-time for Elm Creek Quilts.

2028   Caroline McClure marries Leo Fiore at Elm Creek Manor.

Residents and Visitors

Around the circle the candle went, passed from hand to hand as the violet sky deepened and the stars came out. Women who could barely sew had come for their first lessons; accomplished quilters had come for the opportunity to learn new skills or to work uninterrupted on masterpieces they could as yet only envision. They had come to sew quilts for brides and for babies, to cover beds and to display on walls, for warmth, for beauty, for joy. Through the years Judy had heard similar tales from other women, every summer Sunday as night fell, and yet each story was unique. One common thread joined all the women who came to Elm Creek Manor. Those who had given so much of themselves and their lives caring for others—children, husbands, aging parents—were now taking time to care for themselves, to nourish their own souls.

—*The Winding Ways Quilt*

NOTE: The abbreviations after the characters' names indicate their first appearances in the Elm Creek Quilts series. Please refer to the chapter "The Elm Creek Quilts Library" for a list of the novels and their abbreviations.

THE ELM CREEK QUILTERS

Sylvia Bergstrom Compson (TQA)

Born into a prosperous family in rural central Pennsylvania, young Sylvia Bergstrom cherishes her family estate, Elm Creek Manor, and plans one day to take her place alongside her father in the family horse-breeding business, Bergstrom Thoroughbreds. Tragedy during World War II and a sister's betrayal drive her from her beloved home and force her to choose a new path. A gifted quilter, Sylvia graduates with a degree in art education from Carnegie Mellon University in Pittsburgh. For many years she teaches in the Sewickley, Pennsylvania, area, and she becomes a renowned lecturer at quilt shows and quilt guilds across the country. Upon her return to Elm Creek Manor after a fifty-year absence, Sylvia and her young apprentice, Sarah McClure, transform the manor into Elm Creek Quilt Camp, a retreat for quilters.

Sarah McClure (TQA)

Sarah McClure, a former cost accountant unsatisfied with her career, is hired to help Sylvia prepare Elm Creek Manor for sale. After quilting lessons become the foundation for a blossoming friendship between the two women, Sarah proposes turning Elm Creek Manor into a retreat for quilters. As successful as Sarah is in business matters, she is less adept at navigating the rocky emotional terrain between herself and her mother. She responds with reluctance whenever Sylvia urges her to learn from Sylvia's own mistakes and reconcile with her mother before it's too late.

Anna Del Maso (COQ)

Quilting is a second love for Anna Del Maso, who is working for Waterford College Food Services when she is hired as the chef of Elm Creek Quilt Camp. She and longtime best friend Jeremy Bernstein marry at Elm Creek Manor while he is finishing his Ph.D. dissertation. After he receives his degree, they and their daughter, Gina, leave Waterford so he can accept a faculty position in Virginia, but Anna later returns to Elm Creek Manor when Jeremy is appointed the Abel Wright Professor of American History at Waterford College.

Judy Nguyen DiNardo (TQA)

The daughter of an American serviceman and a Vietnamese translator, Judy immigrates to the United States as a young child, but she does not meet her biological father until she is in her thirties. A professor of computer sciences at Waterford College, Judy enjoys an affectionate marriage and is devoted to her young daughter, Emily, and her husband, Steve, a journalist. Judy prefers hand piecing and quilting, because she finds handwork relaxing after putting in long hours with her computers.

Agnes Emberly (TQA)

As a young woman in the early years of World War II, Agnes marries Sylvia's brother Richard Bergstrom after he enlists in the army. Estranged from her family, who disapproves of the marriage, Agnes remains at Elm Creek Manor after Richard is killed in the South Pacific. She later remarries, bears two daughters, and lives as a homemaker in Waterford, where she still resides when Sylvia returns after her long absence. A founding Elm Creek Quilter, she is also an active member of the Waterford Historical Society, serving as president for two years and founding the society's impressive collection of antique quilts.

Maggie Flynn (COQ)

Sacramento resident Maggie Flynn discovers a love for quilting almost by chance, after a bedraggled sampler quilt she bought at a garage sale for five dollars turns out to be an antique treasure made by Harriet Findley Birch, a former Lowell mill girl who traveled with her husband along the Oregon Trail in the mid-1800s. As she researches the provenance of her find, Maggie becomes a recognized expert on quilt history. She applies to join the faculty of Elm Creek Quilts just as she faces an impending layoff from her longtime job in geriatric care, and it is on her way home from her interview that she meets Russell McIntyre, another candidate for the position and her future husband.

Gretchen Hartley (COQ)

As a high school student in Ambridge, Pennsylvania, Gretchen takes her first quilting lessons from none other than Sylvia herself. Years later, after her husband, Joe, suffers a serious injury at work in a Pittsburgh steel mill, Gretchen supports the family on her modest salary as a substitute home economics teacher. Gretchen helps keep the traditions of quilting alive in the years before the "quilting renaissance" of the 1970s by sharing her knowledge with friends. Eventually that small circle of quilters grows into a thriving guild, and Gretchen becomes so renowned as a teacher that guilds from hundreds of miles away invite her to lecture and teach. Gretchen and a friend found the most successful quilt shop in western Pennsylvania, a position Gretchen leaves in order to join the faculty of Elm Creek Quilt Camp. Her appointment to the faculty of Elm Creek Quilts is the fulfillment of a dream and a well-deserved reward for a lifetime of hard work.

Bonnie Markham (TQA)

As the proprietor of Grandma's Attic, Waterford's only quilt shop, Bonnie Markham provides local quilters with every sort of fabric, notion, pattern, or book they could wish for, but more importantly, she offers them a cozy, friendly gathering place and a sense of community. After her shop goes out of business, Bonnie goes through a difficult divorce and helps an old college friend launch Aloha Quilt Camp in Lahaina on Maui, where she unexpectedly finds new love and new professional opportunities.

Russell McIntyre (COQ)

Russell McIntyre took up quilting as a way of mourning for his wife, a quilter who lost her battle with cancer. Largely self-taught, Russ sidesteps many of the traditions of the craft, but his wholly original, contemporary designs have won him fame. He meets Maggie Flynn on a plane as they return home after interviewing for faculty positions at Elm Creek Quilts, and he subsequently declines the job offer in order to stay on the West Coast near Maggie, unaware that she too has been asked to join the faculty. Later he works for Elm Creek Quilts as a visiting instructor, and eventually joins the permanent faculty.

Diane Sonnenberg (TQA)

Diane was born and raised in Waterford, Pennsylvania, the daughter of a homemaker and a Waterford College professor. A graduate of the University of Pittsburgh, a former middle school teacher, and a onetime part-time employee of Grandma's Attic, Diane is the devoted mother of two boys and the loving wife of Tim, a Waterford College chemistry professor. Diane often finds herself exasperated and frenzied by the multiple demands of her career and family, but she is always the first to extend a hand to a friend in need. An adamant traditionalist, she prefers hand piecing and hand quilting to machine work and has been known to insist that only quilts made entirely by hand are true quilts.

Gwen Sullivan (TQA)

A professor of American studies at Waterford College, free-spirited Gwen is a self-proclaimed former hippie who sees quilting as a feminist act as well as a fulfilling art. A longtime single mother, the stout, auburn-haired founding Elm Creek Quilter enjoys a close, loving relationship with her daughter, Summer.

Summer Sullivan (TQA)

A graduate of Waterford College majoring in philosophy, Summer Sullivan is the youngest founding Elm Creek Quilter and a former employee of Grandma's Attic. Summer is fascinated by quilts as cultural and historical artifacts, and in her own quilts she blends contemporary patterns and techniques with traditional fabrics. Later she leaves Elm Creek Quilts to pursue graduate studies in history at the University of Chicago. She is very beautiful, with long, auburn hair; a slender figure; a ready smile; and hazel eyes.

FRIENDS, FAMILY, RIVALS, AND OTHERS

Aaron (1) (TMQ)

One of Summer Sullivan's flatmates in downtown Waterford.

Aaron (2) (TLQ)

The cruel slave driver at Oak Grove; a mulatto slave who enjoys his own cabin and other privileges.

Julianne Abbot (TWWQ)

One of Summer Sullivan's roommates in Hyde Park; a graduate student in comparative religion at the University of Chicago Divinity School.

Abner (TLQ)

Colonel Robert Harper's groom and coachman at Harper Hall in Charleston.

Adam (TLQ)

A stable boy at Harper Hall in Charleston; a slave.

Grandpa Al (TWWQ)

Bonnie Markham's grandfather.

Mrs. Albrecht (COQ)

Heidi Albrecht Mueller's mother, who employs Gretchen Hartley's mother as a housemaid.

Margaret Alden (TRQ)

A quilt camper from South Carolina who gives a mysterious Birds in the Air quilt to Sylvia Bergstrom Compson. Known by the elders of the Alden family as both *The Elm Creek Quilt* and *The Runaway Quilt,* its deteriorating layers are held together by quilting stitches depicting scenes from the Elm Creek Valley.

Alice (TNYQ)

A friend who gives Sylvia Bergstrom Compson wise advice after her sister passes away.

Mrs. Ames (TLQ)

Robert and Evangeline Harper's next-door neighbor in Charleston.

Anisa Ames (TGQ)

The elder daughter of Noah and Jocelyn Ames.

Jocelyn Ames (TGQ)

Jocelyn is an African-American sixth-grade history teacher at an underfunded public school in the Detroit metro area and a widowed mother of two daughters, Anisa and Rahma. When she assumes leadership of her late husband's after-school academic program, the students and their parents arrange for her to attend Quilts-giving as a token of their thanks.

Noah Ames (TGQ)

The husband of Jocelyn Ames, Noah was a gifted middle school science teacher and track and field coach in Westfield, Michigan. A Detroit native, he was twice named Michigan Teacher of the Year.

Rahma Ames (TGQ)

The younger daughter of Noah and Jocelyn Ames, two years younger than her sister, Anisa.

Major Robert Anderson (TLQ)

The Union army officer who moved his garrison from Fort Moultrie to the more defensible, more strategically placed Fort Sumter in the middle of Charleston Harbor shortly after South Carolina withdrew from the Union. He and his men held the fort until April 14, 1861, when, out of supplies, badly outnumbered, and outgunned, he surrendered after a fierce artillery attack led by one of his former West Point students.

Angela (TWWQ)

One of Gwen Sullivan's few friends from high school, a gifted musician who could play any instrument she touched but could barely spell. When Gwen returns home after dropping out of college, she learns that Angela left town the day after graduation to become a session musician in Nashville.

Susan B. Anthony (TQL)

A founding member of the Women's National Loyal League who hopes to obtain the Union Quilters' assistance in gathering signatures for their petitions calling for Congress to free all the slaves at the earliest practicable date. Years later, Eleanor Lockwood Bergstrom meets Miss Anthony when she tags along with her nanny to a suffragists' meeting.

Ares (TCCQ)

Julia Merchaud's new agent who takes over after Maury Walzer retires; the nephew of one of Hollywood's most powerful directors and as aggressive as his name would suggest.

Asa (TLQ)

Colonel Robert Harper's enslaved valet at Harper Hall in Charleston.

Mr. Ashworth (TLQ)

Joanna North's first master, and her father.

Augustus (TLQ)

A house slave at Oak Grove.

Aya (TAQ)

An employee of Plumeria Quilts in Lahaina, Hawaii.

Ayana (TWQ)

A childhood friend of Caroline McClure's and a member of her bridal party, Ayana is Ethiopian and spent two years in Waterford when her father worked as a visiting professor at Waterford College. She currently lives with her husband in Manhattan, where she works on Wall Street.

Rick Balrud (TMQ)

Judy Nguyen DiNardo's former graduate school classmate who recruits her for a faculty position at the University of Pennsylvania.

Ana Barclay (TQH)

A daughter of Rosa Diaz Barclay and John Barclay, eight years old at the time of *TQH* and *SR*. She suffers from a mysterious wasting illness that has claimed the lives of several of her siblings.

Angela Barclay (SR)

A daughter of Rosa Diaz Barclay and John Barclay, the third of Rosa's children.

Donald Barclay (TQH)

John Barclay's father.

Evelyn Barclay (TQH)

John Barclay's mother.

John Barclay (TQH)

Rosa Diaz Barclay's violent and jealous husband, father to John Jr., Ana, Pedro, and Miguel Barclay. He works as a rye farmer and postmaster in the Arboles Valley until he is tempted by less scrupulous but more lucrative endeavors.

John Barclay Jr. (SR)

The eldest son of Rosa Diaz Barclay and John Barclay.

Lupita Barclay (TQH)

Rosa Diaz Barclay's seventh child and her second by her childhood sweetheart, Lars Jorgensen.

Maria Barclay (SR)

A daughter of Rosa Diaz Barclay and John Barclay.

Marta Barclay (TQH)

Rosa Diaz Barclay's eldest child, twelve years old at the time of *TQH* and *SR*. Everyone in the Arboles Valley assumes that she is the daughter of John Barclay, Rosa's husband, but when Marta is twelve, she discovers that her father is actually her mother's childhood sweetheart, Lars Jorgensen. She is named after Rosa's paternal grandmother.

Pedro Barclay (SR)

A son of Rosa Diaz Barclay and John Barclay.

Rosa Diaz Barclay (TQH)

As a young woman, the beautiful, passionate Rosa Diaz is torn between two rivals for her affection: a hardworking if temperamental Southern California rye farmer who offers her security, and a man who truly loves her but is drawn to drink—and belongs to the family who now owns the ranch her family once cherished, the family her mother cannot forgive. When forced to choose between them in a moment of desperation and fear, Rosa chooses presumed security over love, but the marriage that follows is fraught with unhappiness and tragedy.

Kathleen Barrett (TRQ)

The daughter of Rosemary Cullen and great-great-granddaughter of Thomas Nelson and Dorothea Granger Nelson.

Mrs. Barrows (TUQ)

A middle-aged Union Quilter who runs the Barrows Inn almost single-handedly when her husband and two eldest sons enlist in the Union army.

David Barrows (TUQ)

The second-eldest son of Rufus Barrows, a private in the Forty-ninth Pennsylvania Volunteers, Company L.

Rufus Barrows (TUQ)

The proprietor of the Barrows Inn in Water's Ford, Pennsylvania, and a rather inept private in the Forty-ninth Pennsylvania Volunteers, Company L.

Bartholomew (TLQ)

Miss Evangeline's cousin and Aunt Lucretia's son; a resident of Charleston, South Carolina.

William Bastwick (TUQ)

A gentleman of Washington City and longtime friend of Thomas Nelson's father who assists Gerda Bergstrom and Charlotte Claverton Granger on their journey to Richmond. He is a gray-haired man with thick muttonchops.

Horace Bauer (TUQ)

The mayor of Water's Ford, Pennsylvania, during the Civil War, the successor of Philip Deakins. A red-faced, stocky man with a fondness for his own home-brewed beer, he shattered an ankle in a fall from a horse in childhood and the bones did not heal properly, leaving him with a pronounced limp that precludes him from enlisting in the Union army.

Miss Bauer (TRQ)

A schoolteacher in Creek's Crossing, Pennsylvania; the daughter of Horace Bauer.

Gordon Beck (TUQ)

An unpleasant, angry Copperhead living in the Elm Creek Valley who threatens to set his dogs on Dorothea Granger Nelson and her friends when they visit his farm seeking signatures for the Women's National Loyal League petition calling for the prompt abolition of slavery.

Agnes Bergstrom (TQA)

See Agnes Emberly.

Anneke Stahl Bergstrom (TQA)

The youngest of the three founders of Elm Creek Farm, Anneke marries Hans Bergstrom after her fiancé fails to meet her upon her arrival in America from Germany. Anneke is torn between pleasing her husband, who expects her to fulfill the traditional duties of wife and mother, and pursuing her own dream of running a thriving seamstress's shop. While her devotion to her family is one of her greatest strengths, it also makes her susceptible to deceit when unscrupulous enemies play on her fears for her family's safety.

Clara Bergstrom (TQA)

An aunt of Sylvia Bergstrom Compson who died of influenza at the age of thirteen, two years before Sylvia was born.

David Bergstrom (TQA)

One of two boys known to the people of the Elm Creek Valley as the twin sons of Hans and Anneke Bergstrom.

Eleanor Lockwood Bergstrom (TQA)

The younger of two daughters born to a wealthy department store magnate, Eleanor suffered from poor health as a child and was not expected to survive into adulthood. Virtually ignored by her distant and self-absorbed parents, Eleanor is raised by her nanny, an independent and radical woman who teaches Eleanor to think for herself rather than blindly follow convention. When her elder sister elopes with her father's business rival, Eleanor is expected to secure her family's waning fortunes by marrying her sister's jilted fiancé, but she defies her parents by marrying Frederick Bergstrom for love. Though estranged from her parents, Eleanor never regrets her decision and eventually becomes the mother of three children, including Sylvia.

Elizabeth "Bitsy" Reese Bergstrom (TQA)

Sylvia Bergstrom Compson's paternal grandmother, a woman of Scottish and Welsh heritage given to superstitious beliefs.

Frederick Bergstrom (TQA)

The eldest son of David and Elizabeth Bergstrom, Frederick begins learning the family trade, horse breeding, at an early age. At eleven he meets his future wife, Eleanor Lockwood, while traveling with his father on business for Bergstrom Thoroughbreds; eight years later he helps her escape a hastily arranged, financially motivated marriage by declaring his love—and offering her a ride away from her parents' home. Stationed overseas as a cavalry officer in World War I, he returns home to devote himself to his wife, children, and the family business, eventually succeeding his aging father as the head of Bergstrom Thoroughbreds.

George Bergstrom (TCQ)

The father of Elizabeth Bergstrom Nelson and husband of Millie Bergstrom. At his wife's insistence, he gave up his share of Elm Creek Manor and the family business, Bergstrom Thoroughbreds, in order to work for his father-in-law, a hotelier in Harrisburg, Pennsylvania. Quietly, but not as clandestinely as he believes, George turns to alcohol to numb himself to the sting of life's disappointments.

Gerda Bergstrom (TQA)

In 1856, Gerda Bergstrom leaves her home in Baden-Baden, Germany, for a new life in America after the man she thought was her true love marries another young woman for her wealth. She eagerly takes to the American egalitarian ideal and becomes involved in abolitionism and the women's suffrage movement. Unlike her sister-in-law Anneke, Gerda despises sewing and learns to quilt only so that she might participate in the stimulating political discussions that take place at the home of the leader of the quilting circle. One of the Creek's Crossing Eight arrested and jailed in 1859 for concealing fugitive slaves, she remains undaunted and continues to fight for causes of liberty and social reform throughout her life. Disappointed in love a second time by her best friend's brother, Jonathan Granger, she nevertheless remains steadfast in her affection for him despite his marriage to another.

Hans Bergstrom (TQA)

Confident and independent, Hans prefers to make his own way in the world, but he is not above taking advantage of fools if he believes they deserve their misfortune. Though Hans takes ownership of Elm Creek Farm through somewhat questionable means, his steadfast, industrious efforts to establish himself in America and his devotion to his wife, Anneke, reveal his true strengths of character. An isolationist at heart, Hans prefers to mind his own business and leave the fight for the abolition of slavery to his sister, Gerda.

Lawrence Bergstrom (TQH)

Elizabeth Bergstrom Nelson's elder brother.

Lily Bergstrom (TQL)

The wife of Richard Bergstrom and daughter-in-law of David and Elizabeth Reese Bergstrom.

Louis Bergstrom (TQL)

The second-eldest of the five children of David and Elizabeth Reese Bergstrom, killed in action in France during World War I.

Lucinda Bergstrom (TQA)

Sylvia's great-aunt, the youngest daughter of Hans and Anneke Bergstrom, founders of Elm Creek Farm and the first members of the family to come to the United States from Germany. An accomplished quilter and baker, Lucinda is the caretaker of family history and entrances young Sylvia with her stories of the manor's earliest years, although she does not share all of her secrets. Lucinda never marries, a fact that is of no concern to Sylvia as a child but piques her curiosity in later years.

Lydia Bergstrom (TCQ)

A great-aunt of Sylvia Bergstrom Compson, daughter of Hans and Anneke Bergstrom. Sylvia and Anna Del Maso discover her apron collection sewn from old feed sack cottons as they prepare the kitchen of Elm Creek Manor for remodeling.

Maude Bergstrom (TQL)

The wife of Louis Bergstrom and daughter-in-law of David and Elizabeth Reese Bergstrom.

Millicent "Millie" Bergstrom (TCQ)

Elizabeth Bergstrom Nelson's mother, the wife of George Bergstrom.

Nellie Bergstrom (TQH)

William Bergstrom's wife.

Richard Bergstrom (1) (TQL)

The third-eldest child of David and Elizabeth Reese Bergstrom, killed in action in France in World War I.

Richard Bergstrom (2) (TQA)

Sylvia Bergstrom Compson's younger brother and the first husband of Agnes Emberly, killed in the South Pacific during World War II. He was named for his uncle, a soldier killed in World War I.

Stephen Bergstrom (TQA)

One of two boys known to the people of the Elm Creek Valley as the twin sons of Hans and Anneke Bergstrom.

William Bergstrom (TQA)

An uncle of Sylvia, Claudia, and Richard Bergstrom; Frederick Bergstrom's youngest brother.

William Bernier (TCCQ)

The acclaimed producer of *A Patchwork Life,* a film starring Cross-Country Quilter Julia Merchaud.

Jeremy Bernstein (TRQ)

A Ph.D. student of history at Waterford College. He and Summer Sullivan are romantically involved for a time, but their relationship eventually falls apart when conflicting career goals separate them. Later he falls in love with his friend and neighbor Anna Del Maso. His brown eyes are warm and friendly behind round, wire-rimmed glasses, and his curly dark brown hair usually falls into his eyes. Later in his career, Jeremy is appointed the Abel Wright Professor of American History at Waterford College.

Auntie Bess (TLQ)

An elderly slave who lives with Tavia at Oak Grove.

Beth (TWWQ)

A cousin of Judy Nguyen DiNardo.

David Beuhler (TUQ)

The postmaster of Gettysburg, Pennsylvania, who hosts Gerda Bergstrom, Henry Reinhart, and Harriet Reinhart during their visit to hear President Lincoln deliver an address at the new national cemetery.

Aruna Bhansali (TNYQ)

The current owner of the childhood home of Eleanor Lockwood Bergstrom, a lovely residence on Fifth Avenue in Manhattan across from Central Park.

Bill (TQA)

An older and far more experienced candidate interviewing for the same jobs Sarah McClure is seeking soon after she moves to Waterford, Pennsylvania.

Franklin Birch (COQ)

A Massachusetts man who traveled west along the Oregon Trail in the mid-nineteenth century with his wife, Harriet Findley Birch.

Harriet Findley Birch (COQ)

A gifted quilter and former mill girl who traveled with her husband from Lowell, Massachusetts, to Salem, Oregon, along the Oregon Trail around 1854. She left behind a remarkable quilt, a one-hundred-block sampler Maggie Flynn discovers many decades later at a garage sale in Sacramento.

Jason Birch (COQ)

A great-grandson of Harriet Findley Birch, who provides Maggie Flynn with scant but precious biographic information about the intriguing quilter.

Dottie Blum (COQ)

A resident of Ocean View Hills and member of the Courtyard Quilters.

Mr. Borchard (TCCQ)

A teacher for whom Vinnie Burkholder does mending and sewing to earn money to help out at home.

Steve Boyer (RR)

The husband of Judy Nguyen DiNardo and father of Emily DiNardo-Boyer. Steve is a journalist with the *Waterford Register,* and after the family moves to Philadelphia, he takes a position on the staff of the *Philadelphia Inquirer.*

Brandon (TCCQ)

A medical school student at the University of Minnesota and the fiancé of Donna Jorgenson's eldest daughter, Lindsay.

Annette Brannon (TMQ)

A professor of American studies at Waterford College who is appointed department chair instead of Gwen Sullivan, who was hoping for the job.

Adam Brauer (TCCQ)

The father of Cross-Country Quilter Vinnie Burkholder; the brother of Lynn Brauer.

Frank Brauer (TCCQ)

The elder brother of Cross-Country Quilter Vinnie Burkholder, called Frankie as a boy.

Lynn Brauer (TCCQ)

The aunt of Cross-Country Quilter Vinnie Burkholder and her guardian after her mother's death.

Aaron Braun (TSCQ)

A miller who runs an Underground Railroad station in Woodfall, Pennsylvania; a barrel-chested man with sandy hair and whiskers.

Margaret Braun (TSCQ)

A miller's wife who runs an Underground Railroad station in Woodfall, Pennsylvania; a woman with piercing eyes and streaks of white in her dark hair.

Dr. Bremigan (TSCQ)

A physician in Creek's Crossing, Pennsylvania, who served as Jonathan Granger's first mentor.

Brennan Family, The (TCQ)

The family that owned property along the Craigmiles' north pasture in the Elm Creek Valley.

Brian (1) (COQ)

A former boyfriend of Maggie Flynn, with whom she breaks up just before her twenty-fifth birthday.

Brian (2) (TAQ)

A thin, multi-pierced and multi-tattooed zipline guide with Skyline Eco Adventures in Hawaii.

Brianna (TWQ)

The young receptionist for University Realty during the period when Gregory Krolich, Realtor and nemesis of Sarah McClure, tries to have the Union Hall demolished.

Dr. Bronson (TSCQ)

A physician in Baltimore, Maryland, who serves as Jonathan Granger's mentor.

Henry "Box" Brown (TSCQ)

A slave who famously escaped to freedom by having himself packed into a wooden crate and shipped from Virginia to Philadelphia.

Luther Burbank (SR)

A renowned horticulturalist who developed the Shasta daisy and many other strains and varieties of plants. He was a longtime resident of Santa Rosa and a friend of Beatrice Vanelli.

Lavinia "Vinnie" Brauer Burkholder (TCCQ)

Octogenarian Vinnie Burkholder is one of the first quilters to attend Elm Creek Quilt Camp. A longtime resident of Dayton, Ohio, Vinnie is a member of a quilt guild that meets in her retirement community, where her favorite part of the meeting is the show-and-tell. She often selects a new project based upon the block name rather than its appearance and has a particular affinity for the Wedding Ring, Double Wedding Ring, and Steps to the Altar patterns. Vinnie prefers bright colors, which reflect her sunny outlook on life, and she is always eager to learn a new quilting technique or try out a new gadget.

Lynn Burkholder (TCCQ)

The youngest of Sam and Lavinia Burkholder's three children and their only daughter, named after Vinnie's beloved aunt, Lynn Brauer.

Sam Burkholder (TCCQ)

The late husband of Cross-Country Quilter Lavinia "Vinnie" Burkholder, with whom she has four children.

Dante Cacchione (SR)

A third-generation vintner in Santa Rosa, California, the owner of Cacchione Vineyards. He is a short, powerfully built man in his midfifties, with salt-and-pepper hair, a neatly trimmed goatee, and a deep, rich voice.

Dominic Cacchione (SR)

The twenty-two-year-old eldest child of Dante and Giuditta Cacchione; husband of Mabel, father to infant Sophia; serious, hardworking, and responsible.

Francesca Cacchione (SR)

The eldest daughter of Dante and Giuditta Cacchione who befriends Rosa Diaz Barclay, whom she knows as Rose Ottesen, upon Rosa's arrival in Sonoma County.

Gina Cacchione (SR)

A younger daughter of Dante and Giuditta Cacchione; one of seven siblings.

Giuditta Cacchione (SR)

The wife of Dante Cacchione. She is in her midfifties, with merry eyes and sun-browned face and hands. She wears her hair—so dark brown that it is almost black, except for a patch of white at the crown—pulled back into a loose knot at the nape of her neck, and the lines around her mouth and eyes give evidence to a ready smile. She stands a good three inches taller than her husband, and her solid, sturdy frame conveys strength and comfort.

Mabel Cacchione (SR)

The daughter of a Healdsburg vintner, wife of Dominic Cacchione, and mother of infant Sophia.

Mario Cacchione (SR)

A younger son of Dante and Giuditta Cacchione; one of seven siblings.

Sophia Cacchione (SR)

The infant daughter of Dominic and Mabel Cacchione.

Vincenzo "Vince" Cacchione (SR)

The second-eldest son and third-eldest child of Dante and Giuditta Cacchione, about sixteen years old at the time of *SR*.

Brent Callahan (RR)

The son of Mary Beth Callahan, a former friend of Diane Sonnenberg's youngest son, Todd, and one of the youths who vandalized Bonnie Markham's quilt shop.

Mary Beth Callahan (TQA)

Diane Sonnenberg's next-door neighbor and nemesis, a longtime president of the Waterford Quilting Guild.

Roger Callahan (TMQ)

The husband of Mary Beth Callahan, often impatient with his wife when he isn't ignoring her outright.

Callie (COQ)

Anna Del Maso's favorite work-study student with Waterford College Food Services.

Cameron (TWQ)

A friend and bridesmaid of Caroline McClure, Cameron works as a barista and part-time musician in Chicago.

Mr. Carew (TWWQ)

Bonnie Markham's mother's boss.

Carrie (TWWQ)

A cousin of Judy Nguyen DiNardo.

Carter Family, The (TSCQ)

The Nelson family's tenants who work Two Bears Farm until Thomas Nelson returns to Creek's Crossing.

Mrs. Cass (TNYQ)

A friend of Josephine Compson and a member of the Baltimore Quilting Circle.

Charlie (1) (COQ)

One of Russell McIntyre's best friends from college and the best man at his wedding to Elaine. His wife is Christine, another college friend.

Charlie (2) (SR)

A ranch hand at Sonoma Rose Vineyards and Orchard.

Billy Chester (TLQ)

A younger son of Josiah and Caroline Chester who died of yellow fever.

Caroline Chester (TLQ)

The wife of Josiah Chester, one of the many mistresses Joanna North must endure in her years as a slave.

Elliot Chester (TLQ)

The second-oldest child and eldest son of Stephen Chester and his first wife, besotted with the military and eager to enlist when war breaks out, although he is underage.

Josiah Chester (TRQ)

The owner of Greenfields Plantation in Wentworth County, Virginia, a onetime owner of the slave Joanna North.

Martha Chester (TLQ)

Stephen Chester's second wife, and his children's former governess and tutor. She is only four years older than her eldest stepdaughter, with whom she is frequently in conflict. A native of Philadelphia, she prefers to dress in somber browns and dark blues, wears her hair parted in the middle and pulled back into a smooth knot at the nape of her neck, and studies the world through round spectacles.

Mason Chester (TLQ)

The eldest son of Josiah Chester. When he was a toddler, the slave Joanna North, only five years old herself, was charged with looking after him.

Mother Chester (TLQ)

Josiah Chester's mother, the dowager mistress of Greenfields Plantation.

Stephen Chester (TLQ)

The master of Oak Grove plantation on Edisto Island in South Carolina. He is Josiah Chester's elder, more competent brother and a onetime master of Joanna North. He has dark, curious blue eyes in a heavy face and hair the color of faded corn silk, thin on top, thicker in the beard and sideburns, and flecked with gray.

Agnes Chevalier (TQA)

See Agnes Emberly.

Mr. Childs (TUQ)

The librarian of the Water's Ford Public Library and, later, a soldier with the Forty-ninth Pennsylvania Volunteers, Company L.

Christine (COQ)

One of Russell McIntyre's best friends from college, she is married to Charlie, another of Russell's closest friends.

Claire (TQL)

A young, blond, kindhearted library assistant at Penn State Hazleton who allows Sylvia Bergstrom Compson and Andrew Cooper in from the cold to tour the exhibit *The Art of Women Pioneers,* even though the building is officially closed for winter break.

Angela Clark (TCCQ)

A quilt camper from Erie, Pennsylvania, who wants to make a memorial quilt for her late son's grieving best friend.

Professor Clarke (TQA)

A professor who teaches advanced auditing at Penn State. Sarah McClure and Brian Turnbull are both former students.

Clifford Clarkston (SR)

A neighbor of the Cacchione family who satisfies a long-held grudge by betraying Dante and Giuditta to the Prohibition Bureau.

Millicent Claverton (TRQ)

A Union Quilter whose family lives on the farm adjacent to Jacob Kuehner's in Creek's Crossing, Pennsylvania. She is the mother of Charlotte Claverton, Jonathan Granger's intended.

Clyde (COQ)

A friend of Joe and Gretchen Hartley's from Ambridge, Pennsylvania; a veteran, married to Jan.

Harriet Beals Colcraft (TNYQ)

Born in Chester County, Pennsylvania, to a family of Quakers, Harriet Beals was a lifelong pacifist and abolitionist. She married John Colcraft, the second son of a South Carolina planter who disowned him when he renounced slavery. She and her husband settled in New York, where she worked tirelessly for social justice despite dangers to herself, such as when she valiantly rescued twenty-nine children from the Colored Orphan Asylum when it was looted and burned by angry mobs during the draft riots of July 1863.

John Colcraft (TNYQ)

A South Carolinian by birth, John Colcraft meets a Quaker woman named Harriet Beals while traveling to the North on business for his father's cotton plantation. By 1858, Colcraft has embraced Harriet's faith, renounced slavery, and married her. The couple settle in Philadelphia, where Colcraft embarks upon a remarkable career as an artist and political cartoonist. As his fame—or as some would have it, notoriety—grows, he comes to New York and becomes a regular artist for *Harper's*. Soon thereafter, he and his wife build the Upper East Side brownstone now known as the 1863 House.

Colleen (TGQ)

A high school senior and employee of the String Theory Quilt Shop in Summit Pass, Pennsylvania.

Mrs. Collins (TSCQ)

A member of the Creek's Crossing Library Board and the wife of a banker.

Professor Collins (TCCQ)

One of Lindsay Jorgenson's professors at the University of Minnesota.

James Compson (TQA)

Born in 1918, James Compson is the youngest son of Robert Compson, whose Maryland horse farm is Bergstrom Thoroughbreds' strongest rival. James is twenty when he introduces himself to sixteen-year-old Sylvia at the Pennsylvania State Fair after admiring her riding. Decades later, Sylvia recalls her first impression of James as "quite handsome, tall and strong with dark eyes and dark, curly hair." They meet again the following autumn at the Pennsylvania State College, when Sylvia's father is teaching a course and James is a student. Romance blossoms, and when they marry four years later, James leaves his family business to help Sylvia's father run Bergstrom Thoroughbreds. In March of 1944 he enlists in the army to keep an eye on Sylvia's brother, who impulsively joined with his best friend. He is killed in a tragic "friendly fire" incident in the New Hebrides (now Vanuatu) in the summer of 1945.

Josephine Compson (TNYQ)

Sylvia Bergstrom Compson's mother-in-law, a wise and loving woman who, like her husband, celebrates her son James's happiness when he marries Sylvia Bergstrom and welcomes her into the family with great joy. Upon James's death in World War II, Josephine offers Sylvia comfort and sanctuary at Compson's Resolution, the family horse farm on the Chesapeake Bay in Maryland, and gently encourages her to build a new life for herself. She longs for Sylvia to reconcile with her estranged sister, Claudia, and believes Sylvia's rightful place is home at Elm Creek Manor.

Mary Compson (TNYQ)

The daughter of Robert and Josephine Compson, sister of James Compson. She graduated from the University of Maryland a few months after the attack on Pearl Harbor, and soon thereafter married a congressman and moved to Washington.

Robert Compson (TQA)

A Maryland horse breeder and business rival of Frederick Bergstrom, third-generation leader of Bergstrom Thoroughbreds. He is also the father of James Compson, Sylvia Bergstrom's future husband.

James Conner (TLQ)

A Union soldier with the Sixth Connecticut Infantry whom Joanna North encounters during her attempt to flee Charleston.

Connie (TWWQ)

A frequent Elm Creek Quilt Camper and member of the Flying Saucer Sisters.

Connor (COQ)

A stay-at-home father whose children are in a playgroup with Karen Wise's sons.

Mrs. Cook (TNYQ)

A friend of Josephine Compson and a member of the Baltimore Quilting Circle.

Andrew Cooper (TQA)

Andrew Cooper has admired Sylvia from the time he was her younger brother's boyhood friend. When Andrew and Sylvia reunite after a long separation, their friendship soon grows into mutual affection, and then blossoms into love. He asks Sylvia several times to marry him before she finally agrees, moved by revelations from the journal of her great-grandfather's sister, Gerda Bergstrom, not to let love pass her by. Andrew enjoys the outdoors and travel, and his favorite pastime is fishing. A true gentleman, he is astonished and troubled when his grown children do not welcome the news of his engagement to Sylvia. While he has never made a quilt, he understands and appreciates all the time, energy, and creativity that go into each project.

He is proud of Sylvia's accomplishments and supports her in any way he can, including carrying her bags at quilt shows so she can purchase more fabric.

Angela Cooper (TQL)

The elder daughter of Bob and Cathy Cooper and granddaughter of Andrew and Katy Cooper.

Bob Cooper (TQL)

Andrew Cooper's son, living in the town of Santa Susana in Southern California with his wife, Cathy, and their two daughters.

Cathy Cooper (RR)

The wife of Bob Cooper, daughter-in-law of Andrew Cooper, and mother of Angela and Kayla Cooper.

Katy Cooper (RR)

Andrew Cooper's wife of almost fifty years, a dark-haired, widowed schoolteacher whom he meets after returning home from the service in World War II.

Kayla Cooper (TQL)

The younger daughter of Bob and Cathy Cooper and granddaughter of Andrew and Katy Cooper.

Sally Jane Cooper (TCQ)

Andrew Cooper's younger sister.

Alice Corville (TQL)

The wife of Theodore Corville and mother of Edwin Corville; a friend of Gertrude Drayton-Smith Lockwood.

Edwin Corville (TQL)

The wealthy, jilted fiancé of both Abigail Lockwood Drury and her younger sister, Eleanor Lockwood Bergstrom.

Theodore Corville (TQL)

A prosperous department store magnate who owns shops in Manhattan, Boston, and New Rochelle. Charles Lockwood seeks to forge a partnership with him by marrying one of his daughters to Theodore Corville's eldest son.

Courtney (TWWQ)

Emily DiNardo-Boyer's childhood best friend.

Edith Craigmile (TCQ)

A neighbor of the Bergstrom family during the Great Depression and a particular friend of Eleanor Lockwood Bergstrom.

Malcolm Craigmile (TCQ)

A neighbor of the Bergstrom family during the Great Depression. The Craigmile farm is less than a mile from Elm Creek Farm, and the two families have been friends and loyal neighbors since the 1850s.

Dwight Crowell (SR)

A relentless, unscrupulous Prohibition agent who makes life miserable for grape ranchers and vintners throughout Sonoma County. Except for the thin white scar running from his right earlobe to his jaw and the arrogant gleam in his eye, Agent Crowell bears a strong resemblance to Lars Jorgensen, which Rosa Diaz Barclay finds sharply unsettling.

Robert Cullen (TQL)

An elderly Waterford physician during the Spanish Flu pandemic.

Rosemary Cullen (TRQ)

Great-granddaughter of Thomas Nelson and Dorothea Granger Nelson.

Abner Currier (TSCQ)

A printer in Water's Ford, Pennsylvania, publisher of the *Water's Ford Register,* and private in the Forty-ninth Pennsylvania Volunteers, Company L. He is married to Mary Schultz Currier, one of Dorothea Granger Nelson's dearest friends.

Mary Schultz Currier (TSCQ)

A Union Quilter and one of Dorothea Granger Nelson's dearest friends. A tall, slender woman with light brown hair, she works at her father's shop, Schultz's Printers, in Water's Ford, Pennsylvania.

Danielle (TAQ)

One of the Laulima Quilters in Lahaina, Hawaii.

Gabriel Daniels (TCCQ)

The ex-husband of Grace Daniels and the father of Justine Daniels. He is a carpenter.

Grace Daniels (TCCQ)

Respected worldwide as a quilt artist and historian, Grace Daniels resigned her position as a curator at the de Young Museum in San Francisco to focus on research, consulting, and quilting. Although a diagnosis of multiple sclerosis once threatened the viability of her art, new medications have held the progression of her disease in check, and her newfound hope has brought a remarkable resurgence in her creativity. Grace's quilts have been displayed in museums and galleries across the nation and in several foreign countries. A friend of Sylvia Bergstrom Compson's for more than twenty years, she often helps the Elm Creek Quilters investigate the provenance of antique quilts.

Joshua Daniels (TCCQ)

The son of Justine Daniels and grandson of Grace Daniels, a thoughtful and studious boy who resembles his mother.

Justine Daniels (TCCQ)

The daughter of Cross-Country Quilter Grace Daniels and mother of young Joshua, a law student who volunteers at a women's shelter in San Francisco.

Daria (TGQ)

Pauline Tucker's predecessor as treasurer of the Cherokee Rose Quilters.

Amelia Langley Davis (TQL)

Amelia Langley Davis was born in England, immigrated to the United States, and worked several years as a nanny for the Lockwood family in New York, where she became involved in the workers' rights movement. Upon moving to Boston, and later, to Lowell, Massachusetts, she played a key role in the labor union organizing among garment workers. After serving a prison sentence for "seditious utterings" at a labor rally during World War I, she devoted herself to improving the conditions for incarcerated women, including the establishment of several "residential workhouses," where recently released female convicts lived and learned a trade as they adjusted to life outside prison walls. Although she and Eleanor Lockwood Bergstrom keep in touch through letters after Amelia's dismissal as Eleanor's nanny and often promise to reunite, they never see each other again.

Charles Davis (TQL)

The Boston landlord, and later, husband, of Amelia Langley Davis. In a letter to Eleanor Lockwood Bergstrom, Amelia describes him as her "dear friend and comrade."

Edith Deakins (TSCQ)

A member of the Creek's Crossing Library Board and the wife of Philip Deakins.

Philip Deakins (TSCQ)

The owner of a general store in Creek's Crossing, Pennsylvania, who also served a term as the town's mayor.

Alegra Del Bene (SR)

The strikingly beautiful, Italian-born wife of widowed vintner Paulo Del Bene, who is more than twice her age. They have three young children, one of whom becomes the favorite playmate of Rosa Diaz Barclay's son Miguel.

Gino Del Bene (SR)

The youngest of Paulo and Alegra Del Bene's three children, a favorite playmate of Miguel Barclay.

Paulo Del Bene (SR)

A longtime Santa Rosa vintner who was fortunate enough to secure a sacramental wine permit soon after Prohibition began. Once a grieving widower, he and his second wife, Alegra, have three young children, and he has four adult children from his first marriage.

Gina Del Maso–Bernstein (TWQ)

Gina, the daughter of Anna Del Maso and Jeremy Bernstein, is the assistant chef at Elm Creek Manor and Caroline McClure's maid of honor.

Steven Deneford (TCCQ)

The director who replaces Ellen Henderson on *A Patchwork Life;* a longtime colleague of the producer William Bernier.

Dennis (RR)

Gwen Sullivan's ne'er-do-well boyfriend with whom she travels the country after dropping out of college and the father of her only child, Summer Sullivan. He plays no role whatsoever in Summer's life, but as the years go by Gwen occasionally hears news of him through mutual friends—that he married, divorced, opened a head shop, chained himself to a tree in Oregon to protect it from loggers, and other such adventures.

Carlos Diaz (TQH)

Rosa Diaz Barclay's younger brother and a sixth-generation Californian on his mother's side. During *TQH,* he is employed as a handyman at the Grand Union Hotel in the Arboles Valley.

Isabel Rodriguez Diaz (TQH)

Born in 1870 on El Rancho Triunfo in Southern California, Isabel learns about heartbreak at an early age when her family is forced to sell their once-prosperous lands after suffering through a lengthy drought. She is fifteen when her mother's death forces her to leave school to care for her younger brother and sister. Despite the blessings of a happy marriage and two beloved children, throughout her life Isabel mourns the loss of the ranch—and she cannot forgive those she believes stole it from the Rodriguez family.

Miguel Diaz (TQH)

The husband of Isabel Rodriguez Diaz and the father of Rosa Diaz Barclay and Carlos Diaz.

Dr. Frank DiCarlo (TRQ)

A Penn State archeology professor who examines the ruins of an old cabin on the Bergstrom estate.

Gertrude Diegel (TQH)

The shrewd proprietor of the Grand Union Hotel in the early twentieth century; the employer of Rosa Diaz Barclay and her brother, Carlos Diaz.

Officer Di Marco (TCCQ)

A police officer in Monroe, Ohio, who helps Megan Donohue find her missing son, Robby.

Grandma DiNardo (TWWQ)

Judy Nguyen DiNardo's stepfather's mother. She had a long, thin nose with the slightest hook to it, large gray-blue eyes, and a small mouth. Judy never saw her without her long graying blond hair in a French twist or her delicate pearls around her neck.

John DiNardo (TWWQ)

Judy Nguyen DiNardo's adopted father—her "real father," as she considers him, the man who married her mother when she was still quite young.

Miranda DiNardo (TWWQ)

Judy Nguyen DiNardo's eldest cousin.

Susan DiNardo (TWWQ)

Judy Nguyen DiNardo's cousin and beloved friend.

Tuyet Nguyen DiNardo (RR)

Judy Nguyen DiNardo's mother. Born in Vietnam, she fled Saigon and came to the United States with the infant Judy, her child by an American army doctor, Robert Scharpelsen.

Emily DiNardo-Boyer (TQA)

The daughter of founding Elm Creek Quilter Judy Nguyen DiNardo, Emily begins piecing quilts in the fourth grade, sewing her own clothes in the fifth, and working with a serger in middle school. Favoring an amalgam of quilting, weaving, and sculpture, Emily goes on to earn a BFA from the California College of the Arts in San Francisco and an MFA in fiber and material studies from the School of the Art Institute of Chicago. Professionally, she goes by the name "Emily DiNardo."

Linus Donne (TSCQ)

A county constable who served in the Elm Creek Valley during the antebellum era.

Gina Donohue (TCCQ)

Keith Donohue's second wife, young and pretty and earnestly eager to win over her reluctant stepson, Robby Donohue.

Keith Donohue (TCCQ)

A corporate sales manager and ex-husband of Cross-Country Quilter Megan Donohue. When their young son, Robby, was two years old, Keith confessed to an affair and moved out. He has since remarried and lives in Portland, Oregon.

Megan Donohue (TCCQ)

Megan attends Elm Creek Quilt Camp for the first time after winning a week's stay in a quilting magazine's design contest. The divorced single mother later finds new love and happiness thanks to the encouragement—some might say meddling—of her friend Vinnie Burkholder, who was determined to find a suitable sweetheart for her favorite grandson, Adam. The couple, their young daughter, and Megan's son from her first marriage, Robby, live in the greater Cincinnati area, where Megan is an aerospace engineer and Adam is a high school math teacher.

Robert "Robby" Donohue (TCCQ)

The son of Megan Donohue and Keith Donohue, a quiet and often lonely boy struggling with his parents' divorce and his father's remarriage.

Robert Keith Donohue (TCCQ)

The son of Keith Donohue and his second wife, Gina—her first child, his second. Keith's son from a previous marriage, who is also named Robert, although he goes by Robby, is stunned and hurt that his new half brother has been given his name, and he takes no comfort in his father's reminders that he is Robert Michael, not Robert Keith, so it really isn't the same.

Dora (TLQ)

Aunt Lucretia's maid, a slave.

Father Doug (TWWQ)

Diane Sonnenberg's pastor in Waterford, Pennsylvania.

Lewis Henry Douglass (TLQ)

A sergeant major with the Fifty-fourth Massachusetts Volunteer Infantry, the son of famed abolitionist and former slave Frederick Douglass.

Dove (TLQ)

The housekeeper at Oak Grove plantation and a friend and ally to Joanna North.

Adam Drover (TUQ)

The husband of Abel Wright's younger sister, Frances.

Frances Wright Drover (TUQ)

Abel Wright's younger sister, married to Adam Drover.

Abigail Lockwood Drury (TQL)

The elder sister of Eleanor Lockwood Bergstrom who throws her father's business plans into upheaval when she abandons her fiancé, the son of her father's prospective business partner, in order to elope with Herbert Drury, her father's rival and the father of her best friend.

Herbert Drury (TQL)

Charles Lockwood's chief business competitor and bitter enemy—and later, his son-in-law.

Claire Duffield (TAQ)

Bonnie's friend from college and founder of the Aloha Quilt Camp in Lahaina on Maui. At the time of *TAQ*, she is Bonnie's age, fifty-six—although Bonnie thinks Claire could easily pass for ten years younger—petite and slender, with wheat-brown, shoulder-length hair.

Eric Duffield (TAQ)

Claire Duffield's husband, a retired military officer residing in Lahaina on Maui. He is tall, slender, and tan with hard, wiry muscles from years of calisthenics and blond hair threaded with silvery white.

Ida Mary Dunbar (TLQ)

A Maryland farmwife who protects the runaway Joanna North when she believes her to be a freedwoman illegally held by slave catchers.

Johnny Dunbar (TLQ)

The young son of Maryland farmers Miles and Ida Mary Dunbar.

Miles Dunbar (TLQ)

A Maryland farmer who protects the runaway Joanna North when he believes her to be a freedwoman illegally held by slave catchers.

Ephraim Dunn (TUQ)

The husband of Abel Wright's elder sister, Louisa. In 1863, he was kidnapped and forced into slavery by Confederate troops invading Mercersburg, Pennsylvania.

Louisa Wright Dunn (TUQ)

Abel Wright's elder sister, married to Ephraim Dunn.

Pierre Duval (TQH)

(His name may be Pierre Duvon; accounts disagree.) A man killed in a barroom brawl in the 1880s whose ghost allegedly haunts the Grand Union Hotel. Some guests claim to have woken in the middle of the night to discover a man with a handlebar mustache staring at them from the foot of the bed before suddenly vanishing. He is also blamed for slamming doors, rearranging furniture, and hiding keys and hairbrushes.

Mrs. Eldridge (TWWQ)

A contemporary owner of 714 Juniper Street, a historic residence in the fashionable Society Hill neighborhood of Richardsport, Kentucky.

Elijah (TLQ)

A slave Joanna North encounters at the slave market in Charleston who tries in vain to convince a prospective customer to buy him and his family so they will remain together.

Ellie (TWWQ)

Bonnie Markham's younger sister.

Elspeth (TGQ)

A retired Penn State physics professor and co-owner of the String Theory Quilt Shop in Summit Pass, Pennsylvania.

Joseph Emberly (RR)

Agnes Emberly's second husband, a history professor at Waterford College and an antiques expert.

Laura Emberly (TCQ)

The younger of Joseph and Agnes Emberly's two daughters.

Stacey Emberly (TCQ)

The elder of Joseph and Agnes Emberly's two daughters.

Emma (TGQ)

A junior at St. Andrew's College who befriends Michaela Phillips during cheerleading tryouts.

Hiram Engle (TSCQ)

Violet Pearson Engle's second husband, the owner of a livery stable and a hotel in Creek's Crossing. Before his marriage, his prosperity had made him one of the town's most eligible bachelors despite his ample waistline and facial tic.

Violet Pearson Engle (TRQ)

Violet Pearson Engle considers herself the leader of the town's women and the authority in all matters of propriety and taste. Proud, vain, and scheming, she places her own family's well-being and prosperity above all other considerations but is careful to make it appear as if she is acting for the common good. On the issue of slavery, Violet sympathizes with southern slaveholders and believes that instead of casting their own ballots, women should endeavor to exert moral influence on their sons and husbands and nothing more. Her positions—and her attempts to force others to accept them—create tension between her and Dorothea Granger Nelson.

Enrique (TWQ)

Summer Sullivan's husband, whom she meets in graduate school at the University of Chicago.

Erika (TNYQ)

A German woman whom Sylvia Bergstrom Compson and Andrew Cooper meet during their stay at the 1863 House in Manhattan. She and her husband, Karl, are from a small village not far from Baden-Baden, the ancestral homeland of the Bergstrom family.

Patricia Escher (TWQ)

The president of the Waterford Historical Society during the campaign to save Union Hall.

Edward Everett (TUQ)

A renowned orator who delivered the main address at the dedication of the new national cemetery at Gettysburg, Pennsylvania.

Jason Fielding (TGQ)

Radio talk show host Ezra McNulty's producer.

Leonardo Fiore (TWQ)

Leo, as he prefers to be called, is Caroline McClure's fiancé and a second-grade teacher. He is tall; has thick, wavy brown hair so dark it is nearly black; and has a dimple on one cheek that appears when he smiles. Leo and Caroline met while students at Dartmouth, at a party where he impressed her with his dancing.

Madame Fortescue (TGQ)

Michaela's French professor at St. Andrew's College, a supporter of her right to try out for Tartan Crusader.

Francine (COQ)

A friend of Russell McIntyre's late wife to whom he turns for help in his initial forays into the world of quilting.

Frazier Family, The (TQH)

Farmers who bought Lars Jorgensen's share of the Jorgensen Ranch.

Douglass Frederick (TLQ)

An alias Lenore Harris uses for Joanna North's long-lost son when she writes to Elm Creek Farm on her grandmother's behalf, seeking information about him and his whereabouts.

Asuka Fujiko (TAQ)

An innovative, award-winning quilt artist from Tokyo who specializes in machine quilting techniques, one of the first three teachers appointed to the faculty of Aloha Quilt Camp.

William Lloyd Garrison (TSCQ)

A prominent abolitionist, journalist, and newspaper editor who contributes his signature to Dorothea Granger's *Authors' Album* quilt.

George (TLQ)

The footman at Harper Hall in Charleston, a slave.

Gerald (TQH)

Elizabeth Bergstrom Nelson's former beau from Harrisburg, Pennsylvania.

Gideon (TLQ)

Evangeline Chester Harper's cousin; Aunt Lucretia's youngest son.

Mr. Gilbert (TUQ)

An Elm Creek Valley farmer who worked on the construction of Union Hall and whose wife contributed ten quilt blocks to the *Loyal Union Sampler*. He is one of four men who confront Hans Bergstrom at his home and accuse him of disloyalty to the Union.

Mrs. Givens (TLQ)

Colonel Robert Harper's widowed sister, a vicious woman who beat the young slave Hannah mercilessly for playing with wooden blocks carved with letters of the alphabet.

Dr. Goodwin (SR)

An Arboles Valley physician who is unsuccessful—and is, in fact, harmful—in treating the Barclay children suffering from a mysterious wasting illness.

Gordon (COQ)

Anna Del Maso's pompous boyfriend and a Ph.D. student in English literature at Waterford College.

Charlotte Claverton Granger (TRQ)

A beautiful, dark-haired young woman of Creek's Crossing who marries Jonathan Granger in a match long planned and very much desired by their parents. She resents Gerda Bergstrom for her unabashed admiration and poorly concealed affection for Jonathan, but the two women are often obliged to work together as members of the Union Quilters.

Jeannette Granger (TUQ)

The eldest daughter and second child of Jonathan and Charlotte Granger.

Jonathan Granger (TRQ)

Dorothea Granger Nelson's younger brother and his uncle Jacob Kuehner's heir. Although Jonathan falls in love with Gerda Bergstrom, honor and duty compel him not to break off his long-standing engagement with Charlotte Claverton. A patriot and abolitionist as well as a skilled, respected surgeon, Jonathan enlists as a regimental doctor with the Forty-ninth Pennsylvania Volunteers, Company L, when the Civil War breaks out.

Lorena Kuehner Granger (TRQ)

Jonathan Granger and Dorothea Granger Nelson's mother, a Union Quilter, and one of the founders of the now-defunct utopian community of Thrift Farm.

Malcolm Granger (TQL)

A respected and skilled physician revered for his heroic efforts to treat the residents of Elm Creek Valley during the Spanish Flu pandemic of 1918, although before then he was praised as a modern thinker by some and disparaged for his strange new ideas about the cause and transmission of disease by others.

Robert Granger (1) (TRQ)

Jonathan Granger and Dorothea Granger Nelson's father, a founder of the defunct utopian community of Thrift Farm.

Robert Granger (2) (TUQ)

Jonathan and Charlotte Granger's eldest son, named after his paternal grandfather.

Susan Granger (TWQ)

The ob-gyn on call during Sarah McClure's labor, a great-granddaughter of Dr. Jonathan Granger.

Alexandra Grant (TQL)

A ninety-seven-year-old quilter from Colorado whose works are featured in an exhibit at the Rocky Mountain Quilt Museum.

Greg (TMQ)

One of the youths who vandalized Bonnie Markham's quilt shop, a former friend of Todd Sonnenberg, Diane Sonnenberg's youngest son.

Miss Gunther (TSCQ)

A "sweetly befuddled" schoolteacher in Creek's Crossing, Pennsylvania.

Arlene Gustafson (TAQ)

A traditional quilter from Nebraska and author of three bestselling pattern books; one of the first three teachers appointed to the faculty of Aloha Quilt Camp. Twice divorced and in her late fifties, she looks to Bonnie Markham as if she would be equally comfortable seated at a sewing machine or on a tractor.

Mary Haas (COQ)

A resident of Ocean View Hills and victim of Lenore Hicks's haste.

Dr. Sydney V. Haas (SR)

A physician who developed a strict dietary regimen in the 1920s that revolutionized the treatment of celiac disease.

Dr. Haines (TUQ)

A physician with the Nineteenth Indiana who serves with Jonathan Granger in the battlefield hospital on Seminary Ridge in Gettysburg.

James Hammell (TQH)

The builder of the Grand Union Hotel in Southern California's Arboles Valley.

Archibald Hammock (TUQ)

A skilled boot maker from Dallas County, Alabama, kin to Satterwhite Wilson, and a private with the Twentieth Battalion, Captain Waddell's Company, Alabama Light Artillery.

Hannah (1) (TLQ)

A young slave at Harper Hall in Charleston, rendered mute by early trauma, who emptied chamber pots, scrubbed floors, swept fireplaces, and jumped, wide-eyed, to any other task she was ordered to do.

Hannah (2) (TSCQ)

A fugitive slave passing through the Elm Creek Valley along the Underground Railroad; a daughter of Liza.

Caroline Hanneman (TQH)

An expert horsewoman and trainer at Safari World, a wild animal farm in the Arboles Valley. Married to the founder, George Hanneman.

George Hanneman (TQH)

A trainer of exotic animals for the movies and owner of Safari World, a wild animal farm in the Arboles Valley.

Evangeline Chester Harper (TLQ)

A beautiful blond southern belle with clear blue eyes, Miss Evangeline is the eldest child of Stephen Chester, Joanna North's last mistress, and a compulsive liar.

Colonel Robert Harper (TLQ)

Miss Evangeline's beau and later, her husband, an officer posted to the South Carolina Military Academy in Charleston and heir to the family cotton plantation on James Island.

Thomas Harper (TLQ)

Robert and Evangeline Harper's firstborn child, born in Charleston in August 1861.

Wilberforce Edward Harper (TLQ)

The father of Robert Harper and Mrs. Givens, master of a cotton plantation on James Island near Charleston.

Harriet (TQL)

Gertrude Drayton-Smith Lockwood's maid, confidante, and co-conspirator.

Joe Hartley (COQ)

The dear husband of Elm Creek Quilter Gretchen Hartley and a former steel-worker who suffered a broken back in a terrible accident at the mill. He was not expected to live, much less ever walk again, but his determination and Gretchen's unwavering support compel him to work tirelessly to regain his mobility. Frustrated by his inability to return to his former job and inspired by Gretchen's quilting ventures, he decides to start his own small business repairing and restoring antique furniture and building custom-made pieces.

Officer Hasselbach (TCCQ)

A police officer in Monroe, Ohio, who helps Megan Donohue find her missing son, Robby.

Mr. Hathaway (TSCQ)

A maker of shoes and boots in Creek's Crossing, Pennsylvania.

Dr. Hayd (SR)

A thoughtlessly unkind and chauvinist physician who examines Rosa Diaz Barclay at St. John's Hospital in Oxnard, California.

Helen (TCCQ)

One of Grace Daniels's elder sisters.

Holly Hellerman (COQ)

One of two young sisters who ask Gretchen Hartley to teach them quilting in exchange for doing household chores.

Megan Hellerman (COQ)

One of two young sisters who ask Gretchen Hartley to teach them quilting in exchange for doing household chores.

Augustus Henderson (TCCQ)

The husband of Kansas pioneer Sadie Henderson, and the subject of a film, *A Patchwork Life,* written and directed by their great-granddaughter.

Ellen Henderson (TCCQ)

The writer and director of *A Patchwork Life,* a film based upon the life of her great-grandmother Sadie Henderson, a Kansas pioneer.

Sadie Henderson (TCCQ)

A courageous Kansas pioneer and, decades later, the subject of a film, *A Patchwork Life,* written and directed by her great-granddaughter Ellen Henderson.

Mrs. Hennessey (TSCQ)

Dorothea and Thomas Nelson's housekeeper at Two Bears Farm. When she is hard at work or flustered, her ruddy cheeks flush and frenzied strands of curly gray-streaked auburn hair escape from the bun at the nape of her neck. A long-time employee of Thomas Nelson's parents, she cared for Thomas when he was a boy in Philadelphia and accompanied him to Water's Ford when he came to take over the family estate and to run the town primary school in 1849.

Henry (1) (TQA)

A boyfriend of Carol Mallory's. She speaks of him to her daughter, Sarah Mc-Clure, as "Uncle Henry," a euphemistic title that irritates Sarah.

Henry (2) (TWQ)

The chef hired to replace Maeve, who was hired to replace Anna Del Maso. Habitually late, he eventually wanders off for a smoke and never returns, leaving the

Elm Creek Quilters in rather dire straits in the middle of the summer camp season.

Hester (COQ)

A resident of Ocean View Hills and member of the Courtyard Quilters.

Lenore Hicks (COQ)

A resident of Ocean View Hills, a tall, solidly built woman with a slight stoop to her shoulders. She has a vexing and potentially dangerous habit of knocking over the retirement community's less agile residents, especially when they get between her and pie.

Grover Higgins (TQH)

A Hollywood movie producer with Golden Reel Productions whom Elizabeth Bergstrom Nelson meets while watching a dance marathon in Venice Beach, California.

Pete Hixton (TWWQ)

The former captain of the Brown Deer High School football team who grew up to marry the head cheerleader. He was declared medically ineligible to serve in Vietnam because too many tackles left him deaf in one ear.

Vicky Sinclair Hixton (TWWQ)

One of Gwen Sullivan's former classmates from high school who lived the cliché of the high school cheerleader marrying the captain of the football team. Even when minding her perfect baby at home, Vicky prefers to wear a cashmere twin-set, lipstick, and pearls, with her honey-blond hair swept back in a headband.

Renée Hoffman (RR)

A cardiac specialist at Hershey Medical Center who befriends Carol Mallory at Elm Creek Quilt Camp.

Honor (TLQ)

A half-blind elderly slave at Greenfields whose knowledge of herb lore earns her respect from white and colored folk alike.

Margaret Hoover (COQ)

A resident of Ocean View Hills and victim of Lenore Hicks's haste.

Mr. Hopkins (TQA)

A partner with the small public accounting firm Hopkins and Steele in Waterford who interviews Sarah McClure for a job.

Mrs. Hoskins (TLQ)

A friend of Evangeline Chester Harper, a Meeting Street neighbor and wife of a captain with the Seventh South Carolina Infantry regiment, with whom Miss Evangeline founds the Charleston Gunboat Society.

Brenda Hughley (TGQ)

A particularly recalcitrant and self-absorbed member of the Cherokee Rose Quilters, whose hostility finally forces Pauline Tucker to quit the guild. She is tall and lanky, with sandy blond hair cut boyishly short and angular features.

Isaac (TLQ)

One of two slave catchers who capture Joanna North at Elm Creek Farm and return her to slavery in Virginia.

Isaiah (TGQ)

A carpenter whose son, a seventh grader, is a member of Jocelyn Ames's Westfield Middle School Imagination Quest team.

Jack (1) (RR)

The man with whom Carol Mallory had an extramarital affair when her daughter, Sarah Mallory McClure, was still an infant. He is the nephew of the owner of a bookstore Carol frequents.

Jack (2) (TSCQ)

A fugitive slave passing through the Elm Creek Valley along the Underground Railroad.

Dr. Jamison (TWWQ)

Sarah McClure's ob-gyn during her pregnancy.

Jan (COQ)

A friend of Joe and Gretchen Hartley's from Ambridge, Pennsylvania, married to Clyde.

Janice (COQ)

Karen Wise's best friend, a mother of four, pregnant with her fifth. A former producer of children's public television programs, she decides to return to work as a party planner about the time Karen Wise discovers the Help Wanted ad for Elm Creek Quilts.

Andrea Jarthur (TCCQ)

A television morning news show host who interviews Grace Daniels and asks probing questions about her recent lack of productivity.

Jeannette (TGQ)

Pauline Tucker's friend and neighbor, a gifted art quilter and member of the Cherokee Rose Quilters. She and Pauline meet when their sons are kindergarten classmates.

Jeff (COQ)

A quilter from Nebraska, one of the few male quilters Russell McIntyre meets in his forays into the online quilting community.

Tom Jeffries (TQH)

The Ventura County sheriff investigating the shooting at the Jorgensen Ranch, the discovery of contraband at the Barclay farm, and the disappearances of Lars Jorgensen, Rosa Diaz Barclay, and her children.

Jenny (TLQ)

A slave of Mrs. Ames, Robert and Evangeline Harper's next-door neighbor in Charleston.

Joe (TQA)

An employee of Exterior Architects who assists Matt McClure with the restoration work at Elm Creek Manor.

Joel (TGQ)

A St. Andrew's College student who is Michaela Phillips's stunt partner during cheerleading tryouts. Until she learns his real name, she thinks of him by the nickname "Number Fifty-Eight," his tryout candidate number.

Daniel Johnson (TQL)

A professor of social sciences at Waterford College who is appointed Waterford's health officer during the Spanish Flu pandemic.

Frank Johnson (SR)

A neighbor of John and Rosa Barclay in the Arboles Valley.

Trudie Johnson (COQ)

Gretchen Hartley's friend, for whom she made a crib quilt as a gift for her son.

Annalise Jorgensen (TQH)

The eldest daughter of Oscar and Mary Katherine Jorgensen, a niece of Lars Jorgensen and a classmate of Marta Barclay.

Hannah Jorgensen (TQH)

The mother of Lars and Oscar Jorgensen, Elizabeth Bergstrom Nelson's employer. She was a childhood acquaintance, though not a friend, of Isabel Rodriguez Diaz.

Lars Jorgensen (TQH)

Rosa Diaz Barclay's jilted childhood sweetheart and father of two of her children, Marta and Lupita. When Elizabeth Bergstrom Nelson meets him for the first time at the Simi Valley train station, she sees "a tall, thin man in faded overalls and a plaid shirt wait[ing] beside a wagon, holding the reins of two draft horses. The weathered lines of his face spoke of hard times and disappointment, but his gaze was steady, though unsmiling."

Margaret Jorgensen (TQH)

The younger daughter of Oscar and Mary Katherine Jorgensen.

Mary Katherine Reilly Jorgensen (TQH)

The wife of Oscar Jorgensen and Elizabeth Bergstrom Nelson's first friend in the Arboles Valley.

Oscar Jorgensen (TQH)

Lars Jorgensen's serious, sober younger brother and the owner of the family ranch in the Arboles Valley.

Becca Jorgenson (TCCQ)

The younger of Cross-Country Quilter Donna Jorgenson's two daughters.

Donna Jorgenson (TCCQ)

A homemaker and mother of two from Silver Pines, Minnesota, Donna confesses to being a compulsive fabric shopper with an embarrassingly large accumulation of Unfinished Fabric Objects. Generous with her time and sensitive to the feelings of others, she is sometimes troubled by self-doubt, worrying that she has not set a good enough example for her daughters through her life choices. Her husband and many friends know better.

Lindsay Jorgenson (TCCQ)

The elder of Cross-Country Quilter Donna Jorgenson's two daughters, slender and lovely, with long blond hair. She is a member of the University of Minnesota drama society, with an interest in directing.

Paul Jorgenson (TCCQ)

The husband of Cross-Country Quilter Donna Jorgenson, father of Lindsay and Becca.

Jules (TMQ)

One of Gwen Sullivan's graduate school advisees.

June (TAQ)

One of the Laulima Quilters in Lahaina, Hawaii.

Karen (TMQ)

One of Summer Sullivan's flatmates in downtown Waterford.

Karl (TNYQ)

A German man whom Sylvia Bergstrom Compson and Andrew Cooper meet during their stay at the 1863 House in Manhattan. He and his wife, Erika, are from a small village not far from Baden-Baden, the ancestral homeland of the Bergstrom family.

Katie (TGQ)

Daria's predecessor as treasurer of the Cherokee Rose Quilters. She moved to Texas before Pauline Tucker joined the guild.

Keilana (TAQ)

Midori Tanaka's eldest daughter, the hostess of a glorious Thanksgiving feast to which Bonnie Markham is invited.

William Keller (TMQ)

The chair of the Waterford College Department of American Studies.

William Keller Jr. (TMQ)

The son of the chair of the Waterford College Department of American Studies; one of the youths who vandalizes Grandma's Attic.

Miss Kelley (TCCQ)

A teacher for whom Vinnie Burkholder does mending and sewing to earn money to help out at home.

Kelly (TWWQ)

One of Gwen Sullivan's few friends from high school, an aspiring poet and editor of the school paper. When Gwen returns home after dropping out of college, she learns that Kelly was pursuing a law degree somewhere in New England.

Lee Kessenich (TMQ)

A frequent customer of Grandma's Attic and a member of the Waterford Quilting Guild.

Samantha Key (TCCQ)

The virtually unknown but very attractive young actress cast in the role of Young Sadie in *A Patchwork Life.*

Leonhardt Kraus (TUQ)

A German immigrant allegedly tricked into enlisting in the Union army shortly after his arrival in Castle Garden in New York.

Gregory Krolich (TQA)

An unscrupulous associate at University Realty in Waterford, Gregory Krolich first earned Sarah McClure's enmity by plotting to purchase Elm Creek Manor from Sylvia Bergstrom Compson in order to demolish it and put up a string of condos in its place. Later he conspires with Craig Markham to sell the divorcing couple's condo out from under Bonnie, raises the rent on Grandma's Attic to force the shop out, and orchestrates the attempt to raze Union Hall.

Jacob Kuehner (TSCQ)

Jacob Kuehner's stern demeanor conceals even from those closest to him his deep religious convictions and commitment to justice. Under his strict leadership, the Kuehner farm prospers and his sugar camp gains fame for producing the best maple sugar in the county. When he inexplicably asks his niece Dorothea Granger to stitch him a quilt with unusual patterns of his own design, she reluctantly complies, never suspecting that her uncle is a stationmaster on the Underground Railroad or that the mysterious quilt contains hidden clues to guide runaway slaves to freedom.

Rebecca Kuehner (TSCQ)

Jacob Kuehner's late wife, a Quaker, a passionate abolitionist, and the mother of his two children.

Daniel Kuo (SR)

The young, handsome foreman of Vanelli Vineyards and Orchard in Glen Ellen, California. A skilled grape rancher and winemaker, he cherishes a secret dream to save up enough money to purchase the land his family, of Chinese heritage, has been working for decades.

Adele LaMonte (TNYQ)

A former Wall Street trader, Adele is prompted by crisis to leave her high-powered, high-stress career for a new life as the owner of a bed-and-breakfast on Manhattan's Upper East Side. Adele enjoys exploring her artistic talents and dabbles in quilting, composing poetry, and writing the history of the original owners of her historic brownstone home. She and her husband, Julius, a history professor at Hunter College, take pride in making their guests feel like true New Yorkers no matter how brief their stay in the city.

Arthur and Christine Landenhurst (TQL)

Vaudeville performers who purchase Eleanor Lockwood Bergstrom's Crazy Quilt from a consignment shop while passing through Pennsylvania.

Sophia Lawrence (TLQ)

A curator of the Edisto Island Folk Museum and a longtime friend of Grace Daniels.

Leah (TLQ)

A slave whose quarters Joanna North is ordered to share upon her arrival at Oak Grove; one of the best pickers on the plantation and a favorite of the overseer.

Lena (TCCQ)

The partner of Vinnie Burkholder's aunt Lynn Brauer.

Mr. Lewis (TLQ)

The name—almost certainly an alias—of a Union spy who enlists Joanna North in obtaining information from the home of Colonel Robert Harper, her master.

Amos Liggett (TSCQ)

The first owner of the land that becomes the Bergstroms' Elm Creek Farm, a repugnant, spiteful, vicious, slovenly drunkard occasionally hired to help with the harvest on the Kuehner farm.

Queen Lili'uokalani (TAQ)

The last queen of Hawaii, deposed in 1893 in a political coup led by businessmen and plantation owners with the threat of the far superior military might of the United States Marines. Queen Lili'uokalani relinquished her throne under protest to prevent the loss of life, believing that the international community would denounce the illegal actions of the United States and restore her to her rightful place.

Linda (RR)

A physician's assistant from Erie, Pennsylvania, who befriends Carol Mallory at Elm Creek Quilt Camp.

Mona Lindstad (TGQ)

Linnea Nelson's younger sister, blond, a trifle more slender than her sister, and a few inches shorter. A Quiltsgiving participant, she is an office manager for the Minnesota Department of Transportation, the vice president of her labor union, and the mother of four sons.

Mr. Linney (TLQ)

The overseer at Greenfields Plantation.

Liza (TSCQ)

A fugitive slave passing through the Elm Creek Valley along the Underground Railroad.

Lizzie (TLQ)

A young slave at Oak Grove; a daughter of Leah.

Charles Lockwood (TQL)

The founder of Lockwood's department store, who once enjoyed tremendous success but saw his fortunes dwindle in the Panic of 1893. Ruthless and unsentimental, he is willing to sacrifice his daughters' happiness in order to save his business.

Gertrude Drayton-Smith Lockwood (TQL)

Eleanor Lockwood Bergstrom's imperious, judgmental, bitterly unhappy mother.

Logan (TGQ)

A senior at St. Andrew's College and the captain of the cheerleading squad.

Lois (COQ)

The owner of the Goose Tracks Quilt Shop in Sacramento, California, an early supporter of Maggie Flynn's attempts to learn quilting and her work with the Harriet Findley Birch sampler.

Charmian London (SR)

Jack London's widow and neighbor of Salvatore and Beatrice Vanelli in Glen Ellen, California.

Jack London (SR)

A writer, adventurer, and owner of the Beauty Ranch in Glen Ellen, California. His friendship with his neighbor Salvatore Vanelli suffered an irreparable breach when Vanelli repeatedly refused to sell London his land.

Amy Cooper Lonsdale (TQL)

Andrew Cooper's eldest daughter, who resides with her husband and two children in a historic Queen Anne home in Hartford, Connecticut. A beginning quilter, she takes to Sylvia Bergstrom Compson's lessons eagerly—until Sylvia becomes engaged to her father. Although her father and younger brother might describe her as headstrong and perhaps even bossy, she prefers to consider herself well organized and born to lead. Amy is devoted to her family, but she resists change and cherishes mementos of days gone by.

Alberto Lucerno (SR)

A gangster who claims rather unbelievably to be an employee of Johnson's Bakery in Sonoma, California. He is in his early to midforties; he keeps his short, dark hair oiled and parted down the middle; and he has a penchant for snappy pinstriped suits. Although he is a dangerous man and no stranger to violence, he seems curiously protective of Rosa Diaz Barclay where Agent Dwight Crowell is concerned.

Aunt Lucretia (TLQ)

Miss Evangeline's aunt, her mother's sister, a resident of Charleston.

Lucy (1) (TCCQ)

Julia Merchaud's occasionally hapless assistant.

Lucy (2) (COQ)

A former coworker of Karen Wise's from the Penn State Office of University Development, who seems to embody the life Karen gave up for marriage and motherhood. Lucy is slender and fit, clad in a perfectly tailored suit, childless but intrigued by idealized visions of parenthood, successfully employed, and casually dismissive about the man with whom she had seemed very much in love the last time Karen had seen her, several years before.

Grandma Lucy (TWWQ)

Bonnie Markham's beloved grandmother, her first quilt teacher, tutor, and most steadfast champion.

Mae (TQH)

A woman Elizabeth Bergstrom Nelson meets on the train from Harrisburg to St. Louis. When Elizabeth first sees her in the observation car, she is impressed with Mae's willowy figure, her sleek black bob, her knee-high hemline, and the elegant way she carries her cigarette holder as she pores over a recent issue of *True Story*.

Her thick accent marks her as a native New Yorker. Mae has a way of becoming entangled with unscrupulous men, although she believes herself tough enough to hold her own. Her boyfriend, Peter, works for the mob.

Maeve (TWQ)

Maeve is the first chef hired after Anna Del Maso resigns from Elm Creek Quilts. Her tenure as the chef of Elm Creek Manor is brief, lasting a single summer camp season.

Carol Mallory (TQA)

Sarah Mallory McClure's ofttimes estranged mother. For several years she disapproves strongly of Sarah's marriage to Matt McClure, but thanks to some prompting from Sylvia, she eventually comes to tolerate him, and she and Sarah reconcile. Carol is present at the birth of Sarah and Matt's twins, Caroline and James, and after she retires from nursing, she leaves Uniontown, Pennsylvania, and moves into Elm Creek Manor.

Kevin Mallory (RR)

Sarah Mallory McClure's father, easygoing and indulgent with his daughter, but unforgiving to his wife when she betrays him.

Mr. Maniceaux (COQ)

A resident of Ocean View Hills and sometime polka partner of Dottie Blum.

Marc (TCCQ)

Justine Daniels's ex-boyfriend and the father of her son, Joshua.

Marco (TQH)

A hired hand on the Jorgensen Ranch.

Marcus (TUQ)

An African-American man serving with Abel Wright in the Sixth United States Colored Troops. A native of Philadelphia, he is not yet twenty.

Margot (TGQ)

A retired Penn State mathematics professor and co-owner of the String Theory Quilt Shop in Summit Pass, Pennsylvania.

Mariah (TWQ)

A friend and bridesmaid of Caroline McClure and a student at Yale Divinity School.

Maricela (TWWQ)

One of Summer Sullivan's roommates in Hyde Park, a student at the University of Chicago's Pritzker School of Medicine.

Marjorie (1) (TWWQ)

One of Agnes Emberly's classmates at Miss Sebastian's Academy for Young Ladies in Philadelphia, and later, the maid of honor at Agnes's marriage to Richard Bergstrom.

Marjorie (2) (TWQ)

A recent culinary school graduate hired to replace Henry for the second half of the camp season two years after Anna Del Maso departs. The Elm Creek Quilters like her, but she is clumsy and absentminded and has an unfortunate habit of burning food badly enough to set off the manor's fire alarms, so eventually they have to let her go.

Alice Markham (TAQ)

Craig J. and Julie Markham's daughter and eldest child, four years old at the time of *TAQ.*

Barry Markham (RR)

The youngest of Bonnie and Craig Markham's three children.

Cameron Markham (TAQ)

Craig J. and Julie Markham's son and youngest child, eight months old at the time of *TAQ.*

Craig Markham (TQA)

Bonnie Markham's husband (and future ex-husband) is a proud Penn State gradu-ate and Nittany Lions fan employed by the Office of the Physical Plant at Water-ford College. After he engages in a cyber affair, he and Bonnie attempt to salvage their marriage, but their efforts—halfhearted on Craig's part—ultimately fail. In the acrimonious divorce that follows, Craig maliciously resolves to make Bonnie's life as miserable as he can.

Craig J. Markham (RR)

The eldest son of Bonnie and Craig Markham, also known as Craig Junior or C. J.

Julie Markham (TAQ)

Craig J. Markham's wife; Bonnie Markham's daughter-in-law.

Linda Markham (TAQ)

Bonnie Markham's sympathetic and kind soon-to-be-former mother-in-law from Scranton, Pennsylvania.

Martha (TMQ)

Bill Keller's executive assistant, an unexpected ally when Gwen Sullivan badly needs one.

Sister Mary (SR)

A compassionate nurse who treats Rosa Diaz Barclay's domestic-abuse injuries at St. John's Hospital in Oxnard, California.

Mattie (TLQ)

A slave midwife and nurse from one of the South Carolina barrier islands who is purchased to deliver and care for Evangeline Chester Harper's child. She has sharp, observant eyes and her Gullah talk disguises a keen mind.

Maya (TAQ)

One of the Laulima Quilters in Lahaina, Hawaii.

Irvin Mayer (TWWQ)

An elderly British cardiologist and professor at the University of Chicago's Pritzker School of Medicine whom Summer Sullivan meets while searching for an apartment to rent in Hyde Park.

Noah McCleod (TCCQ)

The actor cast in the role of Sadie Henderson's eldest son in *A Patchwork Life,* a young man with a reputation for being talented, professional, and down-to-earth.

Caroline Sylvia McClure (TAQ)

Sarah and Matthew McClure's daughter, a twin to James. At the time of *TWQ,* she is a Dartmouth graduate attending medical school and engaged to her college sweetheart, Leo Fiore. She is tall, slender, and very pretty, with curly golden hair.

Hank McClure (AQH)

Matt McClure's father, who has long hoped that Matt would quit his job as caretaker of Elm Creek Manor and take over the family construction firm.

James Matthew McClure (TAQ)

Sarah and Matthew McClure's son, a twin to Caroline. He is slender but muscular, with reddish-brown hair the same shade as his mother's. Although nearly everyone assumes that his sister will inherit their mother's love for quilting, James's artistic talents and interest in the family business go unnoticed for years. After graduating from Penn State, James returns home to work for Elm Creek Quilts and quickly becomes one of the most popular teachers on the faculty, while also helping manage the company and pursuing his own art.

Matthew McClure (TQA)

Matt and his wife, Sarah, move to Waterford, Pennsylvania, after Matt obtains a job as a landscape architect with a local company, a position he leaves after the founding of Elm Creek Quilt Camp to become the estate's caretaker. Matt especially enjoys tending the manor's orchards and gardens, and working with agricultural students from Penn State. Like Sylvia, he wishes that Sarah had a better relationship with her mother, and he is willing to ignore his mother-in-law's slights against him for the sake of family harmony.

Amy Cooper McGrath (TQL)

Andrew Cooper's daughter, living in Hartford, Connecticut.

Caitlin McGrath (TNYQ)

The second child and only daughter of Daniel McGrath and Amy Cooper McGrath.

Daniel McGrath (TQL)

The husband of Amy Cooper McGrath.

Gus McGrath (TNYQ)

The eldest child of Daniel McGrath and Amy Cooper McGrath.

Sam McGrath (TNYQ)

The youngest of the three children of Daniel McGrath and Amy Cooper McGrath.

Elaine McIntyre (COQ)

Russell McIntyre's first wife and the mother of two teenagers from a previous marriage. Until her untimely death from ovarian cancer at forty-one, Elaine was a public relations director for a Seattle nonprofit agency and an avid quilter.

Miles McKinney (TGQ)

The coach of the Bloomfield Hills Middle School Imagination Quest team.

Ezra McNulty (TGQ)

A national talk radio firebrand whom Linnea and Kevin Nelson always considered more of a showman than a journalist. He takes the side of an anonymous "concerned citizen" who objects to the Conejo Hills Public Library's collection of "offensive" books and urges his listeners to support the closure of the library.

Peter Gray Meek (TUQ)

The zealous anti-Lincoln publisher of the Copperhead newspaper *Democratic Watchman* and nemesis of Gerda Bergstrom, who publishes pro-Union articles for the *Water's Ford Register*.

Charles Merchaud (TCCQ)

The beloved first husband of the actress Julia Merchaud.

Julia Merchaud (TCCQ)

The winner of four Emmys and a Golden Globe, Julia Merchaud stars as Grandma Wilson on the acclaimed primetime drama *Family Tree*. After the show is canceled, Julia expands her career into feature films. Although she has never sewn, she is offered a role in the historical drama *A Patchwork Life* when her new, young, less-than-honest agent passes her off as an accomplished quilter. With some misgivings, she attends Elm Creek Quilt Camp for a crash course.

Claudia Bergstrom Midden (TQA)

The eldest child of Frederick and Eleanor Bergstrom, Claudia is born in 1918 while her father is serving overseas in World War I. After Claudia nearly dies in the influenza pandemic, her mother becomes especially protective of her, which younger sister Sylvia interprets as favoritism. Sylvia's misguided jealousy, coupled with Claudia's bossiness and vanity, yields intense sisterly friction. Unbeknownst to Sylvia, Claudia's outward confidence and air of superiority mask deep-seated insecurities, for she is painfully aware that she does not possess her younger sister's creative gifts.

Harold Midden (TQA)

A native of Waterford, Pennsylvania, Harold Midden might have been Claudia Bergstrom's high school sweetheart, except he was too shy to do more than admire her from a distance. Harold attends Waterford College briefly, but forgoes earning his degree to take a position at Bergstrom Thoroughbreds—the better to endear himself to Claudia and impress her father. Reserved and taciturn even as a young adult, he is displeased when James Compson marries Sylvia and takes on a more important role in the company—and a higher place in Frederick Bergstrom's esteem. After Richard Bergstrom and James Compson enlist in the army during

World War II, Harold reluctantly follows suit, motivated not by patriotism but by a sullen unwillingness to allow his brothers-in-law to outshine him. After the war, his relationship with his wife fractures over accusations that Harold allowed Richard and James to perish rather than attempt to rescue them. They do not divorce, however, and continue to live together, albeit estranged, in Elm Creek Manor until Harold's death.

Mildred (SR)

The name of John Barclay's grandmother, his choice for the name of Rosa's first child until he realizes that the baby is not his.

Miles (TWQ)

A biology professor at Waterford College dating Emily DiNardo-Boyer, whom he meets when he purchases one of her pieces as a gift from the department for a visiting professor.

Nancy Thorpe Miles (TQL)

The mother of Mary Beth Callahan, who, upon inheriting the *Elms and Lilacs* quilt from Esther Thorpe, sells it to an auction house.

Cameron Miller (TCCQ)

The young actor chosen to play Sadie Henderson's youngest son in *A Patchwork Life*.

Mr. Milton (TQH)

A real estate agent Henry and Elizabeth Nelson meet at the Grand Union Hotel who is eager to sell them a plot in a new Arboles Valley development called Meadowbrook Hills.

Minnie (TLQ)

The housekeeper at Harper Hall in Charleston, a slave.

Mrs. Moore (TWWQ)

Gwen Sullivan's fifth-grade teacher and a member of the Brown Does, a quilt guild in Brown Deer, Kentucky.

Gary Moore (TGQ)

A representative of the Conejo Hills, California, city department of human resources.

Faith Cunningham Morlan (TUQ)

The winner of the *Loyal Union Sampler,* an exquisite quilt raffled off by the Union Quilters to raise money for the war effort. She also contributed a striking block to the quilt, an original design she named Charley Stokey's Star in honor of the first local soldier killed in battle. Her family's farm lies in the foothills of the Four Brothers Mountains in the north of the Elm Creek Valley.

Julius Mortensen (TNYQ)

A history professor at Hunter College in Manhattan; the husband of Adele LaMonte. He is in his late forties, tall, with dark hair streaked with silvery gray.

Chad Mueller (COQ)

Heidi Albrecht Mueller's husband, somewhat tightfisted and suspicious.

Heidi Albrecht Mueller (COQ)

Gretchen Harley's longtime employer, onetime friend, and unexpected rival. From a young age, Heidi had a tendency to latch on to Gretchen's ideas and claim them as her own, including opening a quilt shop in Sewickley, Pennsylvania. They work together at Quilts 'n Things for many years, but she is struck by jealousy when Gretchen is offered an interview with Elm Creek Quilts, and she blatantly lies about Gretchen's work and teaching experience to sabotage her chances.

Wolfgang Kauffmann Mueller (TMQ)

A furniture designer who possessed a unique style drawing from different elements of New England and Pennsylvania history—a little bit of Shaker, some Amish, some German. Scholars often credit him with initiating the Arts and Crafts movement.

Charlene Murray (TQL)

The proprietor of Horsefeathers Boutique, an eclectic shop offering "art from found objects" in downtown Sewickley, Pennsylvania. She is a stout woman with long brown hair that reaches to her waist and a penchant for purple caftans.

Prudence Nadelfrau (TSCQ)

A spinster dressmaker living in Water's Ford, Pennsylvania, a member of the Creek's Crossing Library Board, one of the Union Quilters, and the founder of the Creek's Crossing Abolitionist Society.

Nancy (TWWQ)

President of the Waterford Quilting Guild, successor to Mary Beth Callahan. After she assumes leadership of the local guild, she and Sylvia Bergstrom Compson find many occasions to bring Elm Creek Quilters and Waterford Quilting Guild members together for socializing, advocacy for their mutually beloved art form, and quilting at the manor.

Natalie (TCCQ)

The beautiful but moody and unpredictable fiancée of Adam Wagner, who breaks off their engagement shortly before the wedding. Instead she and her sister go to the Bahamas using the nonrefundable tickets that Adam purchased for their honeymoon. She is an executive with Lindsor's, an upscale department store with a flagship site in downtown Cincinnati.

Abigail Nelson (TRQ)

The only child of Thomas Nelson and Dorothea Granger Nelson.

Dorothea Granger Nelson (TRQ)

In 1849, nineteen-year-old Dorothea Granger lives with her parents on her uncle Jacob's farm, her dreams of furthering her education in an eastern city thwarted by the needs of home. She briefly serves as the teacher of the Creek's Crossing school and is disappointed when she loses the job to the privileged son of a local benefactor—Thomas Nelson, her future husband. A passionate reader, Dorothea initiates a campaign to raise funds for a library and unexpectedly finds herself at odds with some of the town's most prominent ladies. One of the notorious Creek's Crossing Eight, she is devoted to suffragist and abolitionist causes, courageously risking her own life to protect fugitive slaves fleeing north along the Underground Railroad.

Eleanor Nelson (TQH)

The eldest daughter of Henry Nelson and Elizabeth Bergstrom Nelson.

Elizabeth Bergstrom Nelson (TQA)

Though she was raised in Harrisburg, Pennsylvania, rather than at Elm Creek Manor, Elizabeth considers the Bergstrom family estate the true home of her heart and visits as often as she can. She does not understand how her father ever could have given up his stake in the family business to work for his father-in-law and deeply regrets his choice, made before she was born. Beautiful, spirited, and clever, Elizabeth often acts without thinking but can usually charm her way out of trouble. She is Sylvia's favorite cousin, and the younger girl is heartbroken when Elizabeth and Henry Nelson announce their plans to marry and move to California, where Elizabeth faces the first real test of her resourcefulness and moral courage.

Henry Nelson (TQH)

A great-grandson of Dorothea and Thomas Nelson, Henry's roots in the Elm Creek Valley run even deeper than the Bergstroms', which makes his decision to leave the Nelson family farm for a California ranch all the more surprising. Hardworking and steadfast, he upholds high moral standards and has little patience for those who do not. Although he deeply loves his wife, Elizabeth, her flirtatious behavior before their marriage disconcerts him, and he secretly wonders whether she married him out of love or because his family's farm lies adjacent to Elm Creek Manor, which she longs for but cannot have.

Kevin Nelson (TGQ)

Linnea Nelson's husband. A year and a half before Linnea attends Quiltsgiving at Elm Creek Manor, he is laid off from the marketing department of a European luxury car manufacturer's West Coast division, and after that he struggles unsuccessfully to find work. He is distantly related to Sylvia's favorite cousin, Elizabeth Bergstrom Nelson.

Linnea Nelson (TGQ)

Linnea—tall, blond, and sturdily built—is a children's librarian for the Conejo Hills Public Library in Los Angeles County, and a relative by marriage of one of Elizabeth Bergstrom Nelson's descendants. At fifty-four, she is happily married to

Kevin, a former marketing director who lost his job in the recession, and the mother of three children, a son attending college and a son and daughter in high school.

Melissa Nelson (TWQ)

Scott Nelson's sister and a second cousin once removed to Sylvia Bergstrom Compson. She learned to quilt from her grandmother Elizabeth Bergstrom Nelson, Sylvia's beloved cousin, and eagerly accepts Sylvia's invitation to Elm Creek Quilt Camp to meet Sylvia and learn more about their mutual ancestors.

Rosemary Nelson (TQH)

Henry Nelson's sister.

Scott Nelson (AQH)

A grandchild of Elizabeth Bergstrom Nelson and Henry Nelson, and thus second cousin once removed to Sylvia Bergstrom Compson.

Thomas Nelson (1) (TRQ)

The son of a beloved local benefactor, Thomas Nelson returns to Creek's Crossing to take over management of the family farm—as well as Dorothea Granger's teaching position—amidst rumors that he has been banished to Creek's Crossing after suffering a near-fatal illness in prison. Aloof and taciturn, he earns Dorothea's enmity by criticizing her and the other young ladies of the town, unaware that Dorothea is listening nearby. As time passes, Dorothea learns the truth about his questionable past and discovers that he is a better man than she ever suspected. He has a slim, wiry frame; thick, sandy hair; a neatly trimmed beard; and round spectacles.

Thomas Nelson (2) (TQH)

The second child and only son of Henry Nelson and Elizabeth Bergstrom Nelson, named for his great-grandfather.

George New (TUQ)

Surgeon in chief of the First Division; Jonathan Granger's superior officer at the Battle of Gettysburg.

Mrs. Newcombe (TQL)

A friend of Gertrude Drayton-Smith Lockwood in Manhattan.

Mona Niehaus (TQL)

A resident of Silver River, Indiana, who purchases Eleanor Lockwood Bergstrom's Crazy Quilt in an auction of the Landenhurst Theater's extensive prop collections.

Niko (TRQ)

An eighth-grade student at Westfield Middle School and a member of Jocelyn Ames's Imagination Quest team.

Frederick Douglass North (TRQ)

The name Joanna North gives to her firstborn son.

Joanna North (TRQ)

A slave born around 1830 in Wentworth County, Virginia, on a tobacco plantation owned by the Ashworth family. The very fact that she is able to endure the hardships of slavery and the hazards of her journey north prove she is a woman of great fortitude, determination, and courage. Though she is recaptured before she can reach safety in Canada and is sold off to a plantation in South Carolina, her eldest son, born at Elm Creek Farm during her escape attempt, is raised in freedom as a member of the Bergstrom family. Although the Bergstroms who sheltered her never learn what becomes of Joanna, generations later, Sylvia Bergstrom Compson does.

Old Dan (TSCQ)

An elderly fugitive slave passing through the Elm Creek Valley along the Underground Railroad.

Opal (TQL)

An employee of the Rocky Mountain Quilt Museum who helps Sylvia Bergstrom Compson in her search for her mother's long-lost New York Beauty quilt.

Jason Oplichter (TQL)

The proprietor of the shady online company AsIsAuctions.com, who occasionally uses the alias George K. Robinson.

Matthias Ottesen (SR)

A son of Rosa Diaz Barclay and Lars Jorgensen, a.k.a. Rose and Nils Ottesen. He is Rosa's ninth child and Lars's third.

Nils Ottesen (TQH)

The alias Lars Jorgensen adopts after fleeing the Arboles Valley.

Oscar Ottesen (SR)

A son of Rosa Diaz Barclay and Lars Jorgensen, a.k.a. Rose and Nils Ottesen. He is Rosa's tenth child and Lars's fourth, and is named after Lars's younger brother.

Rose Ottesen (TQH)

The alias Rosa Diaz Barclay adopts after fleeing the Arboles Valley.

Owen (TUQ)

An African-American man serving with Abel Wright in the Sixth United States Colored Troops. He is the oldest man in their company, a runaway from Georgia fifteen years free.

Hinano Paoa (TAQ)

A native Hawaiian, a gifted ukulele player, and the owner of the Nä Mele Hawai'i Music Shop in Lahaina. An expert on Hawaiian nature and culture, he becomes Bonnie Markham's guide to Maui at the prompting of his aunt Midori Tanaka.

Kai Paoa (TAQ)

The son of Hinano and Nani Paoa, a talented young ukulele player and student of oceanography at the University of Hawaii on O'ahu.

Nani Paoa (TAQ)

The wife of Hinano Paoa, a biology professor at the University of Hawaii and political activist killed—whether by accident or foul play is uncertain—in a riot at a May Day parade promoting Hawaiian unity.

Paul (TSCQ)

A fugitive slave passing through the Elm Creek Valley along the Underground Railroad.

Monsignor Paul (AQH)

The pastor of Holy Family Catholic Church in Pittsburgh.

Pearl (TLQ)

A young slave woman who works in the cotton fields at Oak Grove; Tavia's daughter and Titus's niece. She is strong and broad shouldered, and her mother frequently cautions her about speaking her mind where the overseer might hear.

Cyrus Pearson (TRQ)

Violet Pearson Engle's grown son from her first marriage. Handsome, witty, and charming, he courts Dorothea Granger, but although she enjoys his company, she is sometimes exasperated by his unwillingness to take anything seriously. Through no fault of Dorothea's, Cyrus mistakenly believes that she will inherit her uncle's farm upon his death. Upon discovering the truth, he abruptly shifts his attention to another girl of more certain fortune, forcing Dorothea to consider that she may have misjudged not only Cyrus, but other men in her life as well.

Peter (1) (TQH)

A man Henry and Elizabeth Nelson meet on the train traveling from Harrisburg to St. Louis. The red-haired man is a few inches shorter than his willowy companion, Mae, with a small mouth, a pencil-thin mustache, and a large mole on his left cheek. Although he claims to be involved in "sales and distribution," in truth, he works for the mob.

Peter (2) (TLQ)

The leader of the two slave catchers who capture Joanna North at Elm Creek Farm and return her to slavery in Virginia.

Michaela Phillips (TGQ)

Blond, pretty, energetic Michaela is a junior at St. Andrew's College whose dreams of becoming a cheerleading coach have recently been cast into doubt. While she is in the hospital being treated for an injury sustained during cheerleading tryouts, she witnesses children receiving Project Linus quilts and is moved by their simple joy and perseverance when confronted with fear and uncertainty, and their courage puts her own pain and disappointment into perspective. She attends Quilts-giving in order to support Project Linus and to fulfill a community service requirement for graduation.

Sharon Phillips (SR)

Rosa Diaz Barclay's landlady during her family's stay in a boardinghouse near Stanford Hospital in San Francisco.

Alex Powell (COQ)

The younger of Elaine McIntyre's two children from her first marriage.

Carly Powell (COQ)

The elder of Elaine McIntyre's two children from her first marriage.

Katherine Quigley (TQL)

A prominent judge in Waterford, Pennsylvania, who officiates at the Christmas Eve wedding of Sylvia Bergstrom Compson and Andrew Cooper.

Rachel (TWQ)

A friend of Caroline McClure's and member of her bridal party, Rachel is the mother of a seven-month-old baby and lives in Boulder, Colorado.

Rebecca (TMQ)

Agnes Emberly's granddaughter, the younger of Laura Emberly's two children.

Harriet Reinhart (TUQ)

The Water's Ford postmaster's nineteen-year-old daughter, a sweet, slender girl with trusting brown eyes and golden hair. Her mother died when she was twelve, so she assumed responsibility for keeping the house and minding her younger brothers and sisters.

Henry Reinhart (TUQ)

The gray-haired widowed postmaster of Water's Ford, Pennsylvania, during the Civil War era.

Leslie Reinhart (TWQ)

The vice president of the Waterford Historical Society and the proud great-great-granddaughter of the town's first postmaster.

Dr. Reynolds (SR)

A physician with Stanford Hospital in San Francisco who correctly diagnoses the mysterious wasting illness afflicting Ana and Miguel Barclay. A native of Santa Rosa, California, he arranges for Lars Jorgensen and Rosa Diaz Barclay, whom he knows as Nils and Rose Ottesen, to live and work at Cacchione Vineyards. He is a short, stocky, humorous man with small, round glasses and a full, bushy black beard.

Grant Richards (TCCQ)

The host of the television program *America's Back Roads*.

Mrs. Richardson (TLQ)

A neighbor of the Josiah Chester family who admired the beautiful gowns Joanna North sewed for Caroline Chester and hired her to make several for herself.

Jason Riegger (TAQ)

Bonnie Markham's son-in-law, the husband of Tammy Markham Riegger.

Tammy Markham Riegger (RR)

The second-eldest of Bonnie and Craig Markham's three children and their only daughter.

George K. Robinson (TQL)

Purportedly the name of the third-generation owner of Brandywine Antiques in Fort Dodge, Iowa, "George K. Robinson" is actually the alias of Jason Oplichter, proprietor of the shady online company AsIsAuctions.com.

Rick Rowen (TCCQ)

The actor cast in the role of Augustus Henderson in *A Patchwork Life,* an arrogant man with whom Julia Merchaud dreads working.

Dr. Russell (SR)

A physician who examines Ana and Miguel Barclay at St. John's Hospital in Oxnard, California, and recommends Rosa Diaz Barclay consult with Dr. Reynolds, a specialist in San Francisco. Dr. Russell's right leg was amputated below the knee after he was wounded while serving as an army medic in World War I.

Ruth (TLQ)

The cook at Greenfields Plantation in Virginia. Ruth's seven children were sold off to Georgia traders years before, and after being assigned to assist her in the kitchen, young Joanna North quickly becomes the unwitting beneficiary of their absence. Upon her thin shoulders Ruth pours the love and attention she is unable to offer her own sons and daughters.

Ruthie (TLQ)

The daughter of Joanna North and Titus. Master Chester does not care for that name, so he records her in his ledger as "Julia." Joanna continues to think of her daughter as Ruthie but must take care to call her Julia whenever the Chesters can overhear.

Theresa Salazar (TGQ)

A first-grade teacher in the Conejo Hills, California, school district who collaborates with Linnea Nelson on the public library's Great Artists program.

Sally (TLQ)

The cook at Harper Hall in Charleston, a slave.

Sam (TLQ)

A slave belonging to Evangeline Chester Harper's aunt Lucretia who runs off during the Great Fire of Charleston.

Edna Schaeffer (TQL)

The wife of Philip Schaeffer.

Frank Schaeffer (TQL)

The postman of Waterford, Pennsylvania, during World War I, husband of Gloria Schaeffer.

Gloria Schaeffer (TQA)

The president of the Waterford Quilting Guild during the 1940s.

Howard Schaeffer (TQL)

The elder son of Frank and Gloria Schaeffer, a former resident of Waterford who moved to Iowa.

Philip Schaeffer (TQL)

The younger son of Frank and Gloria Schaeffer, a onetime sweetheart of Claudia Bergstrom Midden.

Daniel Scharpelsen (RR)

Judy Nguyen DiNardo's half brother, the son of Dr. Robert Scharpelsen and his wife.

Kirsten Scharpelsen (RR)

Judy Nguyen DiNardo's younger half sister, an intern at the University of Wisconsin Hospital in Madison, Wisconsin. She is tall and slender, with chin-length, straight blond hair.

Robert Scharpelsen (RR)

Judy Nguyen DiNardo's biological father, an army doctor who met her mother, Tuyet Nguyen, while serving in Vietnam. He disavowed both mother and child upon returning to the United States, and later relinquished his paternal rights so Judy's stepfather could adopt her.

Sharon Scharpelsen (RR)

Judy Nguyen DiNardo's older half sister, the daughter of Dr. Robert Scharpelsen and his wife, and the mother of two sons.

Reverend Lawrence Schroeder (TRQ)

The minister of the First Lutheran Church on Second Street in Creek's Crossing, Pennsylvania.

Mr. Schultz (TSCQ)

The founder of Schultz's Printers, retired publisher of the *Water's Ford Register,* and father of Mary Schultz Currier.

Shane (TWWQ)

One of Summer Sullivan's roommates in Hyde Park, a graduate student at the University of Chicago.

Mrs. Shepley (TWWQ)

Summer Sullivan's obstinate, mistrustful fifth-grade teacher.

Joan Sheridan (TUQ)

The wife of the owner of a dry goods store on High Street in Water's Ford and a contributor to the *Loyal Union Sampler*.

Shropshire Family, The (TRQ)

Neighbors of the Bergstrom family from the antebellum era to the Great Depression.

Norman Shropshire (TQL)

The flannel-clad, bearded proprietor of the Daily Grind, a popular coffee shop in downtown Waterford, and the grandson of the owner of a now-defunct consignment shop where Claudia Bergstrom Midden sold several of her mother's heirloom quilts.

Doris Simmons (TNYQ)

A friend of Josephine Compson and a member of the Baltimore Quilting Circle.

J. T. Simmons (TQH)

The name, probably an alias, of the con artist who sells Henry Nelson the phony deed to El Rancho Triunfo.

Robert Smalls (TLQ)

An enslaved Charleston Harbor pilot who steals a Confederate transport steamer, the *Planter,* and turns it over to the Union navy. His escape gives hope to slaves throughout Charleston, among them Joanna North.

Alicia Solomon (TCCQ)

One of Lindsay Jorgenson's professors at the University of Minnesota and the faculty advisor of the university drama society.

Sondra (TCCQ)

Grace Daniel's friend and hairdresser.

Michael Sonnenberg (TQA)

The eldest son of Diane and Tim Sonnenberg, Michael struggled with juvenile delinquency, but later achieves success as a computer science major at Waterford College and as a graduate student at MIT. After earning his Ph.D., he turns down several lucrative job offers to work on his own inventions, one of which revolutionizes the world of video games and another of which is likely to do the same for virtual reality and telecommunications.

Tim Sonnenberg (RR)

The husband of Elm Creek Quilter Diane Sonnenberg and a chemistry professor at Waterford College.

Todd Sonnenberg (TQA)

The bright, popular, reliable younger son of Diane and Tim Sonnenberg whose childhood achievements overshadowed those of his troubled elder brother, Michael. A graduate of Princeton, he is an assistant district attorney for the city of Philadelphia and is married with three daughters.

Sophie (TLQ)

The cook on Oak Grove plantation, a slave.

Elizabeth Cady Stanton (TUQ)

A founding member of the Women's National Loyal League who hopes to obtain the Union Quilters' assistance in gathering signatures for their petition calling for Congress to free all the slaves at the earliest practicable date.

Victoria Stark (AQH)

Gwen Sullivan's graduate advisor at Cornell, a Rhodes Scholar and Harvard Ph.D. whose depth and breadth of historical interests and uncanny ability to unearth rich veins of primary source materials from dusty, abandoned archives earn Gwen's admiration.

Mr. Steele (TQA)

A partner with the small public accounting firm Hopkins and Steele in Waterford who interviews Sarah McClure for a job soon after she moves to town.

Dr. Steiner (TCCQ)

A physician who treats Cross-Country Quilter Grace Daniels for multiple sclerosis.

Shelley Stevens (TAQ)

A talented quilter from Michigan who applies for a position on the faculty of Aloha Quilt Camp, known and admired worldwide for her artistry and generosity of spirit.

Charlie Stokey (TSCQ)

A lifelong resident of Water's Ford, Pennsylvania, Charlie Stokey is a classmate of Dorothea Granger, a former hired hand of Jacob Kuehner, the husband of Union Quilter Eliza Stokey, and a private in the Forty-ninth Pennsylvania Volunteers, Company L.

Eliza Stokey (TUQ)

A Union Quilter, originally from Williamsport, married to Charlie Stokey.

Helen Stonebridge (COQ)

The leader of the Courtyard Quilters and unofficial leader of the residents of Ocean View Hills, she is a former professor of anthropology who reads the *Sacramento Bee* daily and the *New York Times* on Sunday.

Mr. Sullivan (TWWQ)

Gwen Sullivan's father.

Mrs. Sullivan (TWWQ)

Gwen Sullivan's mother, a homemaker and member of the Brown Does.

Sunny (TAQ)

An employee of Plumeria Quilts in Lahaina, Hawaii.

Rita Talmadge (COQ)

A resident of Ocean View Hills, three-time hip replacement patient, and victim of Lenore Hicks's haste.

Midori Tanaka (TAQ)

Midori is the manager, cook, and housekeeper of the Hale Kapa Kuiki in Lahaina, a petite woman in her midsixties who usually wears her long black hair in a French twist. Born on O'ahu but a resident of Maui for more than forty years, she is a marvelous cook and the aunt of Hinano Paoa.

Tashia (TGQ)

An eighth-grade student at Westfield Middle School, a member of Jocelyn Ames's Imagination Quest team, and Jocelyn's daughter Anisa's best friend.

Velma Tate (COQ)

A resident of Ocean View Hills and victim of Lenore Hicks's haste.

Authors' Album, 76" x 76", pieced by Jennifer Chiaverini, machine quilted by Sue Vollbrecht, 2005.
Source: *More Elm Creek Quilts*

The Sugar Camp Quilt, 83" x 83", pieced and appliquéd by Jennifer Chiaverini, machine quilted by Sue Vollbrecht, 2009.
Source: *More Elm Creek Quilts*

Christmas Memories, 84" x 112",
pieced, appliquéd, and hand quilted by
Carol Hattan, 2005.
Source: *More Elm Creek Quilts*

Road to Triumph Ranch, 65" x 91",
designed by Jennifer Chiaverini, pieced
by Heather Neidenbach, machine
quilted by Sue Vollbrecht, 2006.
Source: *More Elm Creek Quilts*

New Year's Reflections, 60"x 60",
pieced by Christie Batterman,
machine quilted by Elaine
Beattie, 2007.
Source: *More Elm Creek Quilts*

Winding Ways,
70" x 70", pieced by Jennifer
Chiaverini, machine quilted
by Sue Vollbrecht, 2009.
Source: *Traditions from Elm
Creek Quilts*

Joanna's Freedom, 54" x 72",
designed by Jennifer Chiaverini,
pieced by Heather Neidenbach
and Geraldine Neidenbach,
machine quilted by Sue
Vollbrecht, 2010.
Source: *Traditions from
Elm Creek Quilts*

Pineapple Patch, 54" x 54",
appliquéd by Jennifer Chiaverini,
machine quilted by Sue Vollbrecht,
2010.
Source: *Traditions from Elm Creek
Quilts*

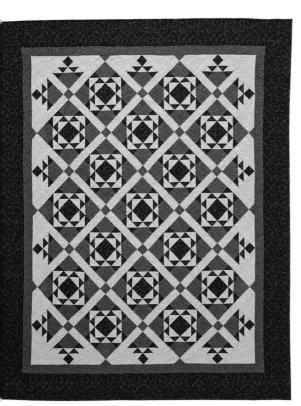

Dorothea's Dove in the Window, 68" x 85.25", designed by Jennifer Chiaverini, pieced by Geraldine Neidenbach, machine quilted by Sue Vollbrecht, 2010.
Source: *Traditions from Elm Creek Quilts*

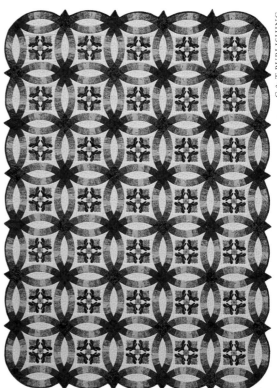

Caroline's Wedding, 58" x 80", pieced and appliquéd by Jennifer Chiaverini, machine quilted by Sue Vollbrecht, 2010.
Source: *Traditions from Elm Creek Quilts*

The Aloha Quilt, 54" x 54", appliquéd by Jennifer Chiaverini, machine quilted by Sue Vollbrecht, 2010.
Source: *Traditions from Elm Creek Quilts*

Elm Creek Medallion, 72.5" x 72.5", pieced, appliquéd, and quilted by Jennifer Chiaverini, 2000.
Source: *Elm Creek Quilts*

Elms and Lilacs, 82" x 82", hand appliquéd by
June Pease, quilted by Deb Randall, 2003.
Source: *Return to Elm Creek*

Loyal Union Sampler, 98" x 98",
pieced and appliquéd by Jennifer
Chiaverini, machine quilted
by Sue Vollbrecht, 2012.
Source: *Loyal Union Sampler*

Sarah's Sampler, 80" x 96", machine pieced, hand appliquéd, and hand quilted by Jennifer Chiaverini, 1998. Source: *Elm Creek Quilts*

The Runaway Quilt, 59" x 76", pieced by Jennifer Chiaverini, machine quilted by Cathy Franks, 2002. Source: *Elm Creek Quilts*

Sylvia's Bridal Sampler, 87" x 115", pieced by Jennifer Chiaverini et al, machine quilted by Sue Vollbrecht, 2004. Source: *Sylvia's Bridal Sampler from Elm Creek Quilts*

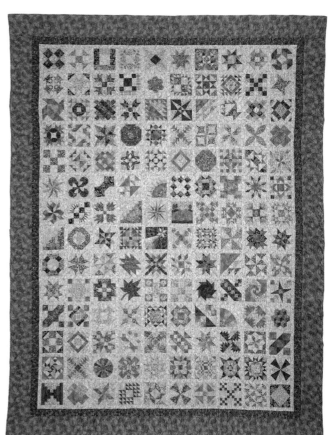

Cross-Country Challenge, 56" x 56",
machine pieced and hand quilted by
Jennifer Chiaverini, 2001.
Source: *Elm Creek Quilts*

Gerda's Log Cabin, 70" x 98",
machine pieced by Jennifer
Chiaverini et al, machine quilted
by Cathy Franks, 2002.
Source: *Elm Creek Quilts*

Tavia (Octavia) (TLQ)

A kind slave woman at Oak Grove who welcomes Joanna North into her cabin in the slave quarters, and into her family. She is the elder sister of Titus and the mother of three children: Ruby, a toddler; Paul, a boy a few years older; and Pearl, a girl almost grown.

Darren Taylor (TQL)

Bonnie Markham's divorce attorney.

Terri (RR)

The woman with whom Craig Markham carries on an extramarital affair, a divorced mother of two working as an office manager in Harrisburg, Pennsylvania.

Miss Thatcher (TRQ)

A schoolteacher in Creek's Crossing, Pennsylvania.

Theresa (COQ)

The roommate and "special friend" of Anna Del Maso's boyfriend Gordon. Theresa, an MFA student in poetry at Waterford College, is shorter than Anna and not much thinner, with waist-length frizzy brown hair and thick glasses set in black plastic frames. Like Gordon, Theresa is pretentious and patronizing, fancies herself an intellectual, and dismisses Anna's interests as archaically feminine.

Esther Thorpe (TQL)

A Waterford woman who bought Eleanor Lockwood Bergstrom's *Elms and Lilacs* quilt from Claudia Bergstrom Midden in 1947, she is also the grandmother of Diane Sonnenberg's neighbor and nemesis, Mary Beth Callahan.

Tia (TAQ)

One of the Laulima Quilters in Lahaina, Hawaii, recently engaged.

Dolores Tibbs (TQL)

A Waterford librarian and one of four founders of the Waterford Quilting Guild, who is placed in charge of the town's volunteer nurses during the Spanish Flu pandemic.

Titus (TLQ)

The groom and coachman of Oak Grove plantation on Edisto Island; Joanna North's husband and father of her daughter, Ruthie; and later a soldier with the Fifty-fourth Massachusetts Volunteer Infantry.

Lieutenant David Humphreys Todd (TUQ)

A warden at Libby Prison in Richmond, Virginia, half brother to Mary Todd Lincoln and brother-in-law to President Abraham Lincoln.

Horace Tomilson (TQH)

A lawyer with the San Francisco legal firm of Tomilson, Hanks, and Dunbar who brings Nils and Rose Ottesen's terms for the sale of the Barclay farm in the Arboles Valley to Henry and Elizabeth Nelson.

Tommy (TLQ)

A young slave at Harper Hall in Charleston, responsible for raking the yard and keeping flies off the food at mealtimes.

Alicia Torres (TGQ)

President of the Conejo Hills Public Library Friends of the Library.

Troy (TAQ)

A dark-haired, handsome zip-line guide with Skyline Eco Adventures in Hawaii.

Colton Tucker (TGQ)

The son of Pauline and Ray Tucker, a middle school student at the time of *TGQ* and the youngest of their two children.

Kori Tucker (TGQ)

The daughter of Pauline and Ray Tucker, a middle school student at the time of *TGQ* and the eldest of their two children.

Pauline Tucker (TGQ)

Pauline is a 911 call center operator from Sunset Ridge, Georgia, and a member of an exclusive quilt guild, the Cherokee Rose Quilters—until friction with a particularly difficult member of the group compels her to attend Quiltsgiving instead of her own guild's retreat. She usually gathers her thick, black, wiry mass of hair in a clip at the nape of her neck, but its length still reaches past her shoulder blades. She wears thick, rectangular lenses with black plastic frames over her green eyes. She is a proud graduate of Georgia Tech, happily married to Ray, and mother of middle schoolers Colton and Kori.

Ray Tucker (TGQ)

The loyal husband of Quiltsgiving participant Pauline Tucker.

Brian Turnbull (TQA)

The owner and CEO of PennCellular who interviews Sarah McClure soon after she moves to Waterford, Pennsylvania.

Major Thomas Pratt Turner (TUQ)

The commander of Libby Prison, a young, clean-shaven man of average height and imperious manner.

Clement Vallandigham (TUQ)

An Ohio congressman and outspoken Copperhead whose request to speak at Union Hall the Republican Union Quilters cordially refuse, provoking the ire of local Peace Democrats, especially the publisher of the Bellefonte *Democratic Watchman.*

Beatrice "Bea" Vanelli (SR)

A woman in her sixties who for nearly four decades grows grapes and makes wine on forty-five beautiful acres in Glen Ellen, California, with her husband, Salvatore Vanelli.

Salvatore "Sal" Vanelli (SR)

A vintner in his early sixties who for nearly four decades grows grapes and makes wine on forty-five beautiful acres in Glen Ellen, California, with his wife, Beatrice Vanelli.

Elizabeth Van Lew (TUQ)

A native Virginian and loyal Unionist who cares for Union prisoners in Richmond and works as a Union spy, although she does not care for that title. She often wears her blond hair pulled back into a French knot with curly wisps framing her face. A petite spinster who has not lost her power to charm, she has a strong nose and chin, and her gaze is steady, clear, and intelligent.

Denmark Vesey (TLQ)

The leader of an ill-fated slave uprising in Charleston in 1822.

Adam Wagner

A teacher at Roger Bacon High School in Cincinnati, the grandson of Cross-Country Quilter Vinnie Burkholder, and the husband of Cross-Country Quilter Megan Donohue.

Megan Wagner (TCCQ)

See Megan Donohue.

Joseph Wainwright (TWWQ)

One of the most prominent citizens of Richardsport, Kentucky, at the turn of the twentieth century. He earned a fortune as a successful lawyer and circuit court judge, and he became a philanthropist in his retirement. In 1890, he built a magnificent home on Society Hill as an anniversary gift for his beloved wife, Martha.

Martha Wainwright (TWWQ)

The wife of Joseph Wainwright, a successful lawyer, judge, and philanthropist in Richardsport, Kentucky, at the turn of the twentieth century.

Thomas Wainwright (TWWQ)

The only son of Joseph and Martha Wainwright; a doctor in Louisville, Kentucky.

Andrea Walker (AQH)

An obstetrics nurse, the wife of Louis Walker, and Louis's partner in the work of Abiding Savior Christian Outreach in Pittsburgh.

Louis Walker (AQH)

The African-American director of Abiding Savior Christian Outreach in Pittsburgh, a Mississippi native and civil rights worker forced to flee the Jim Crow South after his girlfriend was killed by a car bomb meant for him.

Evelyn Walzer (TCCQ)

The wife of Julia Merchaud's agent, Maury Walzer, and her good friend.

Maury Walzer (TCCQ)

Julia Merchaud's agent and her first husband's oldest and dearest friend.

Reverend Webster (TCQ)

The Bergstroms' pastor during the Great Depression with whom Eleanor Lockwood Bergstrom works on numerous charitable endeavors.

Marcia Welsh (TQA)

The director of personnel at PennCellular, whom Sarah McClure meets during a job interview soon after moving to Waterford.

Lawrence Whitehall (TUQ)

The husband of Philippa Whitehall; a tall, thin man who walks with a cane and appears to be ten years older than his wife. The Whitehalls have two daughters, ages five and three, and live near Richmond, Virginia.

Philippa Whitehall (TUQ)

A friend of Elizabeth Van Lew who lives outside Richmond, Virginia, in a spacious, red-brick Georgian home. She and her husband assist Gerda Bergstrom and Charlotte Claverton Granger during their travels to Libby Prison. Before they meet, Gerda expects Mrs. Philippa Whitehall to be a plump dowager, and she is surprised to discover a slender, energetic woman close to her own age, becomingly clad in a subtly made-over dress of blue silk, her only obvious concession to the deprivations of war. The Whitehalls have two daughters, ages five and three.

Charles Wilbur (TRQ)

A Creek's Crossing farmer shot and killed in his own barn by horse thieves.

Daniel Wilbur (TRQ)

The young son of Creek's Crossing farmer Charles Wilbur.

Susanna Wilbur (TRQ)

The ten-year-old daughter of Charles Wilbur, a Creek's Crossing farmer.

Eveline Wilson (TAQ)

A loyal friend of Queen Lili'uokalani, the last monarch of the Kingdom of Hawaii, who shares the queen's imprisonment after she loses her throne in a political coup.

Kawena Wilson (TAQ)

A master of Hawaiian appliqué quilting from the Big Island, one of the first three teachers appointed to the faculty of Aloha Quilt Camp.

Malinda Jane Holmes Wilson (TUQ)

The sweetheart and later wife of Private Satterwhite Wilson.

Satterwhite Wilson (TUQ)

A young, gravely wounded Confederate soldier from Dallas County, Alabama, whom Thomas Nelson saves on the battlefield at Gettysburg.

Thomas Wilson (TQA)

A candidate for the jobs at PennCellular and Hopkins and Steele for which Sarah McClure also applies.

Ethan Wise (COQ)

Karen and Nate Wise's eldest son, age four and a half at the time of Karen's Elm Creek Quilts interview in *COQ,* age ten in *TGQ.*

Karen Wise (COQ)

A loving stay-at-home mom feeling both the joys and the frustrations of her vocation, Karen Wise applies for a position on the faculty of Elm Creek Quilt Camp hoping that her deep understanding of the spirit of Elm Creek Quilts will outweigh her relative inexperience as a quilter. Although she is one of five finalists, ultimately she is not hired because she has no experience teaching quilting. Determined to strengthen her résumé for the next time Elm Creek Quilts has an opening, Karen becomes a valued member of the staff at the String Theory Quilt Shop in Summit Pass, Pennsylvania, where she draws upon her ingenuity and creativity to keep the shop afloat during troubled economic times.

Lucas Wise (COQ)

Karen and Nate Wise's youngest son, eighteen months old at the time of Karen's Elm Creek Quilts interview in *COQ*, seven years old in *TGQ*.

Nate Wise (COQ)

Karen Wise's husband, an ardent environmentalist and a professor of information sciences and technology at Penn State.

Abel Wright (TRQ)

A freeborn dairy farmer in the Elm Creek Valley in the mid-1800s, Abel Wright, one of the Creek's Crossing Eight, runs a station in the Underground Railroad and also works as a conductor, transporting runaway slaves to the North when he returns from his trips to sell cheese in the South. It is on one of these trips that he meets his future wife, Constance; she refuses to risk running away, so he saves enough money to buy her freedom, and they later have two sons. During the Civil War, Abel Wright joins the Sixth United States Colored Infantry Regiment at Camp William Penn in Philadelphia in July 1863 and loses his arm in the trenches at Petersburg about a year later. Obliged to put down the rifle, he takes up the pen, and his first book, an account of his wartime experiences, is published in 1865 to great acclaim.

Constance Wright (TRQ)

A former slave, Constance comes to Creek's Crossing, Pennsylvania, after her husband, Abel, purchases her freedom from a Virginia plantation. Understandably wary of white strangers, Constance initially rejects Dorothea Granger's overtures of friendship but over time comes to trust her. Constance is staunchly loyal to her husband, and knowing the sacrifices he made to bring her to freedom, she rightly never doubts his love for her. The mother of two sons, George and Joseph, she later becomes one of the notorious Creek's Crossing Eight and a founding member of the Union Quilters.

George Wright (TRQ)

The eldest child of Abel and Constance Wright, eleven years old at the time of *TUQ*.

Joseph Wright (TRQ)

The second-eldest child of Abel and Constance Wright, nine years old at the time of *TUQ*.

Joshua Wright (TUQ)

Abel Wright's brother. He serves with Abel Wright in the Sixth United States Colored Troops.

Margaret Wright (TUQ)

Joshua Wright's wife.

Thomas Wright II (TWQ)

A great-grandson of Civil War hero and renowned author Abel Wright, Thomas Wright II is the director of the Abel Wright Foundation, a nonprofit organization dedicated to preserving Abel Wright's legacy and promoting literacy and history education in public schools.

Zachariah (TSCQ)

A runaway slave who finds refuge at the Granger farm soon after it acquires that name.

Zachary (TMQ)

Agnes Emberly's grandson, the elder of Laura Emberly's two children.

The Bergstrom Family Tree

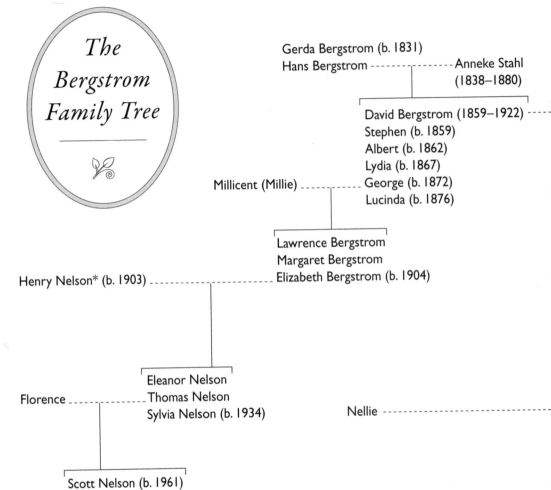

Gerda Bergstrom (b. 1831)
Hans Bergstrom ------------- Anneke Stahl
(1838–1880)

David Bergstrom (1859–1922) -----
Stephen (b. 1859)
Albert (b. 1862)
Lydia (b. 1867)
Millicent (Millie) ------------ George (b. 1872)
Lucinda (b. 1876)

Lawrence Bergstrom
Margaret Bergstrom
Henry Nelson* (b. 1903) ------------------ Elizabeth Bergstrom (b. 1904)

Eleanor Nelson
Florence ------------ Thomas Nelson
Sylvia Nelson (b. 1934)   Nellie -------------------

Scott Nelson (b. 1961)
Melissa Nelson (b. 1965)

*Henry Nelson is a great-grandson of Dorothea Granger Nelson and Thomas Nelson.

Descendants

Descendants

Marriages

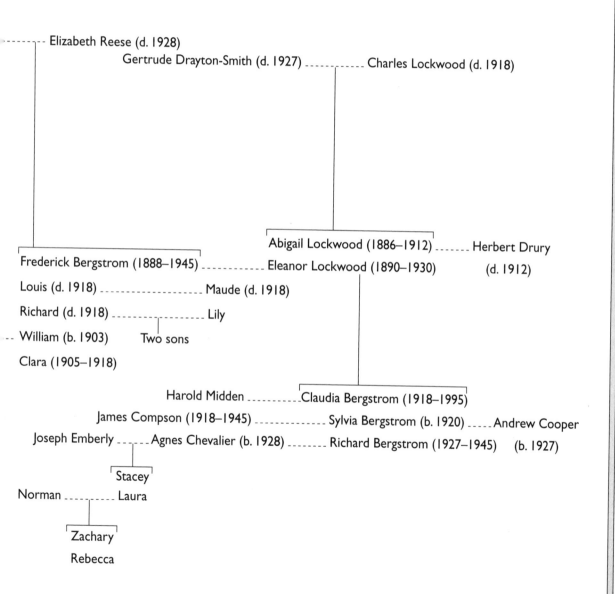

Elizabeth Reese (d. 1928)

Gertrude Drayton-Smith (d. 1927) .... Charles Lockwood (d. 1918)

Abigail Lockwood (1886–1912) .... Herbert Drury

Frederick Bergstrom (1888–1945) .... Eleanor Lockwood (1890–1930)   (d. 1912)

Louis (d. 1918) .... Maude (d. 1918)

Richard (d. 1918) .... Lily

William (b. 1903)   Two sons

Clara (1905–1918)

Harold Midden .... Claudia Bergstrom (1918–1995)

James Compson (1918–1945) .... Sylvia Bergstrom (b. 1920) ..... Andrew Cooper

Joseph Emberly .... Agnes Chevalier (b. 1928) .... Richard Bergstrom (1927–1945)   (b. 1927)

Stacey

Norman .... Laura

Zachary

Rebecca

Places

[Elm Creek Manor] was, for that brief time they lived within its gray stone walls, the world as it should be: women of all ages, from widely varied backgrounds, coming together in harmony to create objects of beauty and comfort. Differences were not merely tolerated, but accepted and even admired. For one week the world was not so much with them, the stress and monotony of daily routines could be forgotten, and they could quilt—or read, or wander through the garden, or take a nap, or stay up all night laughing with friends—as their own hearts desired. Patient teachers stood by willing to pass on their knowledge; friends offered companionship and encouragement. Confidences were shared at mealtime and in late-night chats in cozy suites or on the moonlit verandah. Resolutions were made, promises kept. Quilters took artistic and emotional risks because they knew they were safe, unconditionally accepted.

—*The Winding Ways Quilt*

1863 House

A five-story brownstone bed-and-breakfast on the Upper East Side of Manhattan where Sylvia Bergstrom Compson and Andrew Cooper spend part of their honeymoon. The proprietor, Adele LaMonte, is an occasional guest of Elm Creek Quilt Camp.

Abiding Savior Christian Outreach

A mission serving the residents of an impoverished neighborhood in Pittsburgh, with an emphasis on providing shelter, food, and medical care for pregnant homeless girls.

Agnes Bergstrom Emberly Quilt Gallery

A permanent exhibit of the museum's collection of quilts in the East Gallery of Union Hall in Waterford, Pennsylvania, named after Agnes Bergstrom Emberly, a longtime member and former president of the Waterford Historical Society.

Allen Street Grill

A restaurant on the second floor of the Hotel State College, on the corner of College Avenue and Allen Street in State College, Pennsylvania, across the street from the campus of Penn State University.

Ambridge, Pennsylvania

Gretchen Hartley's hometown, a steel-mill town northwest of Pittsburgh on the Ohio River.

Arboles Grocery

A small grocery store with a single gas pump out front, serving residents of the rural Arboles Valley in Southern California.

Arboles Lodge

A popular place for dining and dancing in the Arboles Valley.

Arboles Valley

A beautiful region of Southern California about forty-five miles northwest of Los Angeles, the birthplace and longtime home of Rosa Diaz Barclay and Lars Jorgensen. Newlyweds Elizabeth Bergstrom Nelson and Henry Nelson move there in 1925, believing themselves the owners of a thriving cattle ranch—but upon their arrival, they discover that they have been swindled.

Arboles Valley School

The public elementary school in the Arboles Valley, a whitewashed building with a bell in a high cupola.

L'Arc du Ciel

The finest restaurant in Waterford, Pennsylvania.

Ashworth Plantation

The tobacco plantation in Wentworth County, Virginia, where Joanna North was born into slavery.

Aurora Borealis

Julia Merchaud's favorite retreat, located in Ojai, California.

Baden-Baden, Germany

The ancestral homeland of the Bergstrom family.

Barrows Inn

A modest hotel in Water's Ford, Pennsylvania.

Bear's Paw Inn

A charming inn in the Poconos where Sylvia Bergstrom Compson and Andrew Cooper spend the first night of their honeymoon.

Belle Isle

An island in the James River west of Richmond used as a Confederate prisoner of war camp for enlisted men. A handful of shacks and tents provided inadequate shelter for the thousands of Union soldiers held captive there. Most prisoners lacked even a blanket to sleep upon and were constantly at the mercy of the sun, wind, and rain.

Bistro, The

A casual restaurant in Waterford; a favorite spot for locals and Waterford College faculty for breakfast and lunch, and a popular student hangout after six.

Books & Company

A wonderful independent bookstore in Dayton, Ohio, where Adam Wagner takes Robby Donohue to meet one of his favorite authors.

Brown Deer, Kentucky

The remote, rural hometown of Gwen Sullivan, west of Lovely, about halfway between Pilgrim and Kermit, population twelve hundred, home to six churches and no movie theaters.

Buffalo Rose

A biker bar in Golden, Colorado.

Cacchione Vineyards

A sixty-acre ranch and winery about five miles south of Santa Rosa, California, founded by the grandfather of Dante Cacchione.

Caffe Florian

An Italian restaurant in Hyde Park near the corner of Blackstone and Fifty-seventh, where Summer Sullivan and Jeremy Bernstein share the best spinach and artichoke heart deep-dish pizza with whole-wheat crust that Summer has ever tasted.

Camp Curtin

A Union army training camp on the outskirts of Harrisburg, Pennsylvania, named in honor of Governor Andrew Curtin.

Camp Meeting Road

During her self-imposed exile from Elm Creek Manor, Sylvia Bergstrom Compson lived in a modest red-brick house on Camp Meeting Road in Sewickley, Pennsylvania.

Carnegie Library

A library in Oxnard, California—one of many across the country by that name founded by wealthy industrialist and philanthropist Andrew Carnegie—where young Ana Barclay enjoys a rare, brief moment of blissful reading after fleeing the Arboles Valley with her mother and siblings.

Centerpiece Art Gallery

An art gallery in Summit Pass, Pennsylvania.

Château Élan

A resort on the outskirts of Atlanta, Georgia, where the Cherokee Rose Quilters hold their renowned annual quilters' retreat. The most important of the guild's many significant charitable activities, the retreat raises money for several homeless shelters and soup kitchens in impoverished Atlanta neighborhoods.

Children's Home, The

An orphanage run by Catholic nuns in Grangerville, Pennsylvania, in a stately, three-story red-brick building not far from the center of town. During the Great Depression, a young Sylvia Bergstrom Compson is inspired to sew quilts for the children residing there.

Chuck's

A diner across the street from the main gate of Waterford College's campus, which Anna Del Maso hopes one day to buy and transform into her own restaurant.

City Quilter, The

A quilt shop in the Chelsea neighborhood of Manhattan, one of Sylvia Bergstrom Compson's favorite places to visit whenever she is in New York.

Cloverdale, California

A town in the Alexander Valley. After Salvatore Vanelli suffers a heart attack, he and his wife decide to sell their vineyard and move to Cloverdale to help Sal's brother and sister-in-law run a resort on the Russian River.

Colored Orphan Asylum

A home for more than two hundred African-American orphans at Fifth and Forty-second in Manhattan, looted and burned by angry mobs in the New York Draft Riots of July 1863.

Commons Coffee House

A popular coffee shop on the campus of Cornell University where Gwen Sullivan and her advisor Victoria Stark often met.

Compson's Resolution

Six hundred acres of neatly fenced pasture, rolling forested hills, and cultivated farmland that have been in the Compson family since the eighteenth century. The name of the farm comes from the settlement of a border dispute with the farmer who owned the acres to the northwest of the Compson property. Well into the 1970s, members of the Compson family still resided within the two-hundred-year-old brownstone farmhouse with a gambrel roof that their first ancestor in Maryland built.

Conejo Hills

A town in Southern California about forty-five miles north of Los Angeles where Quiltsgiving participant Linnea Nelson lives with her family.

Conejo Hills Public Library

The city library where Quiltsgiving participant Linnea Nelson works as a children's librarian.

Corner Room, The

A casual restaurant on the first floor of the Hotel State College, on the corner of College Avenue and Allen Street in State College, Pennsylvania, across the street from the campus of Penn State University, popular with students, alumni, and faculty.

Courthouse Square

A historic section of Lahaina, on Maui, famous for its enormous banyan tree.

Creek's Crossing, Pennsylvania

See Waterford, Pennsylvania.

Daily Grind

A popular coffee shop in downtown Waterford.

Door County, Wisconsin

A beautiful region of northeast Wisconsin where Sylvia Bergstrom Compson and

Andrew Cooper vacation, visiting Peninsula State Park and the towns of Sturgeon Bay, Egg Harbor, and Fish Creek.

Drowned Farm

A disparaging nickname for Thrift Farm, the failed utopian community founded by the Granger family and other idealistic Transcendentalist Christians.

Dutch Mountain

A mountain at the southern edge of the Elm Creek Valley.

Edisto Island Folk Museum

A museum of local art and history in South Carolina that Sylvia Bergstrom Compson visits to learn about Joanna North and the Freedom Quilters.

Eisenhower Chapel

A chapel on the University Park campus of Penn State where Sarah and Matt McClure are wed.

Elm Creek Manor

The ancestral home of the Bergstrom family and the site of Elm Creek Quilt Camp, built in 1858 in the Elm Creek Valley on the outskirts of Waterford, Pennsylvania.

Elm Creek Valley

A beautiful, rural region of central Pennsylvania framed by the Four Brothers Mountains to the north and Dutch Mountain and Wright's Pass to the south. Its largest communities are Waterford and Grangerville, and it is home to Waterford College and Elm Creek Quilt Camp.

Engle's Draper and Fine Tailoring

A shop in Creek's Crossing, Pennsylvania, where Anneke Bergstrom obtains a job sewing for Violet Pearson Engle.

Fabric Warehouse

A massive discount fabric superstore on the outskirts of Waterford, Pennsylvania. Fabric Warehouse contributed significantly to the decline of sales at Bonnie Markham's quilt shop, Grandma's Attic.

Fiddlesticks Quilts

A charming quilt shop in the Old Town district of Boulder City, Nevada, that Sylvia Bergstrom Compson and Andrew Cooper visit on a tip that Eleanor Lockwood Bergstrom's long-lost Ocean Waves quilt was seen there.

First Lutheran Church

A church in Creek's Crossing, Pennsylvania, where the Charles Wilbur family worships.

Four Brothers Mountains

A mountain range framing the northern edge of the Elm Creek Valley.

Glen Ellen, California

In the mid-1920s, Glen Ellen is a small village in a forested valley just north of the town of Sonoma. It is home to Jack London's Beauty Ranch, Vanelli Vineyards, and later, to Sonoma Rose Vineyards and Orchard.

Goose Tracks Quilt Shop

The Sacramento quilt shop where Elm Creek Quilter Maggie Flynn begins her teaching career.

Grandma's Attic

Bonnie Markham's charming quilt shop in Waterford, Pennsylvania, on Main Street across from the Waterford College campus. Bonnie launched her business with funds she inherited from her beloved grandma Lucy.

Grand Union Hotel

An Arboles Valley hotel built in 1876 by James Hammell to serve passengers traveling along the stagecoach route between Los Angeles and Santa Barbara, California. When Elizabeth Bergstrom Nelson and her husband stayed there in 1925, she observed a broad wraparound porch, tall windows, and a second-floor balcony with a railing of turned spindles. Tall, leafy oaks lined the cobblestone drive leading up to the hotel, and the grounds offered guests beautiful groves of magnolia, orange, and lemon trees, with a walking path and a gazebo.

Grangerville, Pennsylvania

The town ten miles east of Creek's Crossing founded by the great-grandparents of Dorothea Granger Nelson, also her birthplace. Many decades later, Elm Creek Quilter Bonnie Markham rents an apartment in Grangerville after separating from her husband.

Greenfields Plantation

A tobacco plantation in Wentworth County, Virginia, where the slave Joanna was owned by Josiah Chester.

Haleakalā

A massive dormant volcano on the island of Maui whose Hawaiian name means "house of the sun." Its crater, roughly the size of Manhattan, offers stunningly beautiful and otherworldly desert landscape views.

Hale Kapa Kuiki

A charming oceanfront Victorian inn in Lahaina on Maui where Claire Duffield and Bonnie Markham establish Aloha Quilt Camp.

Harper Hall

The residence of Colonel Robert and Evangeline Harper in Charleston, a three-story red-brick building on Meeting Street with white stone trim and curved balconies on the second and third floors above the front door. Wrought iron gates open upon a path to the carriage house, and shady, white-pillared piazzas overlook gardens behind the residence. Surrounding the entire property is a solid wrought iron fence whose decorative flourishes cannot disguise the sharp, menacing spikes at the top of each bar, a defense constructed in 1822 following a thwarted slave uprising in the city.

Hazleton, Pennsylvania

The site of the Penn State branch campus where Sylvia Bergstrom Compson and Andrew Cooper take a stealthy, after-hours tour of the New England Quilt Museum's traveling exhibit *The Art of Women Pioneers.*

High Street Tavern

A popular pub in Water's Ford, Pennsylvania.

Holy Family Catholic Church

Gretchen Hartley's grandmother's Croatian parish in Pittsburgh.

Ho'oilo House

A beautiful, luxurious bed-and-breakfast in the foothills of the West Maui mountains where Claire Duffield learns the trade from the proprietors, her friends Amy and Dan.

Horsefeathers Boutique

An eclectic shop offering "art from found objects" in downtown Sewickley, Pennsylvania.

Hotel State College

A hotel built in 1855 on the corner of College Avenue and Allen Street in State College, Pennsylvania, across the street from the campus of Penn State University.

House of Happy Walls

Charmian London's residence on the Beauty Ranch in Glen Ellen, California, now a museum on the grounds of the Jack London State Historic Park.

Institute Hall

The Charleston hall where the Ordinance of Secession declaring the state of South Carolina's withdrawal from the Union was signed and ratified on December 20, 1860.

'Iolani Palace

Built in Honolulu in 1882, the 'Iolani Palace was the official residence of the last two monarchs of the Kingdom of Hawaii. Hinano Paoa takes Bonnie Markham to the palace, now a museum, so she can learn more about the Hawaiian monarchy and see the *Queen's Quilt,* a masterpiece created by Queen Lili'uokalani and her loyal friend Eveline Wilson during the long years of her imprisonment after her kingdom was overthrown.

Johnson's Bakery

A bakery in Sonoma, California, that serves as a front for organized crime.

Kuehner Hall

The building housing the College of Liberal Arts departments at Waterford College, named after an early resident of the Elm Creek Valley whose descendants founded the school.

Lahaina, Hawaii

An oceanfront town on West Maui where Claire Duffield has a quilt shop and where she and Bonnie Markham establish Aloha Quilt Camp in a historic inn. "Lahaina" means "merciless sun" or "a day of calamity" depending upon whom one asks and how one pronounces it. The town was the unofficial royal capital of the Hawaiian islands in the early eighteen hundreds, and King Kamehameha the Great in particular loved Lahaina for its spectacular surfing. Whalers considered it one of the most important ports in the Pacific, and when missionaries began settling in the town, violent conflicts between missionaries and sailors often erupted.

Lake Sherwood

A popular setting for picnics, swimming, and other outdoor recreation in Southern California's Arboles Valley.

Landenhurst Theater

A theater founded in Silver River, Indiana, by vaudeville performers Arthur and Christine Landenhurst.

Libby Prison

A notorious Confederate prison for captured Union officers, a three-story brick warehouse on Tobacco Row in Richmond, Virginia, that held a ship's chandlery and grocery business before the war. The prison takes up an entire block, with Carey Street and the city to the north and the James River to the south. The basement is exposed on the river side, and whitewashed so that any prisoners passing in front of it would stand out in stark relief. The eastern section of the basement contains an abandoned kitchen that was once used by the prisoners, but was closed off due to persistent flooding and an infestation of rats.

Lindsor's

An upscale department store where Adam Wagner's ex-fiancé, Natalie, is an executive.

Lockwood's

The dazzling, modern department store on Fifth Avenue in Manhattan founded by Charles Lockwood, Eleanor Lockwood Bergstrom's father, from which he earns a fortune.

Lutheran Theological Seminary

A Lutheran college high on a ridge in Gettysburg, Pennsylvania, converted into a battlefield hospital where Jonathan Granger labors to save the lives of wounded soldiers, both Union and Confederate, as the battle lines shift and control of the ridge passes from one army to the other.

Meadowbrook Hills

A real estate development in the Arboles Valley.

Meadowbrook Village Retirement Community

Vinnie Burkholder's home in her golden years.

Miss Sebastian's Academy for Young Ladies

The exclusive private school Agnes Emberly attends as a young woman in Philadelphia.

Mon Petit Café

A charming bistro in Manhattan not far from the 1863 House, where Sylvia Bergstrom Compson, Andrew Cooper, Adele LaMonte, and Julius Mortensen enjoy a meal together while Sylvia and Andrew are on their honeymoon.

Nadelfrau Hall of Science

A classroom and laboratory building on the Waterford College campus named after an early resident of the Elm Creek Valley.

New England Quilt Museum

A quilt museum in Lowell, Massachusetts, creators of a remarkable traveling exhibit called *The Art of Women Pioneers.*

North Freedom, South Carolina

A small rural town on Edisto Island founded by former slaves, a corruption of "North's Freedom," the name of the Edisto Island farm owned by Joanna North.

North's Freedom

An Edisto Island farm owned by Joanna North, forty acres of the plantation that once belonged to her former master Stephen Chester. The land was granted to her as part of the Port Royal Experiment, wherein property that had once belonged to rebellious planters was divided up among newly freed slaves.

Oak Grove

A cotton plantation on Edisto Island in South Carolina owned by Stephen Chester.

Oakwood Glen

A real estate development in the Arboles Valley.

Oasis

A day spa and salon in Summit Pass, Pennsylvania.

Ocean View Hills Retirement Community and Convalescent Center

A Sacramento retirement community, home of the Courtyard Quilters and workplace of future Elm Creek Quilter Maggie Flynn.

Old Lahaina Lu'au

The best and most authentic lu'au on Maui, according to Hinano Paoa.

Oxnard, California

A town about sixty-five miles west of Los Angeles where Rosa Diaz Barclay, Lars Jorgensen, and four of Rosa's children hide out for a few days after fleeing from Rosa's abusive husband.

Pheasant Branch, Pennsylvania

A town northwest of the Elm Creek Valley, home to Quiltsgiving participant Michaela Phillips.

Plaza Park

A park in Oxnard, California, where Rosa, Lars, and the children picnic and play in a brief respite from fear the day after they flee the Arboles Valley.

Plumeria Quilts

Claire Duffield's quilt shop in Lahaina on Maui.

Port Royal, South Carolina

A region of South Carolina captured by the Union early in the Civil War. There the United States government and numerous philanthropic and humanitarian groups attempted to prepare former slaves for life as free people.

Quilts 'n Things

Heidi Albrecht Mueller's very successful quilt shop in Sewickley, Pennsylvania, which she launched after essentially stealing Gretchen Hartley's business plan. The success of Quilts 'n Things ends up leading to the closing of Anna Del Maso's aunt's shop, where Anna worked part-time in high school.

Radcliffe Hotel

A hotel in Oxnard, California, where Rosa Diaz Barclay, Lars Jorgensen, and the children hide out after fleeing the Arboles Valley.

Rancho Triunfo, El

A ranch in Southern California in the Arboles Valley about forty-five miles north of Los Angeles. At the time it was granted to Ygnacio Rodriguez by the king of Spain in 1803, its full name was El Triunfo del Dulcísimo Nombre de Jesús, or "The Triumph of the Sweet Name of Jesus." (*See also* Triumph Ranch.)

Richardsport, Kentucky

A town thirty miles west of Brown Deer where Gwen Sullivan investigates a mysterious Pineapple quilt abandoned for decades in a church lost-and-found box.

Riverview Arms

A luxury hotel on the most fashionable street in Harrisburg, Pennsylvania, managed by George Bergstrom but owned by his father-in-law.

Rocky Mountain Quilt Museum

A marvelous quilt museum in Golden, Colorado, that Sylvia Bergstrom Compson and Andrew Cooper visit on a tip that Eleanor Lockwood Bergstrom's long-lost New York Beauty quilt was seen there.

Safari World

A wild animal farm in the Arboles Valley, a tourist attraction and training facility for animal actors.

St. Andrew's College

A small, private, Catholic college in Pennsylvania where Quiltsgiving participant Michaela Phillips majors in secondary education. Instead of school colors, it has a red, black, and white plaid called Crusader Tartan.

St. James of the Valley Catholic Church

The Cincinnati church where Megan Donohue and Adam Wagner marry.

St. John's Hospital

A hospital in Oxnard, California, where Rosa takes Ana and Miguel after fleeing the Arboles Valley. It is a white two-story building on the corner of F Street and Doris Avenue.

Salto Canyon

A wide, often treacherous canyon in the Arboles Valley adjacent to a broad mesa. Local folklore claims that the name derived from a Spanish word meaning "the jumping-off place," because of the many people who accidentally plunged to their deaths there while crossing the mesa in darkness or heavy fog.

Salto Creek

A creek that runs along the bottom of the Salto Canyon in the Arboles Valley. Ordinarily gentle and picturesque, and an important source of water in the dry Southern California climate, it can be prone to flash flooding during heavy rain.

Santa Susana, California

The sunny Southern California town where Andrew Cooper's son, Bob Cooper, lives with his wife and two daughters.

Seminary Co-op Bookstore

Summer Sullivan's favorite bookstore in Hyde Park, Chicago.

Sewickley, Pennsylvania

A residential suburb about twelve miles northwest of Pittsburgh along the Ohio River, where Sylvia Bergstrom Compson makes her home during her fifty-year absence from Elm Creek Manor.

Silver Pines, Minnesota

The hometown of Cross-Country Quilter Donna Jorgenson.

Simi Valley

A valley in Southern California where the nearest train station to the Arboles Valley is located.

Society Hill

The unofficial name for the most fashionable, posh neighborhood in Richard-sport, Kentucky, where the most prominent citizens built their homes so they could enjoy the view of the river.

Sonoma County

A beautiful, fertile county on the Northern California coast in the wine country.

Sonoma Rose Vineyards and Orchard

A beautiful and thriving forty-five-acre vineyard and prune orchard in Glen Ellen, California, nestled in a valley framed by Sonoma Mountain to the northwest and the Mayacamas. Formerly the Vanelli Vineyards and Orchard.

Stanford Hospital

The hospital in San Francisco where Ana and Miguel Barclay undergo treatment for their mysterious wasting illness.

State College, Pennsylvania

The central Pennsylvania college town adjacent to the University Park campus of Penn State, colloquially known as the "Happy Valley."

Stavanger, California

A fictional city in Southern California that Rosa Diaz Barclay, a.k.a. Rose Ottesen, claims as her hometown, well aware that a courthouse fire destroyed its vital records three years earlier, making her assertions difficult to disprove.

String Theory Quilt Shop

A quilt shop in Summit Pass, Pennsylvania, founded by a retired Penn State physics professor, Elspeth, and her mathematician partner, Margot, in a restored one-hundred-and-fifty-year-old carriage house. Karen Wise obtains a job there soon after she is not hired to work at Elm Creek Quilt Camp.

Summit Pass, Pennsylvania

A quaint village halfway between State College and the Elm Creek Valley known for its quirky shops, bed-and-breakfasts, and charming cafés located in restored historic buildings. The String Theory Quilt Shop, where Karen Wise works, is located on a main street.

Sunset Ridge, Georgia

A suburb of Atlanta, home to Quiltsgiving participant Pauline Tucker.

Susquehanna Presbyterian Hospital

The Pennsylvania hospital where Carol Mallory works as a nurse.

Thousand Oaks City Library

A wonderful public library in Thousand Oaks, California, that Sylvia Bergstrom Compson visits on a tip that her mother's long-lost white wholecloth crib quilt has been seen there.

Thrift Farm

A utopian farming community founded in the Elm Creek Valley by a handful of Transcendentalist Christians who were enlightened ethicists and philosophers but poor farmers. When the farm was lost to a flood years later, the denizens went their separate ways, and two of the founders, Robert and Lorena Granger, and their two children, Dorothea and Jonathan, were obliged to move in with Lorena's cantankerous widowed brother, Jacob Kuehner.

Triumph Ranch

The name of the one hundred twenty acres of prime Southern California ranch land Henry Nelson believes he has purchased with his life savings, including more than two hundred head of cattle, a farmhouse, and a bunkhouse. *See also* El Rancho Triunfo.

Two Bears Farm

The Nelson family farm in the Elm Creek Valley, Pennsylvania. It is adjacent to the Bergstrom family property, Elm Creek Farm.

Union Hall

A magnificent meeting hall in Water's Ford, Pennsylvania, constructed in 1862 by the Union Quilters, a local chapter of the United States Sanitary Commission, to host their fund-raising activities in support of the Union war effort, local soldiers, and veterans. The elegant Greek Revival structure boasts a concert hall and two galleries, one ideally suited for art exhibitions, the other for smaller lectures or musical performances. In the twentieth century, after some decades of neglect, the Waterford Historical Society restores the historic structure and reopens it as a local history museum and home to the Agnes Bergstrom Emberly Quilt Gallery.

Union Station

A grand train station in St. Louis where Henry and Elizabeth Nelson abruptly part company with Peter and Mae before continuing on to Los Angeles.

Vanelli Vineyards and Orchard

A secluded ranch in Glen Ellen, California, that boasts a vineyard, winery, and prune orchard. When Rosa Diaz Barclay sees it for the first time, she admires row upon row of trellises covered in lush grapevines nestled into a stream-cut valley surrounded by thickly forested slopes. The high, towering peak of Sonoma Mountain rises in the northwest, and the Mayacamas in the east.

Wainwright Library

A library in Richardsport, Kentucky, founded by judge and philanthropist Joseph Wainwright.

Warrington Prep

The exclusive private school for young gentlemen in Philadelphia that Richard Bergstrom and Andrew Cooper attend.

Waterford Arboretum

A forested nature conservancy adjacent to the campus of Waterford College and to a lovely neighborhood where many faculty members reside.

Waterford College

A small, private college in Waterford, Pennsylvania. Gwen Sullivan, Judy Nguyen DiNardo, and Tim Sonnenberg have served on the faculty, while Summer Sullivan, Michael Sonnenberg, and Jeremy Bernstein have been students. Before joining the staff of Elm Creek Quilts, Anna Del Maso worked for College Food Services on the campus.

Waterford, Pennsylvania

A small, rural college town nestled in the Elm Creek Valley in central Pennsylvania, with a population of about thirty-five thousand permanent residents and fifteen thousand Waterford College students when classes are in session. Downtown

Waterford borders the college campus, and aside from a few city-government offices, it consists mainly of bars, trendy restaurants, and shops catering to the students and faculty. Since its founding, the town has undergone several name changes; first known as Creek's Crossing, it was renamed Water's Ford shortly before the Civil War, which over time evolved into Waterford.

Wentworth County, Virginia

The location of Greenfields Plantation, where Joanna North was once enslaved.

Westfield, Michigan

A town in the Detroit metro area, home to Quiltsgiving participant Jocelyn Ames.

Westfield Middle School

A public school in the Detroit metro area where Jocelyn Ames teaches history and her husband, Noah, teaches science and coaches track and field. Their school colors are orange and blue and their mascot is the Wildcat.

West Grove

Stephen Chester's new plantation, built on acres farther inland than Oak Grove on Edisto Island in hopes of avoiding wartime dangers.

Widow's Pining

A dangerous part of Elm Creek three miles upstream of the ferry, with treacherous currents, sharp rocks, and unexpected undertows, the site of occasional drownings. Among the young men of Creek's Crossing, it was considered a test of courage to swim across Elm Creek at Widow's Pining, but responsible parents forbade their children from setting foot in the water there.

Wild Things

A children's book store in Summit Pass, Pennsylvania.

Wildwood Canyon

A scenic natural feature in Santa Susana, California, not far from the home of Bob and Cathy Cooper.

Wise Owl Teahouse

A charming teahouse and café in Summit Pass, Pennsylvania.

Wolf House

Jack London's magnificent dream home, which took three years to build and mysteriously burned to the ground in 1913 just before the Londons intended to move in. The ruins remain standing to this day on his famed Beauty Ranch.

Woodfall, Pennsylvania

A town eleven miles north of Creek's Crossing where Aaron Braun and his wife maintain a station on the Underground Railroad.

Woodpoppy Inn

A bed-and-breakfast in Summit Pass, Pennsylvania.

Wright's Pass

A southern pass into the Elm Creek Valley, renamed for Abel Wright, who constructed fortifications there to defend against Confederate troops as the Army of Northern Virginia pushed into Pennsylvania. He and other men of the Elm Creek Valley fought off bands of emboldened Copperheads in three skirmishes there.

Elm Creek Manor

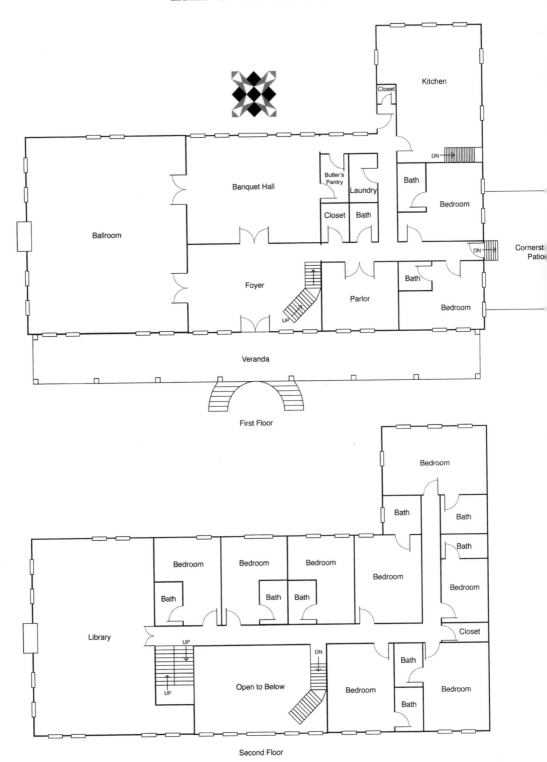

Kitchen

Closet

Banquet Hall

Butler's Pantry

Laundry

Bath

Bedroom

Closet

Bath

DN

Ballroom

Bath

Bedroom

Cornerst
Patio

DN

Foyer

Parlor

Bath

UP

Bedroom

Veranda

First Floor

Bedroom

Bath

Bath

Bath

Bedroom

Bedroom

Bedroom

Bedroom

Bedroom

Bath

Bath

Bath

Closet

Library

Bath

UP

Open to Below

DN

Bath

UP

Bedroom

Bedroom

Bath

Second Floor

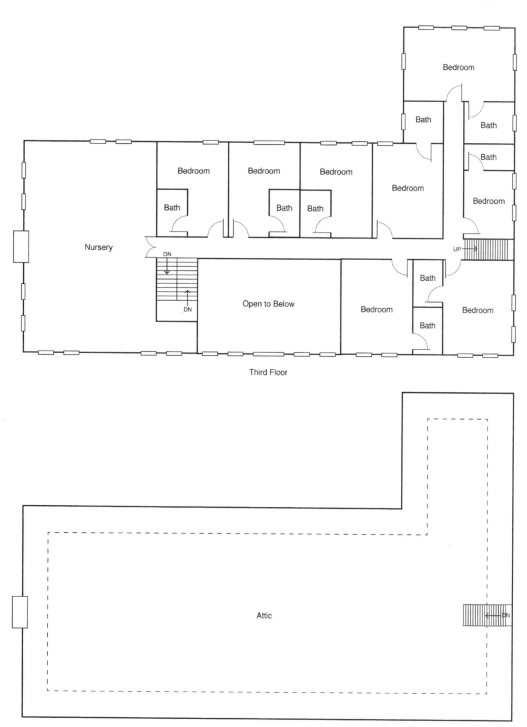

Third Floor

Attic

Artifacts, Souvenirs, and Associations

Sarah and Sylvia greeted Gretchen at the back door when she returned home later that evening, weary from a long day of sorting through dusty artifacts haphazardly packed into cartons and trunks in an upper gallery of Union Hall . . .

About thirty people had turned out for the workday, Gretchen reported, and they had divided themselves into three teams. The first group worked outside, trimming hedges, raking leaves, and yanking weeds from overgrown flower beds. The second, made up of people with carpentry skills or construction experience, fanned out through the building, inspected every room, made a very long list of necessary repairs, and began working on them. Gretchen was assigned to the third team, which took inventory of the storage rooms, sorting, identifying, and cataloging everything from collections of personal documents and shoe boxes stuffed with yellowed newspapers to books and daguerreotypes. It was hard, discouraging work. For each fascinating historical treasure the workers discovered, they found a half dozen so damaged by water, time, or mold that they had to be immediately discarded. "Some papers were so fragile they disintegrated the moment we picked them up," Gretchen lamented. "Others were so blackened by mold that scarcely any of the words remained legible. But someone, years ago, must have thought they were valuable enough to save, or they wouldn't have been stored in the gallery in the first place. I hate to think what knowledge has been lost, all because the building wasn't properly maintained."

"It's a shame," said Sylvia, with a quick upward glance that told Sarah she was thinking of the historical treasures she had found in the manor's attic, clues that had illuminated the mysteries of her heritage. Since her return to Elm Creek Manor after her fifty-year absence, Sylvia,

Sarah, and Summer had investigated many of the trunks and cartons, but much had remained undisturbed.

Thinking of all that they had discovered, Sarah could only imagine what could have been learned from documents and artifacts stored in a public building nearly as old as the town itself, if only they had been properly preserved.

—*The Wedding Quilt*

Abel Wright Foundation

A nonprofit organization dedicated to preserving Abel Wright's legacy and promoting literacy and history education in public schools.

Aloha Quilt, The

A Hawaiian appliqué pattern incorporating birds of paradise motifs, designed by Hinano Paoa as a farewell gift for Bonnie Markham.

Aloha Quilt Camp

A quilters' retreat established by Claire Duffield and Bonnie Markham in the Hale Kapa Kuiki, a historic inn in the town of Lahaina on Maui.

America's Back Roads

A television program that promises to take viewers "down the road less traveled to the heart of America" and produces a feature on Elm Creek Quilt Camp in its early years.

Anabelle Marie

The ship Gerda Bergstrom takes from Germany to America.

Art of Women Pioneers, The

A traveling exhibit from the New England Quilt Museum that Sylvia Bergstrom Compson and Andrew Cooper tour while on their honeymoon.

AsIsAuctions.com

A shady online auction house run by the budding young swindler Jason Oplichter, who occasionally employs the alias George K. Robinson and claims to work for a nonexistent bricks-and-mortar business, Brandywine Antiques.

Authors' Album

A signature quilt created by Dorothea Granger Nelson and the Creek's Crossing Library Board to raise funds to build a lending library.

Baltimore Album

Sylvia Bergstrom Compson works on an elaborate appliqué quilt in this style in December 1943 in anticipation of a friend's wedding. Many years later, Agnes Emberly teaches Baltimore Album classes at Elm Creek Quilt Camp.

Baltimore Quilting Circle

A group of ladies—Sylvia's mother-in-law, Josephine Compson, and Josephine's friends—whom Sylvia Bergstrom Compson teaches to quilt during the postwar years when she resides with her in-laws at Compson's Resolution.

Bergstrom Thoroughbreds

The Bergstrom family horse-breeding business founded by Hans Bergstrom at Elm Creek Farm in 1857 and carried on by his descendants for nearly a century.

Bleigiessen

"Lead pouring," a German New Year's Eve tradition. A small piece of lead is held in an old spoon above a fire until the lead has melted. The liquid metal is then poured into a bowl of cold water, where it swiftly hardens. The shape the lead takes is said to tell the fortune of that person for the coming year.

Blossom

A Bergstrom Thoroughbred and mother of Dresden Rose, the first horse of Sylvia Bergstrom Compson's very own.

Brandywine Antiques

Purportedly an antiques shop in Fort Dodge, Iowa, that contacts Sylvia Bergstrom Compson claiming to have her mother's long-lost Ocean Waves quilt, it is actually the front for a sketchy Internet business, AsIsAuctions.com.

Breadfruit

A traditional Hawaiian appliqué pattern. A turquoise-and-white Breadfruit quilt made by Midori Tanaka adorns the bed in the suite in the Hale Kapa Kuiki where Bonnie resides during her stay.

Brown Does

Gwen Sullivan's mother's quilt guild in Brown Deer, Kentucky.

Bûche de Noël

A special Christmas dessert, a cake rolled and shaped to look like a yule log, often decorated with chocolate frosting shaped to resemble bark and meringue mushrooms. As children, both Eleanor Lockwood Bergstrom and Agnes Emberly enjoyed bûche de Noël at Christmastime.

Bukra

The word the slaves at Oak Grove and elsewhere in South Carolina use to refer to white people, especially slaveholders.

Calennig

A Welsh tradition. Very early on New Year's morning, young boys would each procure a fresh evergreen twig and a pail of water. From dawn until noon the boys traversed the village, dipping the twig into the water and sprinkling the faces neighbors out and about. In return, they would be rewarded with *calennig,* or "small gifts" of coins or fruit. If they came to a house where the occupants were still asleep, they sprinkled the doorways instead, singing songs or reciting chants welcoming the New Year.

Cancer Quilt

While undergoing treatment for ovarian cancer, Elaine McIntyre works on an abstract quilt of angry reds, sickening greens, and blacks as deep as oblivion, in jagged shapes. Her husband Russell McIntyre finishes the project, her last quilt becoming his first.

Candlelight

A welcoming ceremony on Sunday evening of quilt camp in which campers express their hopes and goals for the week ahead, a revered Elm Creek Quilts tradition.

Castor and Pollux

Two beautiful, perfectly matched horses Hans Bergstrom wins in a horse race from Amos Liggett, along with the deed to his farm in Pennsylvania.

Celtic knotwork

Bonnie Markham makes a blue-and-gold Celtic knotwork quilt for the Waterford Summer Quilt Festival, earning a first place in the appliqué/large bed quilt division.

Certain Sewing and Suffrage Faction of Creek's Crossing, Pennsylvania, The

The name of Dorothea Granger Nelson's politically minded sewing circle before the Civil War, called the Certain Faction for short.

Chain of Progress

A quilt the young sisters Sylvia Bergstrom Compson and Claudia Bergstrom Midden collaborate on and enter in a quilt competition at the 1933 World's Fair in Chicago.

Charleston Gunboat Society

An organization founded by Evangeline Chester Harper and her friend Mrs. Hoskins, whose mission was to raise money to purchase a gunboat to protect Charleston Harbor from a Union attack.

Charleston Soldiers Relief Association

An organization dedicated to raising funds for the Confederate soldiers' needs. As an active member, Evangeline Chester Harper helps arrange charity concerts and association fairs, with the proceeds going to buy provisions for the soldiers at the front.

Charlie

A fourteen-year-old African lion, a former movie star who has retired to Safari World, a wild animal farm and training facility in the Arboles Valley.

Charm Quilt

A style of quilt in which no two pieces are made of the same fabric, although they may be (and often are) the same size and shape. Megan Donohue's watercolor charm quilt wins first prize in *Contemporary Quilting* magazine's annual design contest.

Cherokee Rose Quilters

The most acclaimed, exclusive quilt guild in Georgia, for which Quiltsgiving participant Pauline Tucker serves for many years as treasurer. The Cherokee Rose Quilters are tireless champions of the quilting arts, respected ambassadors for the state of Georgia in the art world, and dedicated benefactors of numerous worthy causes. Their annual quilt retreat at the Château Élan is universally acknowledged to be worth every penny spent, every mile driven, and every seam ripped out and resewn in order to impress their perfectionist teachers.

Christmas Quilt, The

A red, green, gold, and white Christmas quilt worked upon by several generations of Bergstrom women and finally completed by Sylvia Bergstrom Compson and Sarah McClure.

Close the Book, California

The state chapter of a national organization of parents and citizens dedicated to removing books they deem offensive from school and public libraries.

College Food Services

Anna Del Maso's employer before she becomes the chef of Elm Creek Manor.

Conejo Hills Call

The local newspaper of Linnea Nelson's hometown, Conejo Hills, California.

Contemporary Quilting

A popular quilting magazine that sponsors an annual design contest. One year, Megan Donohue's watercolor charm quilt takes first prize, a week at Elm Creek Quilt Camp.

Copperheads

Northern Democrats who opposed the Civil War and advocated for an immediate peace settlement with the Confederates, even if it meant allowing those states to withdraw from the Union and perpetuate slavery. Although their political enemies understood their name to denote their similarity to the poisonous snake, it actually came from the Liberty heads they cut from copper pennies and wore as badges.

Cornucopia

Claudia Bergstrom Midden made a woven cornucopia as a schoolgirl. The Bergstrom family used it as a centerpiece for their Thanksgiving feast, and decades later, it came to serve an important role in the Elm Creek Quilters' Quilter's Holiday celebrations. Each quilter would sew a quilt block, one that by either name or imagery represented something for which she wished to give thanks, and place it in the cornucopia. As they enjoyed their potluck lunch, they would remove the blocks from the cornucopia one by one and share their stories of gratitude, the inspiration for their handiwork.

Courtyard Quilters

A quilting bee made up of residents of the Sacramento retirement home where Elm Creek Quilter Maggie Flynn formerly worked.

Creek's Crossing Agricultural Society

A group of progressive farmers in the Elm Creek Valley who work together for mutual benefit, including the hiring of a horse-powered thresher during the harvest.

Creek's Crossing Album

A masterpiece of the Agnes Bergstrom Emberly Quilt Gallery, the *Creek's Crossing Album* is reminiscent of the Baltimore Album style. Discovered during the restoration of Union Hall, it contains sixteen large appliqué blocks about eighteen inches square, with calico flowers, leaves, and figures sewn by hand into soft muslin. The blocks are arranged in four rows of four blocks apiece, with Turkey-red cornerstones and an appliqué border of elegant swags gathered by roses framing the whole. One of the blocks bears the embroidered inscription "Creek's Crossing, Elm Creek Valley, Pennsylvania, 1849," while on the back is embroidered, "Appliquéd by Miss Dorothea Granger, 1849. Quilted by Mrs. Abel Wright, 1850. Presented to Mrs. Wright by Miss Granger in celebration of her marriage, 1847, on the occasion of her arrival to her new home."

Creek's Crossing Eight

Eight residents of the Elm Creek Valley—Dorothea and Thomas Nelson, Gerda and Hans Bergstrom, and Abel, Constance, George, and Joseph Wright—who worked as stationmasters on the Underground Railroad. In 1859, they were betrayed, but although they were imprisoned for breaking the Fugitive Slave Act, all eight were released after a few days and none were ever brought to trial. The nationwide outcry over the notorious incident led to the changing of the town's name from Creek's Crossing to Water's Ford.

Creek's Crossing Informer

A newspaper serving the residents of Creek's Crossing, Pennsylvania, in the antebellum era.

Cross-Country Quilters' Challenge Quilt

A sampler quilt made by Vinnie Burkholder, Grace Daniels, Megan Donohue, Donna Jorgenson, and Julia Merchaud. On their last day of Elm Creek Quilt Camp, the new friends chose a single piece of fabric, divided it into equal shares, and resolved to use it in a quilt block that each woman would piece to symbolize her personal goals. They planned to reunite at Elm Creek Manor the following summer to sew their blocks together, complete the quilt, and renew their cross-country friendship.

Crowns and Kahili

A stunning yellow-and-red Hawaiian appliqué quilt designed by Hinano Paoa and made by Midori Tanaka for the grandest suite in the Hale Kapa Kuiki. The crowns honor Hawaiian kings and queens, and the *kahili* are feather standards displayed in throne rooms and carried in royal processions.

Curandera

A traditional healer. At age fifteen, Isabel Rodriguez seeks help from a *curandera* in San Mateo to cure her mother's breast cancer.

Daisy Bouquets

Grandma DiNardo's appliqué bridal quilt, a precious heirloom made by her mother.

Democratic Watchman

A Copperhead newspaper published by the firebrand Peter Gray Meek out of Bellefonte, Pennsylvania.

Diamond

A Bergstrom Thoroughbred belonging to Herbert Drury.

Dinner for One

A comical skit written in the 1920s for the British cabaret, but best known to Germans from the black-and-white version filmed in the early 1960s in front of a live audience in Hamburg. It has been shown on German television every New

Year's Eve since the 1970s, and watching the program—and sometimes shouting the dialogue along with the characters, serving the same meal as the one served in the play, or finishing a beer every time a certain line is repeated—is considered an integral part of a German New Year's Eve celebration.

Dresden Rose

The Bergstrom Thoroughbred Sylvia Bergstrom Compson rides competitively as a young woman, a Christmas gift from her father at the suggestion of Santa Claus.

Drys

A nickname for those who supported Prohibition, in contrast to their opponents, known as Wets.

Elm Creek Medallion

A round robin quilt the Elm Creek Quilters make as a surprise for Sylvia in *Round Robin*. It is proudly displayed from the second-floor balcony in the grand front foyer of Elm Creek Manor.

Elms and Lilacs

An exquisite appliqué quilt Eleanor Lockwood Bergstrom makes as a gift for her husband, Frederick Bergstrom, on the occasion of their twentieth anniversary. The *Elms and Lilacs* quilt is Sylvia Bergstrom Compson's favorite of all her mother's quilts; indeed, it is quite possibly her favorite out of all the quilts she has ever seen. A masterpiece of appliqué and intricate, feathery quilting, the *Elms and Li-*

lacs quilt displays her mother's skills at their finest. The circular wreath of appliquéd elm leaves, lilacs, and vines in the center gives the quilt its name; a graceful, curving double line of pink and lavender frames it. The outermost border carries on the floral theme with elm leaves tumbling amidst lilacs and other foliage, and intertwining pink and lavender ribbons finish the scalloped edge. The medallion style allows for open areas, which Eleanor Lockwood Bergstrom quilts in elaborate feathered plumes over a delicate background crosshatch.

Explore Summit Pass

An organization founded by Karen Wise whose mission is to sustain the economic viability of the village of Summit Pass, Pennsylvania, by educating residents and visitors about the importance of supporting local small businesses.

Exterior Architects

The Waterford firm where Matt McClure works as a landscape architect.

Family Tree (1)

Julia Merchaud's long-running, acclaimed television series, for which she received two Emmys and a Golden Globe for her portrayal of Grandma Wilson.

Family Tree (2)

Mother and daughter Gwen and Summer Sullivan collaborate on this quilt, which incorporates piecing, appliqué, and photo-transfer techniques. They receive second place in the innovative division at the Waterford Summer Quilt Festival.

Farewell Breakfast

The closing event of Elm Creek Quilt Camp held on Saturday mornings on the Cornerstone Patio (weather permitting), featuring a delicious breakfast, a campers' show-and-tell, and the sharing of favorite memories of the week.

Fawns

The daughters of the Brown Does, too young to be considered guild members but welcome and encouraged to attend guild meetings with their mothers. Daughters of Brown Does are considered Fawns from birth regardless of their own inclinations.

Festa di San Silvestro, La

An Italian New Year's Eve celebration, with music, dancing, games, and a feast featuring dishes made from lentils, which traditionally represent riches, abundance, and good fortune in the New Year.

Feuerzangenbowle

"Fire tongs punch," a traditional German hot beverage made from red wine, rum, lemon, orange, cinnamon, allspice, and cardamom that the Bergstrom family enjoyed on New Year's Eve.

First Footing

A Scottish New Year's Eve tradition that holds that the first person who crosses the threshold after the stroke of midnight will determine the luck of the household for the coming year. The year will be especially prosperous if a tall, dark-haired, handsome man is the first to enter the house on the first day of the New Year. A new bride or an expectant mother is also believed to bring good luck, but a blond man is thought to bring bad luck, possibly because in the eighth century, when the Vikings invaded Scotland, a dark-haired man was assumed to be a fellow Scot, but a blond could be a Viking, come to pillage and plunder.

Flying Saucer Sisters

A group of three quilters, frequent Elm Creek Quilt Campers, whose closets are stuffed full of UFOs (Unfinished Fabric Objects). They have made a pact not to begin any new quilts until they have cut their UFO backlogs in half. Unbeknownst to them, Diane Sonnenberg refers to them as Team Fuchsia for the signature hue of their multiple sets of matching clothes.

Forty-ninth Pennsylvania Volunteers, Company L

The Union regiment and company in which the soldiers from the Elm Creek Valley serve during the Civil War.

Freedom Quilt

In the nineteenth century, a quilt presented to a young man upon the occasion of his twenty-first birthday.

Freedom Quilters

A quilting circle founded by Joanna North in the small rural town of North Freedom, South Carolina, shortly after the end of the Civil War.

Garden Maze

Sarah McClure uses a Garden Maze setting for her first quilt, a twelve-block sampler.

Giving Quilt

A Quiltsgiving project designed especially for giving, quick to put together but as beautiful and warm as any more complicated pattern. The pattern is taught in an optional, weeklong class, designed for beginners but suitable for anyone who wants to learn a new, simple, attractive pattern that can be assembled with relative ease. The Elm Creek Quilters design a new Giving Quilt each Quiltsgiving to encourage volunteers to return year after year to build up a repertoire of patterns. Sylvia designs the first Giving Quilt using the Bright Hopes block. Sarah designs the second using the Rail Fence block. For the fourth Quiltsgiving and third Giving Quilt, Gwen teaches the Stacked Coins pattern. For the fifth Quiltsgiving and fourth Giving Quilt—the project featured in the novel *The Giving Quilt*—Gretchen designs a quilt using the Resolution Square block.

Golden Reel Productions

Grover Higgins's movie production company in Hollywood.

Grandma Wilson

Julia Merchaud's character in the acclaimed television series *Family Tree,* a role for which she received two Emmys and a Golden Globe.

Haku La'ape

A quilt made by Midori Tanaka in the traditional Hawaiian style, jade green appliqué on white, in the likeness of a monstera plant.

Harvest Dance

An annual community celebration held every autumn in Creek's Crossing, Pennsylvania.

Hell Dance

One element of the tryouts for the St. Andrew's College cheerleading squad, a complex four-minute dance routine that the female candidates are required to learn in one afternoon, practice all night, and perform the following day.

Ho 'ā Ahi

A Hawaiian phrase meaning "to kindle fire," the name of the Aloha Quilt Camp welcoming ceremony, which takes place on the first evening of camp. Campers gather on the beach at sunset, sit on grass mats in a circle around a bonfire, and pass a pair of *'uli 'uli* around the circle. When a camper receives the feathered gourd rattles, she explains why she came to Aloha Quilt Camp and what she hopes to achieve that week. When she is finished speaking, she shakes the *'uli 'uli* and passes them on to the next camper.

Hogmanay

The Scottish word for the last day of the year. As Sylvia Bergstrom Compson's grandmother describes Hogmanay in her Scottish mother's household: "We had to clean the house thoroughly before we could give any thought to a celebration. Before midnight on New Year's Eve, the fireplaces had to be swept clean and the ashes carried outside. All debts had to be paid, too. Sometimes my mother would send one of my brothers running to a neighbor's house after supper with a coin or two to pay off a debt, even though most of our neighbors weren't Scottish and wouldn't mind if she waited another day. The purpose was to prepare yourselves and your home to begin the New Year with a fresh, clean slate, with all the problems, mistakes, and strife of the old year forgotten."

Holiday Boutique

An annual holiday fair held by Sylvia Bergstrom Compson's church to raise money for a local food pantry.

Ho'oilo

The Hawaiian winter, a four-month rainy season. In ancient times, priests would watch the night skies from temples on the western sides of the Hawaiian islands. When the *Makali'i*—the Hawaiian name for the star cluster known as the Pleiades or the Seven Sisters—began to rise at sunset and set at dawn, *ho'oilo* had begun.

Hopkins and Steele

A small public accounting firm two blocks from Grandma's Attic in downtown Waterford, Pennsylvania. Sarah McClure applies for a job with the company, but she turns down their offer in favor of launching Elm Creek Quilts with Sylvia Bergstrom Compson.

Humility block

A block pieced with a deliberate error so the quilter may avoid the sin of pride, since only God can create perfection.

iFabricShop

An online fabric retailer whose new price-check-and-purchase smart-phone app threatens the economic viability of independent bricks-and-mortar quilt shops.

Imagination Quest

A national, nonprofit educational organization dedicated to promoting creativity, problem solving, and teamwork beyond the classroom. Teams of five to eight students work together over the course of several months to choose one of five challenges, solve it, and present their solution at a regional competition. Depending upon the challenge, the students might be required to build a device that can perform specific tasks within a certain time frame, write and perform a skit, or—most often—a combination of the two. Although each team has a parent or teacher acting as advisor, the work is explicitly required to be the students' own.

Imu

A traditional Hawaiian underground oven.

Jungle Vengeance

An action movie set in South America starring Julia Merchaud's arrogant *A Patchwork Life* costar, Rick Rowan.

Jupiter

Charles Lockwood's bold, black stallion that was said to have acquired a taste for blood in the Spanish-American War.

Kalikimaka

The Hawaiian word for "Christmas."

Kanaka maoli

"Native Hawaiian."

Kapa

A traditional Hawaiian cloth made from the bark of the paper mulberry tree.

Kapa moe

A traditional Hawaiian bed covering made by sewing together several layers of *kapa* with large running stitches and decorating the top with traditional patterns made from natural dyes.

Kapu

A word used to describe something absolutely forbidden in traditional Hawaiian culture.

Kau

The Hawaiian summer.

Knecht Ruprecht

In the German tradition, on the eve of St. Nicholas's Day, St. Nicholas traveled with a helper named Knecht Ruprecht. He carried St. Nicholas's bag of treats for him, and it was he who went up and down the chimneys filling the shoes of good little children with candy, nuts, and fruit. But he also carried a sack and a stick. He used the stick to beat naughty children, and if a child was very, very bad, Knecht Ruprecht would stuff him in the sack and carry him off, never to see his family again.

Ladies' Aid Society

A philanthropic organization in Creek's Crossing, Pennsylvania.

Laulima Quilters

Midori Tanaka's quilt guild in Lahaina, Hawaii.

Left-Armed Corps

The name given to the scores of right-handed veterans who lost their right arms to war wounds and who, upon their return to civilian life, were obliged to adapt to using their left arms and hands for writing, work, and other tasks of daily life.

Lei

(1) A traditional Hawaiian garland of flowers, recognized around the world as a symbol of Hawaii and the aloha spirit. (2) The border of a traditional Hawaiian appliqué quilt. The lei of a quilt can symbolize the lands beyond Hawaii, with the center of the quilt representing Hawaii itself. Since the leis are unbroken, they also represent the circle of life, and life continuing into eternity, even after death.

Library Board, The

A group of ladies of Creek's Crossing, Pennsylvania, led by Violet Pearson Engle who organize to raise funds to build a lending library. Other members include Mrs. Deakins, the mayor's wife; Mrs. Collins, married to the banker; Miss Nadelfrau, a timid dressmaker; Mrs. Claverton, a prosperous farmer's wife; and Dorothea Granger, a former schoolteacher, abolitionist, and suffragist.

Lowell Offering

A monthly magazine that from 1840 to 1845 published poetry and fiction written by mill girls, the young women who worked in the textile mills of Lowell, Massachusetts. Harriet Findley Birch contributed a short story, probably autobiographical, about a mill girl who married and left Lowell to accompany her husband west along the Oregon Trail.

Loyal Union Sampler

A unique masterpiece organized by the Union Quilters to raise money to construct Union Hall, where they intend to hold fund-raisers to support the Union war effort, and especially to provide for the Forty-ninth Pennsylvania Volunteers, Company L, and the Sixth United States Colored Troops.

Maile

A Hawaiian flower often used to make leis. Bonnie Markham finds it wonderfully fragrant, reminiscent of vanilla and fresh woodland air, sweet and spicy and woodsy.

Makahiki

A four-month season of peace and celebration marking the beginning of the new year in the Hawaiian calendar.

Meadows of Middlebury, The

A film based upon the classic children's novel featuring Julia Merchaud as Mrs. Dormouse, her first major role. Despite strong critical acclaim, the film quickly slipped into obscurity.

Mele Kalikimaka

The Hawaiian phrase for "Merry Christmas."

Merrimack Manufacturing Company

The maker of more than twenty of the cotton prints in the Harriet Findley Birch sampler and her presumed employer.

Modern Quilter

A magazine that carries the fateful Help Wanted ad from which numerous aspiring quilt camp teachers learn about two vacant positions on the Elm Creek Quilts faculty.

Mrs. Dormouse

Julia Merchaud's character in *The Meadows of Middlebury,* a film based upon the classic children's novel. It is her first major role.

My Journey with Harriet

Maggie Flynn's replica of the Harriet Findley Birch sampler, the inspiration for her bestselling pattern book of the same name.

Na Huihui o Makali'i

The Hawaiian name for the star cluster known as the Pleiades or the Seven Sisters. In ancient times, priests would watch the night skies from temples on the western sides of the Hawaiian islands. When the *Makali'i* began to rise at sunset and set at dawn, it marked the beginning of winter, *ho'oilo,* the rainy season. *Ho'oilo* lasted about four months, until the *Makali'i* began to rise in the east at sunrise and were no longer visible at night, marking the start of *kau,* or summer.

National Quilting Day

An annual celebration of the art and history of quilting established on the third Saturday in March by the National Quilting Association in 1991.

New Year's Reflections

A quilt Sylvia Bergstrom Compson makes as a tribute to the memories and lessons of New Years past.

Norwegian Grade

An improved road connecting the Arboles Valley and the Simi Valley, named in honor of the Norwegian immigrants who donated the land and constructed the difficult route through the hills.

Ohana

The Hawaiian word for "family."

Old Butterfield Road

A dangerous, steep, and often muddy road farmers in the Arboles Valley used to haul their crops over the grade into the Camarillo Valley to the train station, before the Norwegian Grade was constructed in the Simi Valley.

A Patchwork Life

A film based upon the life of Kansas pioneer Sadie Henderson, written and directed by her great-granddaughter Ellen Henderson and starring Cross-Country Quilter Julia Merchaud.

PennCellular Corporation

A mobile phone company in Waterford, Pennsylvania, where Sarah McClure applies for a job soon after moving to town.

Phylloxera

A relentless, voracious species of louse that devastated California vineyards in the late 1800s.

Piko

The center of a traditional Hawaiian appliqué quilt. A *piko* can be solid or open, but it must be balanced so that love and energy can flow freely. A solid *piko* may represent the family, the strong core of a person's life, or Mother Earth. An open *piko* represents the gateway between the physical world and the spiritual.

Pineapple Patch

Bonnie Markham's first quilt made in the Hawaiian style.

Planter

The Confederate transport steamer an enslaved Charleston Harbor pilot named Robert Smalls steals and turns over to the Union navy in a daring escape to freedom.

Potluck Pals

Friends of Aunt Lynn and Lena who gather twice a month for a potluck supper and wild games of gin rummy. Young Vinnie Burkholder is very impressed by them.

Prohibition

The banning—with a few specific exceptions—of the manufacture and sale of liquor within the United States from 1920 to 1933.

Project Linus

A national organization dedicated to providing love, warmth, and comfort to children in need through the gifts of homemade quilts, blankets, and afghans.

Queen's Quilt

A masterpiece of crazy quilting and embroidery created by Queen Lili'uokalani, the last monarch of the Kingdom of Hawaii, and her loyal friend Eveline Wilson during the long years of her imprisonment after her kingdom was overthrown.

Quilter's Holiday

A special holiday celebrated by the Elm Creek Quilters on the Friday after Thanksgiving. While others throughout their rural central Pennsylvania valley are sleeping in or launching the Christmas shopping season, the Elm Creek Quilters gather at Elm Creek Manor for a sewing marathon to work on holiday gifts or decorations. At noon they break for a potluck lunch of dishes made from leftovers from their family feasts the previous day.

Quilts from the Kitchen

Anna Del Maso's somewhat tongue-in-cheek name for a series of quilts she has made that unintentionally turned out to resemble such culinary delights as strawberry pie, eggs Benedict, chocolate soufflé, and blueberries falling from a bucket into cream.

Quiltsgiving

The Elm Creek Quilters' annual winter camp session devoted to creating quilts for charity, held on the week after Thanksgiving.

Quilts of North Freedom, The

An exhibit featuring the work of the Freedom Quilters, a quilting circle founded in the small rural town of North Freedom, South Carolina, shortly after the end of the Civil War. The scrap quilts are improvisational rather than carefully planned, with bold colors and striking arrangements of squares, bars, and triangles.

St. Nicholas Day

A holiday celebrated by the Bergstrom family on December 6. At bedtime, each child within the household leaves a shoe by the fireplace. When they wake the next morning, if they have been good children all year, they find their shoes filled with candy, nuts, and fruit. If they have been naughty, they might find coal or twigs.

Salto Creek

A creek running through the bottom of the Salto Canyon in the Arboles Valley. While it is usually a gentle, picturesque waterway, it is prone to flash flooding in heavy downpours.

Sarah's Gold

A new breed of apple cultivated by Matt McClure and named in honor of his wife, Sarah. It is very popular at the Waterford town square farmer's market.

Schultz's Printers

A print shop in Creek's Crossing (later Water's Ford) and the publisher of the *Water's Ford Register.*

Sewickley Sunrise

Sylvia's best-known quilt. It was featured in the American Quilter's Society's calendar for May 1982 and is included in the Museum of the American Quilter's Society's permanent collection.

Sheik Bandits, The

A gang of three or four sharply dressed men who robbed post offices and banks in Los Angeles County and preyed on unwary travelers in the 1920s.

Silver Lake Quilters' Guild

A South Carolina quilt guild where Sylvia Bergstrom Compson meets Margaret Alden after a speaking engagement.

Sixth United States Colored Troops

The African-American Union regiment to which Abel Wright belongs.

Skyline Eco Adventures

A zipline adventure company in Ka'anapali, Hawaii, that gives Bonnie Markham the ride of her life.

Soldier's Friend

A Civil War–era magazine dedicated to helping veterans adapt to civilian life.

Star of the West

A steamship sent by the United States government to deliver supplies and reinforcements to Major Anderson's Union troops holding Fort Sumter in Charleston Harbor. It was fired upon by cadets from the South Carolina Military Academy stationed on Morris Island and turned back without relieving the Union garrison.

Stitch Witches

Grandma Lucy's quilting bee.

Sunset Ridge Quilt Guild

The first quilt guild Georgia quilter and Quiltsgiving participant Pauline Tucker joins, before she is invited to join the exclusive Cherokee Rose Quilters.

Susquehanna Militia, African Descent

A volunteer regiment of African-American men that formed out of Mercersburg, Pennsylvania, in the early months of the Civil War. Although the men organized their ranks, made their own uniforms, appointed officers, and trained under the guidance of retired white army veterans, the United States government refused to allow them to enlist. They eventually disbanded.

Sylvester Ball

A celebration held on New Year's Eve in honor of Holy St. Sebastian, featuring the gathering of friends and family, delicious food and drink, and games.

Sylvia's Bridal Sampler

Sylvia's Bridal Sampler is a 140-block sampler quilt the Elm Creek Quilters secretly make for Sylvia Bergstrom Compson and her new husband, Andrew Cooper, in *The Master Quilter*. The Elm Creek Quilters and many of Sylvia's other friends, colleagues, and former students contribute sampler blocks that represent what Sylvia means to them.

Tangled Web Quilters

A group of six quilters Sarah McClure meets soon after moving to Waterford, Pennsylvania, who soon become her dearest friends and colleagues. Several years before, they seceded from the Waterford Quilting Guild mostly because of the animosity between their friend Diane Sonnenberg and longtime guild president Mary Beth Callahan.

Tartan Crusader

The mascot of St. Andrew's College.

Tartan Times

The St. Andrew's College student newspaper.

Team Fuchsia

A group of three inseparable friends and dedicated Elm Creek Quilt Campers who enjoy wearing matching attire in their signature hue. Diane invented the nickname, which the Elm Creek Quilters use privately. They call themselves the Flying Saucer Sisters for their many UFOs (Unfinished Fabric Objects).

Thompkins County Quilt Guild

Gwen Sullivan's quilt guild while she is a graduate student at Cornell.

Trouble at Rocky Ranch

A Western filmed in the Arboles Valley.

Tulip Bouquets

An unquilted but exquisite appliqué quilt top Grandma DiNardo's mother intended as a bridal quilt for Grandma DiNardo's sister, who died unexpectedly before she could marry.

Ua Mau ke Ea o ka aina i ka Pono

The motto of the Kingdom of Hawaii and, later, the state of Hawaii, meaning, "The life of the land is perpetuated in righteousness."

UFO

An Unfinished Fabric Object, a quilt that is not yet complete. The connotation is that the project has been abandoned, in contrast to a WIP, a work in progress.

'Uli 'uli

Traditional Hawaiian gourd rattles used by hula dancers, often decorated with feathers, flowers, and leaves.

Underground Railroad

A clandestine network of safe houses and secret routes used by fugitive slaves to escape from the South to free northern states and Canada in the years leading up to the Civil War. The language of the railroad was adopted to help maintain secrecy. Safe houses were known as "stations" or "depots," and those who kept them were "stationmasters"; allies who guided runaways along secret, often purposely indirect routes were called "conductors"; and the runaways were spoken of as "passengers" or "cargo."

United States Sanitary Commission

A private relief agency created by federal legislation in 1861 to support soldiers and veterans of the Union army during the Civil War. Its mission was to tend to the soldiers' "sanitary needs" by promoting healthy conditions in the army camps, and to provide care for the ill and wounded by staffing field hospitals and educating officers and government officials on matters of health and sanitation. All across the North, volunteers—many of whom were women—organized local chapters to raise money for the war effort and to provide essential supplies, and it is estimated that they contributed $5 million in cash and $15 million in donated goods to the Union cause.

University Realty

The Waterford real estate agency of Gregory Krolich, who is determined to buy Elm Creek Manor from Sylvia Bergstrom Compson.

Veteran Reserve Corps

During the Civil War, a corps of wounded Union soldiers who, though no longer able to fight, could perform other necessary duties, freeing up more able-bodied men for field duty. Members assigned to the First Battalion could still hold a rifle and withstand the rigors of guard duty, and often served as guards at prison camps or railroads, or as details for provost marshals escorting new recruits and prisoners to and from the front. The Second Battalion was comprised of men who had been more seriously injured, and they generally served as cooks, orderlies, or nurses. It was honorable service, benefiting both the country and the patriotic men who remained eager to serve the Union despite their injuries.

VirtualMaterial.biz

An online fabric retailer whose huge volume sales enable it to offer steep discounts independent bricks-and-mortar quilt shops cannot match.

Volger Academy

The private boarding school in Walterboro about fifty miles west of Charleston and twenty-five miles from Stephen Chester's new plantation, West Grove, where young Elliot Chester is a student.

Vote Yes for Libraries

An organization created by Kevin Nelson and Alicia Torres to promote a city referendum on a dedicated millage to fund the Conejo Hills Public Library.

Waterford College Chamber Ensemble

A group of musicians, students of nearby Waterford College, who occasionally perform at Elm Creek Quilt Camp's evening programs.

Waterford Historical Society

An organization dedicated to preserving the history and heritage of Waterford, Pennsylvania, and the Elm Creek Valley.

Waterford Quilting Guild

A guild serving the quilters of the Elm Creek Valley. Their approximately one hundred members meet monthly on the campus of Waterford College and break into smaller groups for weekly quilting bees.

Waterford Register

The newspaper serving Waterford, Pennsylvania, and the Elm Creek Valley region.

Waterford Summer Quilt Festival

An annual quilt show put on at the Waterford College Library by the Waterford Quilting Guild.

Waterford Zoning Commission

A city commission tasked with enforcing building and construction codes, with a special emphasis on preserving historic sites and neighborhoods.

Water's Ford Register

A pro-Union newspaper serving the Elm Creek Valley during the Civil War era.

Water's Ford Sanitary Commission and Union of Loyal Quilters

A chapter of the United States Sanitary Commission based in the Elm Creek Valley, known, for short, as the Union Quilters.

Wednesday Night Stitchers

Gretchen Hartley's quilting circle, which evolved from the class she taught to her friends and neighbors. Heidi Albrecht Mueller joins to learn quilting (and, as Joe Hartley predicts, to yet again take over something Gretchen has that she covets), and before long she turns it into a formal guild with bylaws and elected officials.

Welcome Banquet

A grand feast that marks the commencement of each new session of Elm Creek Quilt Camp, held on Sunday evenings in the banquet hall of Elm Creek Manor.

Wets

A nickname for those who opposed Prohibition, in contrast to its advocates, known as Drys.

Wholecloth Crib Quilt

An intricately hand-quilted masterpiece Eleanor Lockwood Bergstrom makes while expecting her first child, but never uses.

Wildrose

A bay mare Charles Lockwood gives to his daughters' nanny, Amelia Langley Davis, for Christmas, much to his wife's consternation.

Women's National Loyal League

The first national women's political organization in the United States, organized in 1863 to lobby Congress for an amendment to the Constitution abolishing slavery.

Quilt Blocks

Eleanor had so longed to make a patchwork quilt to brighten her own room. The patterns with their charming names—Royal Cross, Storm at Sea, Dutch Rose—evoked romantic times and far-off places, and she longed to learn them all.

—*The Quilter's Legacy*

Advent Wreath

A block featured on the endpapers of *The Christmas Quilt*.

Album

A popular block for signature quilts that Dorothea Granger Nelson chooses for the *Authors' Album* quilt. The block is also used by the clients of Abiding Savior Christian Outreach to make a signature quilt for their teacher, Gretchen Hartley.

American Beauty Rose

A lovely appliqué block that is a particular favorite of Agnes Emberly.

Apple Core

A block featured on the endpapers of *The Quilter's Kitchen*.

Arboles Valley Star

A quilt pieced from the scraps of cherished garments by Isabel Rodriguez Diaz, Rosa Diaz Barclay's mother.

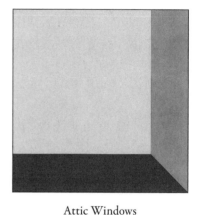

Attic Windows

Sylvia Bergstrom Compson and Andrew Cooper view an Attic Windows quilt pieced of vintage cotton feed sacks in an exhibit of agriculture quilts at the Rocky Mountain Quilt Museum.

Augusta

Gwen Sullivan completes a quilt made from this block that was begun by her academic advisor, Victoria Stark.

Autumn Leaf

A block Gwen Sullivan uses to teach her advisor, Victoria Stark, how to piece and appliqué. The Cross-Country Quilters add a border of Autumn Leaf blocks to their Challenge Quilt.

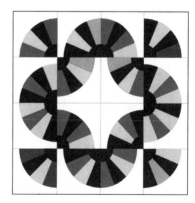

Baby Bunting

Judy Nguyen DiNardo makes a Baby Bunting crib quilt for her daughter, Emily, with the unexpected help of the future Tangled Web Quilters.

Bachelor's Puzzle

The sixth block Sarah McClure learns under Sylvia Bergstrom Compson's tutelage, and the inspiration for a joke between Sylvia and her sister, Claudia Bergstrom Midden, at the expense of Agnes Emberly. In a sly admission that she knew about the joke, Agnes contributes a Bachelor's Puzzle block to *Sylvia's Bridal Sampler*.

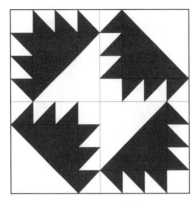

Barrister's Block

A block contributed to *Sylvia's Bridal Sampler*.

Bear's Paw

Sylvia Bergstrom Compson suggests this block for a quilt she and Claudia are to make for their new brother or sister, but she is overruled. Donna Jorgenson contributes a Bear's Paw block to the Cross-Country Quilters' Challenge Quilt.

Best Friend

The block Anna Del Maso places in the cornucopia on a Quilter's Holiday, representing her thankfulness for the kindness and generosity of her friend Jeremy Bernstein.

Birds in the Air

Quilt camper Margaret Alden gives Sylvia Bergstrom Compson a mysterious antique quilt composed of Birds in the Air blocks.

Blazing Star

A block contributed to *Sylvia's Bridal Sampler*.

Blockade

A block featured on the endpapers of *The Lost Quilter,* a nod to the Union blockade of Charleston Harbor during the Civil War.

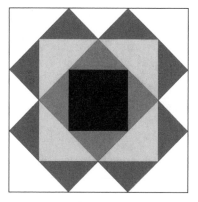

Boy's Nonsense

A traditional block, a variation of which appears in the *Loyal Union Sampler.*

Bridal Wreath

A block contributed to *Sylvia's Bridal Sampler.*

Bride's Bouquet

A block contributed to *Sylvia's Bridal Sampler.*

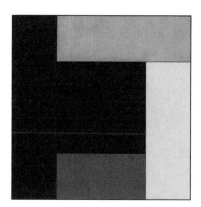

Bright Hopes

A simple, traditional block Sylvia Bergstrom Compson chooses for the first Giving Quilt. During the Great Depression, Sylvia and her great-aunt Lucinda piece Bright Hopes quilts for the orphans residing in the Children's Home in Grangerville.

Broken Dishes

A block used in a quilt Sylvia and Anna piece from Great-Aunt Lydia Bergstrom's old feed sack apron collection.

Broken Path

A block featured on the endpapers of *The Lost Quilter*, symbolic of Joanna North's thwarted attempts to escape from slavery.

Broken Star

A purple-and-green quilt Sylvia Bergstrom Compson makes as she recovers from a stroke, proudly displayed from the second-floor balcony in the grand front foyer of Elm Creek Manor.

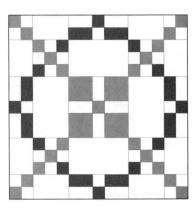

Burgoyne Surrounded

A quilt block named to commemorate British general John Burgoyne's defeat in the Revolutionary War, and a clue in the quilt block anagram word game the Cross-Country Quilters play at Elm Creek Quilt Camp.

California

Sylvia Bergstrom Compson places a California block in the Quilter's Holiday cornucopia one year to celebrate reconnecting with the California branch of her family, the descendants of Elizabeth Bergstrom Nelson.

Campfire

A block Union Quilter Eliza Stokey designed and contributed to the *Loyal Union Sampler* in honor of her husband, Charlie Stokey, and the other men of the Forty-ninth Pennsylvania Volunteers, Company L.

Candleglow

A block featured on the endpapers of *The Giving Quilt* in a nod to the Elm Creek Quilt Camp welcoming ceremony, Candlelight.

Carpenter's Wheel

The block Grace Daniels makes for the Cross-Country Quilters' Challenge Quilt.

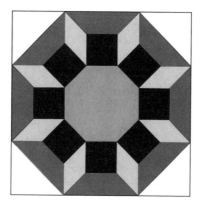

Castle Wall

Agnes Emberly and Claudia Bergstrom Midden work together on a Castle Wall memorial quilt for Sylvia Bergstrom Compson using pieces of clothing that belonged to James Compson, Sylvia's late husband.

Charlie Stokey's Star

A block designed by Faith Cunningham Morlan and contributed to the *Loyal Union Sampler* in honor of Charlie Stokey, a lifelong resident of the Elm Creek Valley and the first soldier of the Forty-ninth Pennsylvania Volunteers, Company L, killed in battle.

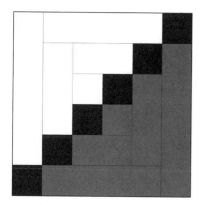

Chimneys and Cornerstones

A popular traditional pattern. Lucinda Bergstrom makes a Chimneys and Cornerstones scrap quilt for her grandniece, Elizabeth Bergstrom Nelson, as a wedding gift. The block also appears in Sarah McClure's first quilt, a twelve-block sampler.

Chimney Sweep

A block included in the Harriet Findley Birch sampler.

Christmas Cactus

A block featured on the endpapers of *The Christmas Quilt*.

Christmas Eve

A block featured on the endpapers of *The Christmas Quilt*.

Christmas Star

A block featured on the endpapers of *The Christmas Quilt*.

Churn Dash

Gerda Bergstrom pieces a quilt using this traditional block as she awaits the confirmation of bad news from Jonathan Granger.

Commencement

Sarah McClure makes a Commencement block quilt for her daughter, Caroline, as a graduation gift, using the green and white colors of her alma mater, Dartmouth.

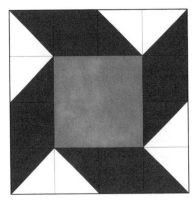

Contrary Husband

A block contributed to *Sylvia's Bridal Sampler*.

Contrary Wife

The fourth sampler block Sarah McClure makes under Sylvia Bergstrom Compson's tutelage.

Corn and Beans

Sylvia Bergstrom Compson and Andrew Cooper view a Corn and Beans quilt with a Farmer's Daughter border in an exhibit of agriculture quilts at the Rocky Mountain Quilt Museum.

Cornerstone

A simple block Gerda Bergstrom designs for the *Loyal Union Sampler* and names in honor of the Union Quilters' ambitious plans to build Union Hall.

Cornucopia

A quilt block Anna Del Maso includes in a quilt she and Sylvia Bergstrom Compson make for the newly remodeled kitchen of Elm Creek Manor, an amusing tribute to the woven cornucopia centerpiece that Sylvia's sister made as a schoolgirl.

Cotton Boll

A block featured on the endpapers of *The Lost Quilter,* reminiscent of Joanna North's work sorting cotton at Oak Grove on Edisto Island.

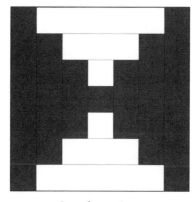

Courthouse Steps

A traditional block similar in construction to Log Cabin that Joanna North uses in a quilt she makes at North's Freedom during Reconstruction.

Courtyard Quilters

The title Maggie Flynn gives to a block she discovers in the Harriet Findley Birch quilt, named after a quilting circle at the retirement community where she works.

Crazy House

A quilt block Elizabeth Lockwood Bergstrom decides is unsuitable for a bride's quilt because of its unfortunate name.

Crazy Quilt

Gwen Sullivan uses Crazy Quilt blocks as the border for the round robin quilt the Elm Creek Quilters make for Sylvia Bergstrom Compson. Amelia Langley teaches Eleanor Lockwood Bergstrom how to quilt by making a Crazy Quilt.

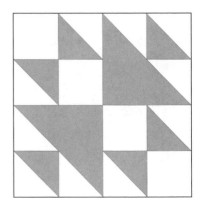

Crosses and Losses

Maggie Flynn identifies a Crosses and Losses block in the *Loyal Union Sampler* after it is discovered in a steamer trunk in Union Hall by a member of the Waterford Historical Society.

Cut Glass Dish

A block used in a quilt Sylvia Bergstrom Compson and Anna Del Maso piece from Great-Aunt Lydia Bergstrom's old feed sack apron collection, a fond reminder of Sylvia's mother's favorite potluck serving piece.

Delectable Mountains

Dorothea Granger Nelson uses this traditional quilt pattern to make a quilt for her cantankerous uncle Jacob Kuehner, varying the design according to his extremely particular and rather unusual instructions.

Devil's Claws

A quilt block Elizabeth Lockwood Bergstrom decides is inappropriate for a bride's quilt because of the negative connotations of its name.

Dogtooth Violet

Gretchen Hartley teaches a class at Quilts 'n Things using her own Dogtooth Violet quilt pattern.

Double Four-Patch

Maggie Flynn identifies a Double Four-Patch block in the *Loyal Union Sampler* after it is discovered in a steamer trunk in Union Hall by a member of the Waterford Historical Society.

Double Nine-Patch

The second sampler quilt block Sarah McClure makes as Sylvia Bergstrom Compson's pupil.

Double Pinwheel

Vinnie Burkholder works on a Double Pinwheel quilt in a Quick Piecing class at Elm Creek Quilt Camp.

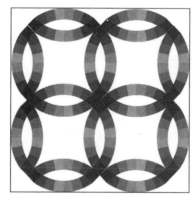

Double Wedding Ring

The women of the Bergstrom family make a beautiful Double Wedding Ring quilt embellished with floral appliqués for Elizabeth Bergstrom when she marries Henry Nelson. Decades later, Sylvia Bergstrom Compson makes another version for Caroline McClure.

Dove in the Window

Dorothea Granger Nelson uses this traditional quilt pattern to make a Turkey red, Prussian blue, and muslin quilt for her husband, Thomas, in honor of their sixth wedding anniversary. Summer Sullivan makes a Dove in the Window quilt for a fifth-grade history project.

Dresden Plate

Sarah McClure, Matt McClure, and Sylvia Bergstrom Compson admire a Dresden Plate variation at the Waterford Summer Quilt Festival. A blue-and-white Dresden Plate quilt is on the bed of Donna Jorgenson's room at Elm Creek Quilt Camp.

Drummer Boy

A block designed by Water's Ford quilter Deborah Madigan and contributed to the *Loyal Union Sampler* in honor of her son, who serves as a drummer boy with the Forty-ninth Pennsylvania Volunteers, Company L.

Drunkard's Path

A block Megan Donohue recommends that Julia Merchaud make in order to practice piecing curved seams.

Dutch Rose

Eleanor Lockwood Bergstrom admires a quilt her nanny, Amelia Langley Davis, makes with this block, especially its enchanting name, which evokes thoughts of romantic times and far-off places.

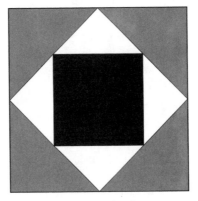

Economy Patch

Joanna North spots a quilt made from this block hanging on a clothesline on a Maryland farm where she takes momentary refuge after escaping from slave catchers.

Emancipation

Maggie Flynn identifies an Emancipation block in the *Loyal Union Sampler* after it is discovered in a steamer trunk in Union Hall by a member of the Waterford Historical Society.

Farmer's Daughter

Sylvia Bergstrom Compson and Andrew Cooper view a Corn and Beans quilt with a Farmer's Daughter border in an exhibit of agriculture quilts at the Rocky Mountain Quilt Museum.

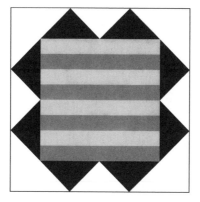

Farm in the Valley

One of the blocks Dorothea Granger Nelson contributes to the *Loyal Union Sampler* in honor of her beloved home.

Feathered Star

A complex traditional pattern based upon the eight-pointed star. Judy Nguyen DiNardo, Joanna North, and Lucinda Bergstrom have made Feather Star quilts.

Flower of Christmas

A block featured on the endpapers of *The Christmas Quilt*.

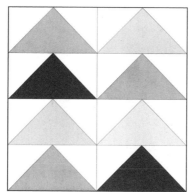

Flying Geese

Claudia Bergstrom Midden slept beneath a Flying Geese quilt in Elm Creek Manor.

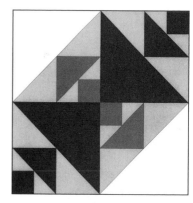

Fond Farewell

A quilt block Sylvia Bergstrom Compson includes in a quilt she and Anna Del Maso make for the newly remodeled kitchen of Elm Creek Manor, to remind them of the Farewell Breakfasts that conclude each week of quilt camp.

Fool's Puzzle

Dorothea Granger Nelson believes that one of the unusual blocks her uncle Jacob Kuehner designs for his Delectable Mountains quilt resembles Fool's Puzzle.

Fort Sumter

Maggie Flynn identifies a Fort Sumter block in the *Loyal Union Sampler* after it is discovered in a steamer trunk in Union Hall by a member of the Waterford Historical Society.

Four-Patch

Isabel Rodriguez Diaz and Eleanor Lockwood Bergstrom both make Four-Patch quilts for beloved children in their lives. During the Great Depression, Sylvia Bergstrom Compson and her great-aunt Lucinda piece Four-Patch quilts for the orphans residing in the Children's Home in Grangerville.

Franklin's Choice

The title Maggie Flynn gives to a block she discovers in the Harriet Findley Birch sampler, named in honor of Harriet's husband, Franklin Birch.

Friendship Knot

A pretty pink-and-yellow Friendship Knot quilt is on Pauline Tucker's bed at Elm Creek Manor during her Quiltsgiving visit.

Friendship Square

A quilt block Sylvia Bergstrom Compson includes in a quilt she and Anna Del Maso make to decorate the newly remodeled kitchen of Elm Creek Manor, chosen in honor of National Quilting Day.

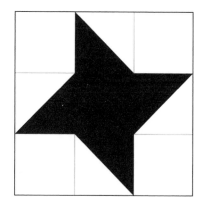

Friendship Star

A simple block Julia Merchaud learns to make in Diane Sonnenberg's Beginning Piecing class at Elm Creek Quilt Camp. Later she makes another version to contribute to the Cross-Country Quilters' Challenge Quilt.

Georgia

A block featured on the endpapers of *The Giving Quilt,* in honor of Georgia resident and Quiltsgiving participant Pauline Tucker.

Gettysburg

A block contributed to the *Loyal Union Sampler.*

Girl's Joy

Using Girl's Joy blocks she brought from home, Linnea Nelson makes an extra quilt for Project Linus during her Quiltsgiving visit to Elm Creek Manor.

Glorified Nine-Patch

Grandma Lucy plans to use the Glorified Nine-Patch pattern for Bonnie Markham's bridal quilt. Sylvia Bergstrom Compson makes a Glorified Nine-Patch quilt for Bob and Cathy Cooper.

Good Fortune

A block Sylvia Bergstrom Compson includes in her quilt *New Year's Reflections.*

Grace's Friendship

An original appliqué block Grace Daniels contributes to *Sylvia's Bridal Sampler*.

Grandmother's Delight

A block Carol Mallory places in the cornucopia on one Quilter's Holiday.

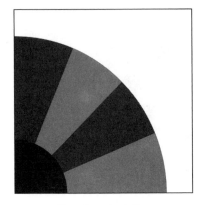

Grandmother's Fan

A traditional block used in the quilt block anagram word game the Cross-Country Quilters play at Elm Creek Quilt Camp. A Grandmother's Fan quilt conceals the television in the formal parlor of Elm Creek Manor when it is not in use.

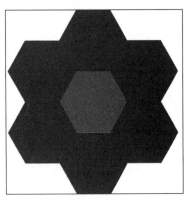

Grandmother's Flower Garden

During World War II, the Waterford Quilting Guild, including members Sylvia Bergstrom Compson and Claudia Bergstrom Midden, makes a Victory Quilt from this pattern to raise money for the war effort.

Grandmother's Pride

A block contributed to *Sylvia's Bridal Sampler* by Cross-Country Quilter Vinnie Burkholder.

Grape Basket

A small pink, white, and yellow Grape Basket quilt hangs on the wall of one of the suites in Elm Creek Manor. A yellow-and-white Grape Basket quilt is spread upon a bed with a cherry headboard in one of the smaller bedrooms of the Jorgensen farmhouse.

Gretchen

A block featured on the endpapers of *The Giving Quilt* in honor of Elm Creek Quilter Gretchen Hartley.

Guiding Star

The block Gwen Sullivan places in the cornucopia on one Quilter's Holiday, representing her thankfulness for the teachers and mentors who have guided her throughout her life.

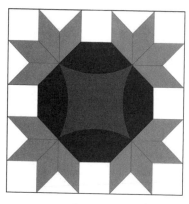

Hands All Around

One of the blocks Sarah McClure includes in her first quilt, a twelve-block sampler.

Handy Andy

A block Judy Nguyen DiNardo contributes to *Sylvia's Bridal Sampler* in honor of Andrew Cooper, Sylvia's husband.

Happy Home

Rosa Diaz Barclay plans to make a quilt for her daughter Lupita using this block, a symbol of her prayers that her daughter will learn to love their new home in Sonoma County and not mourn for the unhappy, broken home they left behind in the Arboles Valley.

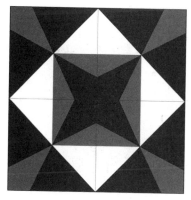

Harriet's Favorite

The name Maggie Flynn gives to an unfamiliar block she discovers in the Harriet Findley Birch sampler.

Harvest Home

A quilt block Anna Del Maso and Sylvia Bergstrom Compson include in a quilt they make for the newly remodeled kitchen of Elm Creek Manor, to remind them of the Bergstrom women's contributions to many community Harvest Dances throughout the decades.

Hatchet

A block Sylvia Bergstrom Compson includes in her quilt *New Year's Reflections* to remind her of the fortune her sister cast while playing *Bleigiessen* one New Year's Eve long ago.

Hen and Chicks

A block Donna Jorgenson considers making for the Cross-Country Quilters' Challenge Quilt.

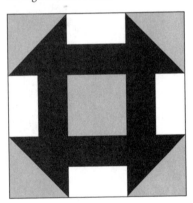

Hole in the Barn Door

A traditional block used in the quilt block anagram word game the Cross-Country Quilters play at Elm Creek Quilt Camp.

Homecoming

Sarah McClure considers making a Homecoming block for *Sylvia's Bridal Sampler* before choosing Sarah's Favorite.

Home Sweet Home

Sarah McClure places a Home Sweet Home block pieced from red, blue, and tan fabrics in the cornucopia on the Quilter's Holiday following the birth of her twins.

Honeybee

A block used in a quilt Sylvia Bergstrom Compson and Anna Del Maso piece from Great-Aunt Lydia Bergstrom's old feed sack apron collection.

Hunter's Star

Sylvia Bergstrom Compson gives a blue-and-white Hunter's Star quilt to Carol Mallory as a Christmas gift.

Irish Chain

Claudia Bergstrom Midden made a green-and-white Irish Chain quilt for her grandfather when she was eight years old.

Jack in the Pulpit

Summer Sullivan's grandmother made her a Jack in the Pulpit quilt for her third birthday.

Jacob's Ladder

A block Agnes Emberly urges Judy Nguyen DiNardo to choose instead of Turkey Tracks, which is also known as Wandering Foot and is supposedly bad luck.

Jewel Box

Gwen Sullivan's mother made her a candy-colored Jewel Box quilt when she was a young girl, and it remains on the bed in her old room to this day.

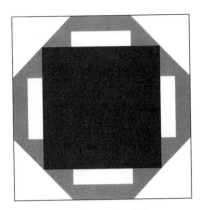

Jonathan's Satchel

A block designed by Union Quilter Charlotte Claverton Granger and contributed to the *Loyal Union Sampler* in honor of her husband, Jonathan Granger, a physician serving with the Forty-ninth Pennsylvania Volunteers, Company L.

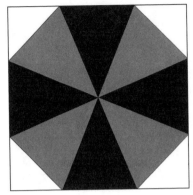

Kaleidoscope

A block Summer Sullivan teaches in a piecing workshop at Elm Creek Quilt Camp.

Lancaster Rose

The eighth sampler block Sarah McClure makes with the guidance of Sylvia Bergstrom Compson.

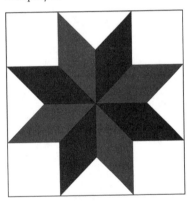

LeMoyne Star

The fifth sampler block Sarah McClure makes under Sylvia Bergstrom Compson's tutelage. Donna Jorgenson includes a LeMoyne Star block in a quilt she makes for her daughter Lindsay, and Harriet Findley Birch included it in her sampler.

Lincoln

A block featured on the endpapers of *The Lost Quilter* in honor of President Abraham Lincoln, the Great Emancipator.

Lincoln's Platform

A block Diane Sonnenberg contributes to *Sylvia's Bridal Sampler.*

Little Giant

A block contributed to *Sylvia's Bridal Sampler* in *The Master Quilter*.

Little Red Schoolhouse

The third quilt block Sarah McClure makes for her first sampler. Gretchen Hartley adds a Little Red Schoolhouse to the middle of her Oak Leaf variation for the sample block she makes for her interview with Elm Creek Quilts.

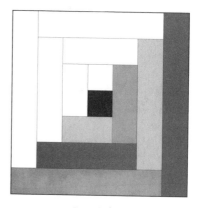

Log Cabin

Sylvia Bergstrom Compson finds her great-great-aunt Gerda Bergstrom's memoir in a trunk in the attic wrapped in a Log Cabin quilt with alternating light and dark rectangles encircling a black center square.

Lone Star

One of Sylvia Bergstrom Compson's favorite patterns. Her red-and-green Lone Star quilt hanging in the front window of Grandma's Attic catches Sarah McClure's eye and kindles her desire to learn to quilt.

Lost Children

A block featured on the endpapers of *The Lost Quilter* in tribute to the many enslaved parents who were cruelly separated from their children.

Lowell Crossroads

The name Maggie Flynn gives to a block she finds in the Harriet Findley Birch sampler.

Loyal Daughter

Rosa Diaz Barclay plans to make a quilt for her eldest daughter, Marta, using this block, because the name suits the steadfast, loving girl perfectly.

Manassas

A block contributed to the *Loyal Union Sampler* by Dorothea Granger Nelson.

Mariner's Compass

Sarah McClure makes a Mariner's Compass quilt for her son's inspiring eighth-grade art teacher. Gwen Sullivan uses the pattern for her daughter Summer's high school graduation gift, and Summer contributes a Mariner's Compass block to *Sylvia's Bridal Sampler*.

Memory

A block contributed to the *Loyal Union Sampler* by Millicent Claverton.

Memory Album

Sarah McClure and the Elm Creek Quilters collect signatures and good wishes for the bride and groom on Memory Album blocks to sew into a quilt for her daughter and new son-in-law.

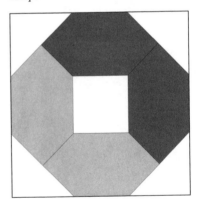

Memory Chain

Sylvia Bergstrom Compson includes this block in her quilt *New Year's Reflections* so she will never forget the hard lessons learned from the unexpected course her life took.

Michigan Beauty

Jocelyn Ames's grandmother made her a Michigan Beauty quilt, which she uses in her living room.

Mill Girls

The name Maggie Flynn gives to a block she discovers in the Harriet Findley Birch quilt.

Mother's Choice

A quilt block featured on the endpapers of *Circle of Quilters,* a tribute to the choices Elm Creek Quilts applicant Karen Wise makes as she balances work and motherhood, and her needs and her family's.

Mother's Delight

A block contributed to *Sylvia's Bridal Sampler* by Cross-Country Quilter Megan Donohue Wagner.

Mother's Favorite

A block Sylvia Bergstrom Compson adapts to suit her quilt *New Year's Reflections.* A Mother's Favorite block is also contributed to *Sylvia's Bridal Sampler.*

New York Beauty

Eleanor Lockwood Bergstrom uses this block, which is also known as Crown of Thorns and Rocky Mountains, in a quilt she intends as a wedding gift for her sister, but which unexpectedly becomes her own bridal quilt.

Nine-Patch

An easy, traditional block a young Sylvia Bergstrom uses to make her first quilt. Because of its simplicity and charm, many quilters throughout the series use the Nine-Patch block to teach others to quilt.

North Star

A block featured on the endpapers of *The Lost Quilter* in honor of the many slaves who, like Joanna North, followed the North Star in their difficult, courageous attempts to escape bondage.

Oak Leaf

Gretchen Hartley uses a variation of the Oak Leaf block in her original design for her Elm Creek Quilts interview, altering the appliqués so they resemble elm leaves.

Ocean Waves

Eleanor Lockwood Bergstrom makes an Ocean Waves quilt for her husband while he is serving overseas in World War I.

Odd Fellow's Chain

Claudia Bergstrom Midden chooses Odd Fellow's Chain blocks for the border of a quilt she and her sister, Sylvia Bergstrom Compson, enter in a quilt competition at the 1933 World's Fair in Chicago.

Ohio Star

The eleventh block Sarah McClure makes for her first sampler. Grace Daniels uses the block in a special gift she makes at Elm Creek Quilt Camp for Vinnie Burkholder. Years later, Vinnie—hoping for a girl—makes a pink-and-white Ohio Star crib quilt for a grandchild.

Orange Peel

A block Sylvia Bergstrom Compson includes in her quilt *New Year's Reflections* as a tribute to Elizabeth Bergstrom Nelson and her husband, Henry Nelson, who Sylvia hoped had been blessed with true love and all the sweetness life had to offer.

Oregon Trail

A block Maggie Flynn finds in the Harriet Findley Birch quilt.

Path Through the Woods

A block featured on the endpapers of *The Giving Quilt,* a nod to the morning walks taken by Quiltsgiving participants Pauline Tucker, Linnea Nelson, and Mona Lindstad.

Peace and Plenty

Sylvia Bergstrom Compson includes this block in her quilt *New Year's Reflections* in tribute to her mother-in-law, Josephine Compson.

Pennsylvania

A block contributed to the *Loyal Union Sampler.*

Pickle Dish

Sylvia Bergstrom Compson and Andrew Cooper view a Pickle Dish quilt pieced from cow-print fabrics in an exhibit of agriculture quilts at the Rocky Mountain Quilt Museum. Karen Wise makes a foundation paper pieced Pickle Dish quilt.

Picnic Basket

A block featured on the endpapers of *The Quilter's Kitchen*.

Pineapple

Gwen Sullivan finds a fascinating navy blue, brick red, and forest green foundation paper pieced Pineapple quilt long abandoned in the lost-and-found of the church where her mother's quilt guild meets.

Pine Burr

Donna Jorgenson makes a Pine Burr table runner as a Thanksgiving decoration.

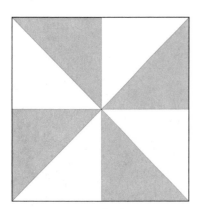

Pinwheel

Bonnie Markham adds a border of Pinwheel blocks to the *Elm Creek Medallion* quilt. During the Great Depression, Sylvia Bergstrom Compson and her great-aunt Lucinda piece Pinwheel quilts for the orphans residing in the Children's Home in Grangerville.

Pinwheel Star

A block Rosa Diaz Barclay chooses for a quilt for her ninth child, Matthias Ottesen.

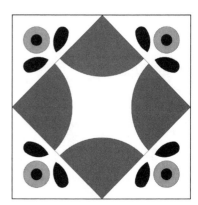

Posies Round the Square

The seventh sampler block Sarah McClure makes for her first quilt.

Postage Stamp

An overall design composed of many small squares in either a planned or random arrangement. Melissa Nelson gives Sylvia Bergstrom Compson a scrap Postage Stamp quilt with a leafy vine border made by Sylvia's beloved cousin Elizabeth Bergstrom Nelson.

Prosperity

A block Gretchen Hartley places in the cornucopia on a Quilter's Holiday, representing her thankfulness for her new job with Elm Creek Quilts.

Providence

May Beth Callahan's award-winning quilt made from Providence blocks, *Springtime in Waterford,* inspires her longtime rival, Diane Sonnenberg, to learn to quilt. Sylvia Bergstrom Compson places a Providence block in the cornucopia on a Quilter's Holiday.

Queen Charlotte's Crown

A block contributed to *Sylvia's Bridal Sampler.*

Quilter's Dream

A block contributed to *Sylvia's Bridal Sampler.*

Rail Fence

A simple, traditional block Sarah McClure chooses for the second Giving Quilt. Summer Sullivan made her first quilt using a Rail Fence block.

Railroad Crossing

Rosa Diaz Barclay makes a quilt for her son Miguel using this pattern in hopes that he will sleep as peacefully beneath it as he did on the train from Oxnard to San Francisco.

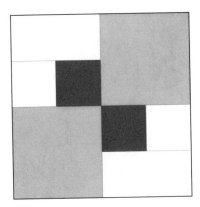

Resolution Square

A simple, traditional block Gretchen Hartley chooses for the fourth Giving Quilt. Sylvia Bergstrom Compson includes a Resolution Square block in her quilt *New Year's Reflections*.

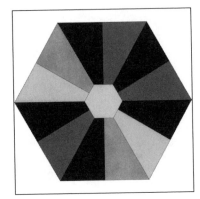

Road to Triumph Ranch

A hexagonal quilt made by Rosa Diaz Barclay's great-grandmother and discovered years later in a ramshackle cabin on the Jorgensen Ranch by Elizabeth Bergstrom Nelson.

Rocky Road to Dublin

A block contributed to *Sylvia's Bridal Sampler*.

Rocky Road to Salem

The name Maggie Flynn gives to a block she discovers in the Harriet Findley Birch sampler.

Rosebud

A quilt camper displays a beautiful Rosebud quilt at a Farewell Breakfast show-and-tell.

Rose of Sharon

A beautiful traditional appliqué pattern that Agnes Emberly uses to make a farewell gift for Judy Nguyen DiNardo. Joanna North spots a Rose of Sharon quilt hanging on a clothesline at a Maryland farm. A Rose of Sharon block appears in the Harriet Findley Birch quilt.

Royal Cross

Eleanor Lockwood Bergstrom admires a quilt her nanny, Amelia Langley Davis, makes with this block, especially its enchanting name, which evokes thoughts of romantic times and far-off places.

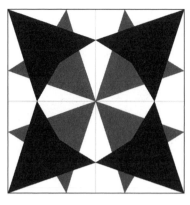

Russell's Way

An original block featured on the endpapers of *Circle of Quilters* and inspired by the work of quilt artist Russell McIntyre.

Saint Louis Star

A variation of the LeMoyne Star that Sylvia Bergstrom Compson has often used in her quilts.

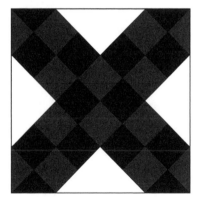

Sarah's Favorite

A block Sarah McClure makes for *Sylvia's Bridal Sampler*.

Sawtooth Star

The first sampler block Sarah McClure sews for her first quilt, evoking memories of the pink-and-white Sawtooth Star quilt her grandmother made for her. Years later, Carol Mallory makes a pair of Sawtooth Star quilts for her grandchildren.

Schoolhouse

Rosa Diaz Barclay plans to make a quilt using this block for her daughter Ana, her little scholar, who loves books, libraries, and reading, even though she has been too ill to attend school.

Shepherd's Light

A block featured on the endpapers of *The Christmas Quilt*.

Shoo-Fly

Dorothea Granger Nelson teaches Gerda Bergstrom how to quilt using a Shoo-Fly block, although Gerda is a reluctant pupil.

Shooting Star

A block Gwen Sullivan contributes to *Sylvia's Bridal Sampler*.

Signs of Spring

The block Agnes Emberly places in the cornucopia on a Quilter's Holiday, representing her thankfulness for hope in difficult times.

Sister's Choice

The ninth block Sarah McClure makes for her sampler under Sylvia's tutelage. Agnes Emberly contributes a Sister's Choice block to *Sylvia's Bridal Sampler*.

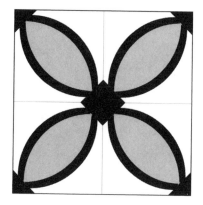

Slave Chain

A block featured on the endpapers of *The Lost Quilter*.

Snail's Trail

A block that catches Russell McIntyre's eye when he begins delving into his wife Elaine's pattern books.

Snow Crystals

The block Megan Donohue makes for the Cross-Country Quilters' Challenge Quilt.

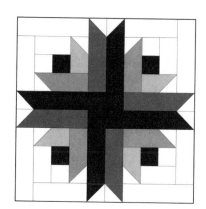

Sonoma Rose

An original quilt block inspired by Rosa Diaz Barclay and the Sonoma Rose Vineyards and Orchard.

South Carolina

A block featured on the endpapers of *The Lost Quilter* in recognition of the many years Joanna North lived in the state, in bondage and in freedom.

Spiderweb

Dorothea Granger Nelson believes that one of the unusual blocks her uncle Jacob Kuehner designs for his Delectable Mountains quilt resembles the Spiderweb block.

Spinning Hourglass

A block contributed to *Sylvia's Bridal Sampler.*

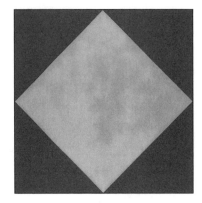

Square in a Square

Sarah McClure adds a border of Square in a Square blocks to the *Elm Creek Medallion,* a round robin quilt the Elm Creek Quilters make for Sylvia.

Stacked Coins

A strip-pieced block Gwen Sullivan chooses for the third Giving Quilt.

Stamp Baskets

A block Megan Donohue recommends that Julia Merchaud make in order to practice her new sewing skills.

Star of Bethlehem

A variation of the LeMoyne Star that Sylvia Bergstrom Compson has often used in her quilts.

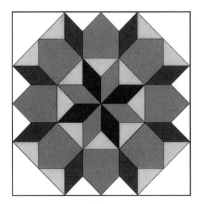

Star of the Magi

Sylvia Bergstrom Compson uses a Star of the Magi block in a quilt she makes for the silent auction at her church's Holiday Boutique.

Steps to the Altar

A traditional block used in the quilt block anagram word game the Cross-Country Quilters play at Elm Creek Quilt Camp.

Storm at Sea

Sylvia Bergstrom Compson and Gwen Sullivan discover a bundle of Storm at Sea blocks in the attic of Elm Creek Manor, pieced from pastel cottons common to the 1920s and 1930s, the construction suggestive of Claudia Bergstrom Midden's work.

String Pieced Star

Constance Wright makes a String Pieced Star scrap quilt for her husband, Abel, on the occasion of their marriage.

Sunburst

A block included in a charity quilt made by the Waterford Quilting Guild in 1918 to raise money for the Red Cross.

Sunflower

Salvatore Vanelli uses a green-and-gold Sunflower quilt on the daybed of his front porch while recovering from a heart attack. Maude Bergstrom wants to make a Sunflower quilt for her husband, Louis Bergstrom, as a gift for their first anniversary.

Swamp Patch

A pattern Gretchen Hartley uses to make a quilt for Project Linus.

Sylvia's Choice

A block featured on the endpapers of *The Giving Quilt* in honor of Master Quilter Sylvia Bergstrom Compson.

Tea Leaves

A block featured on the endpapers of *The Quilter's Kitchen*. Maggie Flynn identifies a Tea Leaves block in the *Loyal Union Sampler* after it is discovered in a steamer trunk in Union Hall by a member of the Waterford Historical Society.

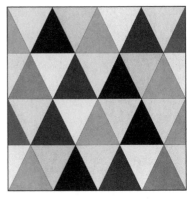

Thousand Pyramids

Adele LaMonte discovers a quilt made from a variation of this pattern in an Upper East Side brownstone.

Three Cheers

A block contributed to *Sylvia's Bridal Sampler*.

Tree of Life

A block featured on the endpapers of *The Lost Quilter*. Although this was not the inspiration for the quilt block name, the pattern of scars on a whipped slave's back was sometimes called the Tree of Life.

Trip Around the World

A simple, traditional pattern and one of the first quilts Bonnie Markham made as a child. A Trip Around the World block is among those contributed to *Sylvia's Bridal Sampler*.

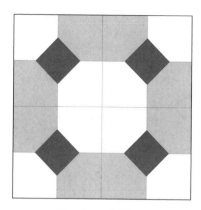

True Lover's Knot

Jeremy Bernstein places a sketch of a True Lover's Knot block in the Quilter's Holiday cornucopia as part of his proposal to Anna Del Maso. Sylvia Bergstrom Compson includes the block in her quilt *New Year's Reflections* in honor of her parents.

Tumbling Blocks

Sylvia Bergstrom Compson works on a Tumbling Blocks baby quilt during her pregnancy, while her husband, brother, and future brother-in-law are at war.

Turkey Tracks

Claudia Bergstrom Midden's suggestion for the quilt she and Sylvia Bergstrom Compson are to make for their new sibling. Sylvia protests because her superstitious grandmother has convinced her that the pattern, also known as Wandering Foot, brings bad luck.

Twin Star

The block Sarah McClure places in the cornucopia on a Quilter's Holiday, representing her thankfulness for the good health of her unborn twins, for her uneventful pregnancy, and for her husband's steadfast support.

Twin Star Log Cabin

Sarah McClure makes a Twin Star Log Cabin quilt as a Christmas gift for her father-in-law, Hank, hoping he will come to appreciate the mission of Elm Creek Quilts.

Underground Railroad

A block featured on the endpapers of *The Lost Quilter*.

Union

A block featured on the endpapers of *The Lost Quilter*.

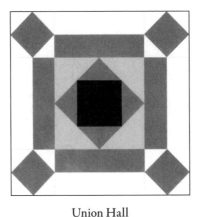

Union Hall

A block designed by Water's Ford quilter Joan Sheridan and contributed to the *Loyal Union Sampler* in honor of the Union Quilters' "noble enterprise," the building of Union Hall.

Variable Star

Gerda Bergstrom's second quilt is comprised of Variable Star blocks. Claudia Bergstrom Midden contributed Variable Star blocks to the Bergstrom women's Christmas Quilt.

Virginia Star

A variation of the LeMoyne Star that Sylvia Bergstrom Compson has often used in her quilts.

Wandering Foot

Another name for the block Turkey Tracks, which Claudia Bergstrom Midden proposes she and her sister, Sylvia Bergstrom Compson, use to make a crib quilt for their new brother or sister.

Wedding Bouquet

A block featured on the endpapers of *The Wedding Quilt* in honor of the beautiful flowers that Matt McClure grows and gathers for his daughter, bride-to-be Caroline McClure.

Wedding March

The Elm Creek Quilters use the Wedding March block to make a wedding quilt for Bonnie Markham and Hinano Paoa, using floral and solid fabrics in tropical hues.

Wedding Ring

The block Vinnie Burkholder makes for the Cross-Country Quilters' Challenge Quilt.

Whig Rose

An intricate floral appliqué block that is a particular favorite of Agnes Emberly.

Windblown Square

A quilt made from this block is on the bed of the suite at Elm Creek Manor Bonnie Markham moves in to when she finds herself between more permanent homes during her divorce proceedings.

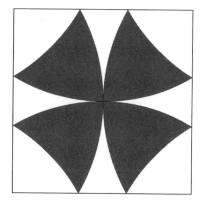

Winding Ways

A traditional quilt block with curved pieces that Sylvia selects for a special quilt for her friends the Elm Creek Quilters, ever mindful of the many winding paths they will follow throughout their lives.

Year's Favorite

Sylvia Bergstrom Compson includes the block in her quilt *New Year's Reflections* in honor of her brother's birth, and to remind her of her mother's patience and endurance and the great happiness that was her reward.

A Stitch in Time:
Behind the Scenes at Elm Creek Quilt Camp

In honor of the tenth anniversary of the world's most popular and renowned quilters' retreat, *Contemporary Quilting* sat down with the Elm Creek Quilters in the parlor of the historic manor in rural Pennsylvania, where each summer hundreds of quilters from around the world gather for quilting, fellowship, and fun. On a sunny September afternoon, with the forested hills of the Elm Creek Valley just beginning to don their vibrant autumnal hues, the Elm Creek Quilters—founder and matriarch Sylvia Bergstrom Compson; cofounder Sarah McClure; inaugural faculty members Bonnie Markham, Gwen Sullivan, Agnes Emberly, Diane Sonnenberg; newcomers Gretchen Hartley and Maggie Flynn; and former instructors Summer Sullivan and Judy DiNardo—reflected upon the first ten seasons of Elm Creek Quilt Camp, their enduring friendships, and the challenges they have overcome, separately and together. The twists and turns of their journey—and their plans for the future—may surprise you.

By Ellen Henderson

Elm Creek Quilts has just wrapped up its tenth successful season of quilt camp. How does that make you feel?

DIANE: Tired!

GRETCHEN: Grateful.

SYLVIA: Astonished. Where does the time go? It seems like only yesterday we were planning for the new season with all those balmy, busy weeks of summer awaiting us, and here it is autumn already.

SARAH: Proud. It might sound like bragging, but I'm very proud of all we've accomplished.

I think your many satisfied quilt campers would agree that you have good reason to be proud. After all, over the past decade, you've transformed a neglected country estate into a thriving retreat beloved by quilters worldwide. How did you make this happen?

GWEN: Well, looking back . . . [Pause] I honestly have no idea how we pulled it off.

DIANE: That's okay, I've got this. [Leans forward and addresses interviewer seriously] It's actually quite simple. Anyone can do it. First, you start with a gorgeous manor on a multimillion-dollar estate owned by an eccentric, reclusive master quilter—

SYLVIA: I beg your pardon?

DIANE: Then gather up a group of friends who love to quilt and teach, and after that, everything falls into place.

GWEN: [Rolling her eyes] Sure, that's exactly how it went.

AGNES: I certainly don't remember it that way! We all worked many long, hard hours over the course of nearly a year preparing for our first guests, and then we spent the entire summer learning on the job, and all autumn and winter deciding what to do differently the next year. Of course, it all began with Sarah.

SARAH: I wouldn't say that.

GWEN: Oh, don't be so modest. Elm Creek Quilts was your idea.

SARAH: But I couldn't have done any of this alone.

DIANE: Well, obviously. You wouldn't have gotten anywhere without us.

My understanding is that Gwen is right, Sarah, and that Elm Creek Quilts was your idea. What inspired you to create a quilt camp all those years ago, especially considering that at the time, only a few weeks had passed since your first quilting lesson?

SARAH: [Laughs] Believe me, I definitely didn't intend to teach, not as a novice with only one quilt to my credit! I always saw myself in a more administrative role. [Pause] I first met Sylvia when my husband, Matt, brought me along when he came out to inspect the Bergstrom estate.

SYLVIA: I had hired the landscaping firm where he worked to help me get the grounds and gardens in order. They had been neglected for decades and were in a terrible state.

SARAH: It seems unimaginable now, but at the time, Sylvia was preparing the manor for sale. She hired me to help her tidy up inside.

SYLVIA: "Tidy up"? She makes it sound like a mere afternoon's worth of work, but it was much more than that. My late sister had left the interior of the manor in an even sorrier state than the grounds. When Sarah agreed to take on the arduous task of putting everything in good order, she asked me to teach her to quilt as part of her compensation. So after we would put in a good day's work, I would show her a few things.

SARAH: Quilting together gave us ample opportunity to chat, and to become friends. As the weeks went by and I discovered how much Sylvia truly loved her ancestral home despite her determination to sell it, I couldn't bear the thought of the manor without her, and I tried to convince her to stay. She told me that if I could find a way to bring the manor back to life and fill it with happiness again, she would never sell it. So I thought, what better way to do that than to open it up to quilters?

SYLVIA: Along the way, Sarah also discovered that the real estate agent who had offered to buy the manor intended to raze it and put up condominiums in its place. Well, I certainly couldn't let that happen. My Bergstrom ancestors would have haunted me forevermore. So when Sarah came to me with her proposal to transform Elm Creek Manor into a quilters' camp, I was intrigued—and also tremendously relieved. I wanted a reason to stay, you see, so although Sarah's plan seemed utterly preposterous, really quite impossible, I was willing to take a chance.

SARAH: [To Sylvia] You never told me you thought my plan was preposterous or impossible.

SYLVIA: Of course not. That would have been terribly impolite. I should add that I was quite happy to be proven wrong.

SARAH: Well . . . I'm glad to hear it! [Laughs]

It all began with Sarah's idea and Sylvia's resources, but soon thereafter, you invited your quilting friends to become the faculty of Elm Creek Quilts. Most of your original teachers are still with the company, although two founding members have left to pursue other professional interests and a few new teachers have joined you.

GRETCHEN: I'm one of the very fortunate Elm Creek Quilters whom they welcomed into the fold.

MAGGIE: And I'm the other one.

SYLVIA: A wonderfully talented chef named Anna Del Maso also joined us for a time, but eventually her husband finished graduate school and took a position in Virginia, and so she moved away.

DIANE: We will never forgive him. Never. Be sure to put that in your article.

I'll do that.

JUDY: I might as well admit that I'm one of the founding members who left Elm Creek Quilts. I still receive e-mails from former students questioning my sanity.

SUMMER: [Laughs] I've received a few of those too!

DIANE: Why *did* you two leave? Now's your chance to put it on the record.

JUDY: How could I have turned down my dream job at an Ivy League school?

DIANE: You could have told them, "I'm sorry, but I'm perfectly happy where I am." Would that have been so difficult?

JUDY: Since it would have involved turning down my dream job, yes, actually, it would have been!

SUMMER: For me, I simply felt that the time had come to pursue other professional interests. I had worked at Bonnie's quilt shop from the time I was in high school until it closed. I joined the faculty of Elm Creek Quilts while I

was still in college, and I had been working there full-time since graduation. Remember, too, that I had lived in Waterford almost my entire life. I
love quilting and I always will, but it's not all that I am, and I was ready to
move on.

GWEN: Before you interject any pithy remarks, Diane, I want to say that as her
mother, I fully support her decision.

SUMMER: Thanks, Mom.

*Contemporary Quilting readers were invited to submit questions for this interview,
and several of them touch on Elm Creek Quilters who have recently left or joined
your circle. The first is for you, Judy. Faith Morlan of Aurora, Colorado, asks, "I
know you took your dream job in Philadelphia. Do you have any regrets about leaving such a wonderful group of friends? Would you consider coming back to teach a
class at camp if you could?"*

JUDY: Hmm. [Pause] Let me put it this way: I regret that joining the faculty of
the University of Pennsylvania meant that I had to leave my friends, but I
don't regret my choice. Of course I miss the Elm Creek Quilters, and no one
will ever replace them in my heart, but my work is every bit as satisfying and
rewarding as I had hoped it would be. As for returning to teach a class, I'd
love to, if I could fit it into my schedule. Why not?

SARAH: I'm going to hold you to that!

JUDY: Let's compare calendars later.

*Faith has a similar question for Summer. "Now that you are in graduate school at the
University of Chicago, do you ever teach your classmates or roommates the art of quilting? Do you see yourself ever returning to Waterford and the Elm Creek Quilters?"*

SUMMER: [Smiles] I'm here now, aren't I?

GWEN: Only for a visit, sadly.

SUMMER: That's better than nothing, right, Mom? As for teaching my friends
in Chicago how to quilt, I'd be happy to if any of them had the time and the

interest. We're all so unbelievably busy with classes and research, though, that I don't see that happening any time soon.

DIANE: No time for quilting? That's tragic.

SUMMER: I can't disagree.

Bonnie, several of our readers are interested in your new venture, Aloha Quilt Camp in Lahaina on Maui. Cheryl Odle from Michigan City, Indiana, wants to know how it's working out for you, spending part of the year in Hawaii and part of the year in Pennsylvania.

BONNIE: It's absolutely heavenly. I get to spend the spring and summer in the beautiful Elm Creek Valley with my best friends, and when the camp season is over, I get to escape to paradise before the winter snows and icy winds strike. And throughout the year, I'm blessed to share my love of quilting with fun, motivated quilters from all parts of the world. I've never been happier.

AGNES: You've earned every bit of that happiness, dear.

DIANE: Wait. You're going to leave it at that? You expect—what was her name?—Cheryl from Indiana to believe that you're thrilled with the arrangement just because you can quilt three hundred sixty-five days a year in fair weather? You expect us to believe that your newfound joy has nothing to do with a certain handsome Hawaiian ukulele player?

BONNIE: I freely admit that part of the appeal of returning to Maui every autumn is that I'll get to see Hinano again.

[Laughter]

Bonnie, a question from Geri Schick of Eaton, Ohio, will suit nicely as a follow-up: "Do you plan to remain in Hawaii, or will you return to the mainland and bring some Hawaiian quilt history and technique into a new store?"

BONNIE: Oh, I don't plan to open a new store. I loved Grandma's Attic, and I loved every day I worked there. I got it off the ground with an inheritance I received from my grandma Lucy, and every moment of joy and satisfaction it brought me and my customers was a tribute to her. It was a glorious adventure, but that chapter of my life is over, and I accept that. I'm happy to continue as an Elm Creek Quilter, and I've really enjoyed the excitement and challenge of launching another new business and watching it grow. But I can't see myself opening a new quilt shop.

Do you plan to continue to spend half the year at Elm Creek Manor and half at the Hale Kapa Kuiki?

BONNIE: Well, sure. Elm Creek Quilt Camp is in season only from the end of March through Labor Day, so why not spend the rest of the year in Hawaii, since I'm not needed here?

AGNES: Not needed for work, perhaps, but always wanted and always missed.

BONNIE: I miss all of you too, while I'm in Hawaii—and when I'm here, I miss my coworkers at Aloha Quilt Camp.

DIANE: And Hinano.

BONNIE: Especially Hinano. I admit that he and the Aloha Quilters have told me time and time again that they'd like me to stay in Hawaii all year round, since we hold quilt camp in every season, but I can't really foresee myself doing that unless . . .

GWEN: Don't leave us in suspense. Unless what?

BONNIE: [Pause] At this point I don't think I'll need to make that decision, so let's leave it at that. [Laughs]

Why don't we turn to one of the newest Elm Creek Quilters? Maggie, as someone very interested in antique quilts and women's roles in American history, I find your research about the Harriet Findley Birch quilt absolutely fascinating.

MAGGIE: Oh, thank you. I found the research fascinating too! [Laughs] I only wish I could have uncovered even more details about Harriet's life. For those among your readers who aren't familiar with my work—

GRETCHEN: I can't imagine there would be many of those.

MAGGIE: You're sweet, Gretchen, but just in case there are a few, I should explain that the Harriet Findley Birch quilt is an extraordinary one-hundred-block sampler made by a former Lowell mill girl who traveled with her husband along the Oregon Trail in the mid-1800s. I found it at a garage sale, worn and dirty and looking every bit its age, and as I examined it and learned all I could about it, I decided to make my own version of her quilt to spare the original any more wear and tear.

Countless thousands of quilters have been inspired to follow your example thanks to your bestselling pattern book, My Journey with Harriet. *Several years have passed since it was published. Do you foresee any more pattern books in your future?*

MAGGIE: Oh, I wish. My editor definitely wants one, but there's a problem.

GRETCHEN: How often does one stumble upon a fascinating antique sampler at a garage sale?

MAGGIE: Exactly. So unless I have another amazing stroke of good fortune—and the odds are against it—I don't think I'll publish another pattern book.

AGNES: Don't give up hope. You never know. You might make another discovery as wonderful as the Harriet Findley Birch quilt—perhaps even more so. State quilt documentation projects uncover forgotten antique quilts all the time. Even now there might be one waiting for you, forgotten beneath someone's bed or packed up in an old box at the back of a closet.

SYLVIA: Or upstairs in my attic. You're welcome to search through my ancestors' trunks and cartons any time you like.

MAGGIE: I might do that. Thanks, Sylvia.

SYLVIA: Under no circumstances should my generosity be interpreted as a clever ploy to trick you into organizing my attic.

[Laughter]

Gretchen, you joined Elm Creek Quilts a few months before Maggie, and you're known for your devotion to the rich heritage of traditional quilting, as well as for your many charitable endeavors.

GRETCHEN: Oh, dear. I'm known for that? Really? I thought I was fairly anonymous.

GWEN: Sorry, my friend, but the secret's out: You're a sincerely good and generous person.

SUMMER: There are far worse things to be known for.

One of our readers wrote in to say, "You showed so much compassion to pregnant homeless girls when you volunteered for Abiding Savior Christian Outreach in Pittsburgh. Do you ever wonder how those young mothers are doing? Are they still using the beautiful quilts you taught them to make?"

GRETCHEN: I think about them often, and occasionally I do hear from some of them. A few of the girls still write to me from time to time. Some have gone on to build successful, safe, happy lives for themselves and their children. Some of them have returned to volunteer at the shelter where they once lived, offering guidance to the younger girls as only people who have walked in their shoes can. Others—well, I'm afraid some slipped through the cracks despite our best attempts to help them help themselves, and that breaks my heart. [Pause] I like to think that most of the girls I met at Abiding Savior continued to quilt, and that it brought them comfort and happiness.

AGNES: Gretchen's adopted a new favorite cause in her new hometown—our local chapter of Project Linus. They're a national organization dedicated to providing love, warmth, and comfort to children in need through the gifts of homemade quilts, blankets, and afghans.

GWEN: Gretchen also suggested Quiltsgiving, our annual winter camp session devoted to creating quilts for charity. Gretchen never stops giving, and I truly admire her for that.

GRETCHEN: You're taking this a bit too far. You make me sound like a saint, and I'm far from that.

SUMMER: You don't have to be a saint to give of your time and talent, and you do both in abundance.

GRETCHEN: Now you're embarrassing me. Please stop, or I'll have to leave the room, really.

Let's give Gretchen a break and embarrass someone else for a while. Agnes, Cyd Runde from St. Charles, Illinois, asks, "Why do you wear rose-tinted glasses? Eye condition, fashion statement, or perhaps to reflect an optimistic personality?"

[Laughter]
AGNES: That wasn't a real question, was it?
[More laughter]

Yes, absolutely.

AGNES: Oh, dear. Do you think she means that my glasses are a little out of style? I suppose they are.
SYLVIA: Nonsense. They've been in style for thirty years. Sarah, why are you and Summer grinning like that?
SARAH: No reason.
AGNES: Well, goodness. I hardly know what to say. I suppose I should choose something more fashionable, but my prescription hasn't changed, and these glasses are comfortable—
GWEN: Don't worry about it. Styles come and go. If you wait another ten years, pink-tinted glasses with huge lenses will probably be the height of fashion again.
DIANE: I think your rose-colored glasses *do* reflect your optimistic personality, and I don't think there's anything wrong with that.
AGNES: Thank you, dear.
DIANE: However, if you ever decide to update your look, I'd be happy to introduce you to my optometrist.

On a more personal note, Agnes, Linda Bazemore from Mustang, Oklahoma, wants to know how you felt when Sylvia left Elm Creek Manor. Did you try to find Sylvia to reunite with her back then? What was your initial reaction when Sarah wanted to reunite the two of you after Sylvia returned to Elm Creek Manor?

AGNES: Oh, my. I'd almost prefer another question about my fashion choices. [Pause] Of course I was terribly disheartened when Sylvia left Elm Creek Manor. I prayed that she would return soon, but I honestly thought I might never see her again. Claudia [Sylvia's estranged sister] and I watched from the library window as Sylvia carried her suitcase outside, climbed into a taxi, and drove away. I'll never forget what Claudia said to me then—"She'll be back. She loves Elm Creek Manor more than she hates me. She'll come home within a week." I didn't believe her, but I was too upset to argue.

SYLVIA: I truly regret that you got caught up in the animosity between my sister and me. I'm sorry you suffered any unhappiness on my account.

AGNES: I know, dear, and even at the time I understood why you left. I did try to find you, and after a while, Claudia joined in the search. We tracked you to your aunt and uncle in Harrisburg, and then to your in-laws' farm in Maryland, but the trail faded there, and eventually we gave up. When I heard that you had finally returned to Waterford after decades without a word, I almost couldn't believe it. When Sarah urged me to meet with you in the garden that day, I admit I was quite anxious, and I almost backed out at the last minute.

SARAH: What made you go through with it?

AGNES: Diane reminded me that I might not get another chance.

Sylvia, the story of your fifty-year estrangement from your sister and sister-in-law has resonated with so many quilters who are aware of the tumultuous history of Elm Creek Manor, and I know you've inspired countless people to seek reconciliation in their own broken relationships. Jen Zimmerman from Grand Rapids, Michigan, wonders if, during those long years apart, you ever felt your heart softening toward Claudia—perhaps when a particular quilt pattern reminded you of your childhood—or if those memories were simply too painful?

SYLVIA: I admit that in those first years, I was too angry and hurt to think about my sister at all. Later, I was filled with so much regret that I couldn't bear to dwell upon the past. Whenever I felt my heart softening, I hardened it again by sheer force of will rather than risk new and sharper hurt. By the time I returned to Elm Creek Manor, I was very hard and bitter indeed, as Sarah can attest.

SARAH: You weren't that bad.

SYLVIA: Oh, yes, I was. How fortunate I was that you were able to see through the dark, brittle walls I had built all around myself. I'll be forever thankful that you arranged that surprise reunion for Agnes and me in the garden that day.

AGNES: And I'll be forever grateful that Diane insisted upon driving me out here to meet you!

Speaking of Diane, we have a question for her too. Faith Morlan, who asked a couple of questions earlier, says, "You have sons, but unfortunately, we think of traditional quilting as a woman's art form. Are you sorry you didn't show your sons how to quilt?

DIANE: Not at all.

[Pause]

GWEN: That's it?

Yes, please do elaborate.

DIANE: For most of my life, I've lived in a house full of men. Sports on the TV, skateboards on the mudroom floor, every toilet seat left up, impassioned dinner conversations about how to survive the zombie apocalypse. Quilting is the one thing in my life that's just me and the girls. I'm quite happy to keep it that way.

AGNES: Did your boys ask for quilting lessons?

DIANE: Not once, which was another good reason not to bother teaching them.

SUMMER: My mom taught me to quilt, and I'm very glad she did.
GWEN: I'm very glad you wanted to learn!

Gwen, you're known not only for your unique artistic style, but also for your research of historic quilts and other textiles as a professor at Waterford College. Tracey Baumgarten of Philipsburg, Pennsylvania, wants you to tell us about the most interesting or important quilt you've researched.

GWEN: It's difficult to choose since there have been so many—much to the chagrin of my department chair—but for purely personal reasons, I'd have to choose the foundation paper pieced Pineapple quilt I discovered in the lost-and-found box at my parents' church in Brown Deer, Kentucky, back in the midseventies. As I explored library archives and historic sites in an attempt to establish the quilt's provenance, it kindled my desire to learn to quilt, and it also inspired me to return to college and earn my degree.
SUMMER: And a few more degrees after that.

You published an intriguing and moving account of this experience in Contemporary Quilting *a few years ago, and it certainly struck a chord with readers. In fact, Pam Leach of Winnemucca, Nevada, wanted us to ask you whatever became of that quilt.*

GWEN: I still have it, and I assure you, I take excellent care of it.

It probably won't surprise you that many of our readers have questions about other significant quilts in the lives of the Elm Creek Quilters, especially you, Sylvia. Anita Soltis from Walkerton, Indiana, asks, "Which quilt holds the most meaning for you?"

DIANE: *Sewickley Sunrise.* That has to be her most famous quilt. It was featured in the American Quilter's Society's calendar for May 1982 and it's in the Museum of the American Quilter's Society's permanent collection.

SYLVIA: No, Diane, you've got it wrong. Of all my quilts, that's the one that seems to hold the most meaning for other people, but it's not the most meaningful to me. My choice is less impressive, perhaps, but far more personal. Of the quilts I've made, my Broken Star is the most meaningful to me because it was the first project I attempted after my stroke. My friends know all too well how I struggled through it, but when I look upon it now, I can trace the path of my progress from those first awkward, painful stitches to those I made well into my recovery, which were nearly as small and neat as before. Every time I see it, which is often since it hangs in the front foyer, it reminds me anew of the rewards of perseverance and determination. It reminds me how far I've come.

There must be a project on the opposite end of the spectrum. Elizabeth Benducci from Oakland, New Jersey, wants to know which of your quilts is your least favorite and why.

SYLVIA: Hmph. Pick any quilt my mother forced me to make with my sister when we were girls.

SARAH: What about the crib quilt you and your sister made when your mother was expecting your younger brother? You got to choose the colors and Claudia the pattern, but when she chose the Wandering Foot block, you protested because your grandmother told you it was bad luck to use that block in a child's quilt.

SYLVIA: As strange as it may seem, I wouldn't choose that quilt as my least favorite because my darling baby brother adored it. I still remember cuddling him in it. . . . [Shakes her head] No, I have too many happy memories of my brother with his quilt to ever consider it my least favorite.

DIANE: So if not that quilt, which one?

SYLVIA: Well, if I have to choose, I'll admit that my first attempt at a rotary-cutter quick-pieced quilt was something of a disaster. I finished the top in a matter of hours, just as the pattern promised, but it was so quick and expedient, so impersonal and unsatisfying, that I immediately tossed it aside and tried to forget about it. I abandoned it on my guild's swap table, and if someone picked it up, finished it, and made good use of it, well, more power to her.

Our last question is for Sarah. Julie Delano of Newtown, Pennsylvania, writes, "Sarah, your life was so different before you arrived at Elm Creek Manor. Meeting Sylvia and starting Elm Creek Quilts was integral to your amazing adult life. What do you think your life would be like if you had never met Sylvia?"

SARAH: Oh, wow. I don't know. What a horrible thought, to have never met Sylvia!

SYLVIA: I'm sure you would have survived somehow, dear.

SARAH: Survived, maybe, but far less happily. Well, let me think . . . Shortly before Sylvia and I agreed to launch Elm Creek Quilts, I had been offered an accounting job with a small public accounting firm, Steele and . . . something. No, Hopkins and Steele. It would have been a great job for the right person, but not for me, not really. If had never met Sylvia, I probably would have accepted that job anyway, and I'd probably still be toiling away at it, crunching numbers in a cubicle, thoroughly unfulfilled and longing for something more. I probably never would have learned to quilt.

AGNES: Perish the thought!

MAGGIE: It's scary to think that Elm Creek Quilts might not have existed.

GRETCHEN: Indeed it is. I don't know where I'd be if Sylvia and Sarah hadn't met and dreamed up this wonderful venture. Joe and I would be facing a very bleak, lean, and worrisome future, that's for sure. This job has been such a blessing to us both, a true blessing from God. I firmly believe that.

BONNIE: Without Elm Creek Quilts, I don't know what I would have done after my shop went bankrupt. Elm Creek Manor was my safe harbor in a terrible storm.

DIANE: You would have had Aloha Quilt Camp.

BONNIE: No, I wouldn't have, because Claire chose me as her partner because of my experience with Elm Creek Quilts. So I wouldn't have gone to Maui, I wouldn't have started Aloha Quilt Camp, I wouldn't have met Hinano—

DIANE: And you would have been completely miserable.

BONNIE: Absolutely. Thoroughly and utterly miserable.

SYLVIA: As for me, if I hadn't met Sarah, I almost certainly would have sold Elm Creek Manor to that unscrupulous real estate fellow and moved back to Sewickley. I probably would have heard about the razing of the manor long after the fact, too late to do anything to prevent it. I wouldn't have reconciled with Agnes, nor would I have reunited with Andrew—Oh, my goodness, it really is too dreadful to contemplate.

MAGGIE: Elm Creek Quilts helped me find new love too. If not for Elm Creek Quilts, Russell and I never would have met.

GRETCHEN: It's evident we all owe you a great deal, Sarah.

SARAH: You don't owe me a thing. Everything I've given to you and to Elm Creek Quilts has been repaid to me a thousandfold.

GWEN: This is beginning to sound like a quilter's version of *It's a Wonderful Life.*

SUMMER: It really has been, hasn't it? A wonderful life.

AGNES: It has been, and still is.

SYLVIA: And long may it continue to be, for all of us.

◆ ◆ ◆

Ellen Henderson is a writer and director who first garnered fame for her acclaimed PBS series *A Patchwork Life,* which won four Emmys and a Peabody. Her most recent series, *Oregon Trail,* was recently renewed for a third season on HBO and has earned her two Emmys for Outstanding Drama Series, two for Directing for a Drama Series, and three for Writing for a Drama Series. She lives in Santa Barbara, California, with her husband and two children.